"Years ago my daughters and wife were inhaling Robin Gu[...] [...]ing them, so I had to take a peek myself to find out why [...] [...]acters are believable, and her stories have just the right bl[...] hearts, disappointments, lighthearted fun, joy, and an eter[...] Lord Jesus always plays a role, whether behind the scene[...] things. Robin lives the faith that's so evident in her books. [...] tell a story—and the stories she tells make an eternal diffe[...]"

RANDY ALCORN, AUTHOR OF DEADLINE

"When you read a Robin Gunn book, you know you're goi[...] der lesson in what it means to belong to Christ—and you wi[...]"

FRANCINE RIVERS, AUTHOR OF REDEEMING LOVE A[...]
THE MARK OF THE LION SERIES

"Gratefully Robin's warmth, insight, and humor spill over from her heart onto the written page. She delights us with the well-woven fabric of a well-told tale and I'm certain Robin delights the Lord with her obvious passion for him."

PATSY CLAIRMONT, AUTHOR OF GOD USES CRACKED POTS AND
SPORTIN' A 'TUDE

"Robin Jones Gunn cares. She cares about her characters, she cares about her readers, and most of all, she cares about their mutual search for a life that pleases the Lord. Her novels are a delight to read—perfectly crafted, heart-warming, and fun. I'm always thrilled when one of Robin's books appears on the top of my to-be-read stack!"

LIZ CURTIS HIGGS, AUTHOR OF MIXED SIGNALS, BOOKENDS, AND BAD GIRLS OF THE BIBLE

"Robin Jones Gunn is one of those rare and wonderful writers who infuses her stories with bountiful doses of humor, wisdom, and warmth. Her books have touched and changed countless hearts and given a whole generation of read-ers a host of fictional characters who feel like dear friends!"

CAROLE GIFT PAGE, AUTHOR OF HEARTLAND MEMORIES SERIES

"Whenever I think of stories that touch the heart, I think of Robin Jones Gunn. They touch my heart and leave me wanting more. Reading a novel by Robin Jones Gunn is like spending time with a good friend…troubles are lighter and joys are deeper."

ALICE GRAY, AUTHOR OF STORIES FOR THE HEART BOOK COLLECTION

"Robin Jones Gunn writes from a heart of love. Her tender stories honor the Savior and speak truth to a world desperately eager to hear it."

ANGELA ELWELL HUNT, AUTHOR OF THE TRUTH TELLER

"Robin Gunn is a gifted and sincere storyteller who gets right to the heart of matters with her readers."

MELODY CARLSON, AUTHOR OF HOMEWARD

THE GLENBROOKE SERIES

Woodlands

ROBIN JONES GUNN

Multnomah®Publishers *Sisters, Oregon*

WOODLANDS
published by Multnomah Publishers, Inc.
© 2000 by Robin's Ink, LLC

International Standard Book Number: 1-59052-237-0

Cover design and images by Steve Gardner/His Image PixelWorks

Scripture quotations are from *The Holy Bible,* King James Version
New American Standard Bible (NASB) © 1960, 1977 by the Lockman Foundation

The Holy Bible, New International Version (NIV) © 1973, 1984 by International Bible Society, used by permission of Zondervan Publishing House.

Printed in the United States of America

For information:
MULTNOMAH PUBLISHERS, INC.
P. O. BOX 1720
SISTERS, OR 97759

Library of Congress Cataloging-in-Publication Data
Gunn, Robin Jones, 1955–
    Woodlands/by Robin Jones Gunn. p.cm.–(The Glenbrooke series; bk. 7)
    ISBN 1-57673-503-6 (alk. paper) I. Title.
        1-59052-237-0
PS3557.U4866 W66 2000
813'.54–dc21   99-051803

04 05 06 07 08 09 — 10 9 8 7 6 5 4 3

To my exceptional friend, Anne de Graaf, who prayed.
And to Liz Curtis Higgs,
with whom Anne and I shared cheesecake
at 2 A.M. in a Toronto hotel room
when heaven broke through.

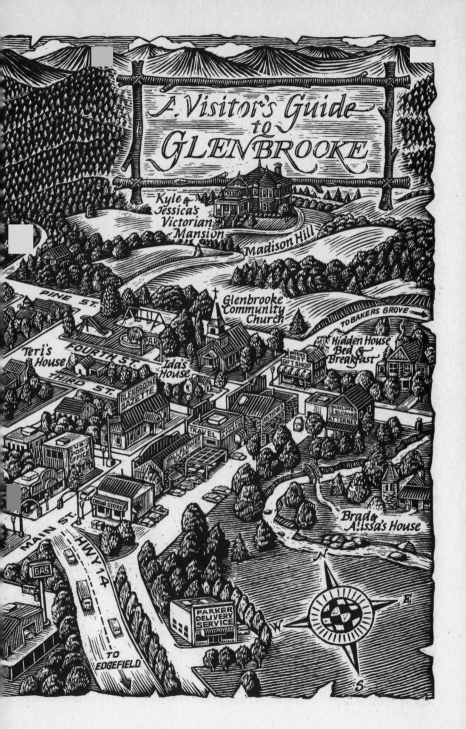

"The LORD thy God in the midst of thee is mighty, he
will save, he will rejoice over thee with joy, he will rest in his love,
he will joy over thee with singing."

ZEPHANIAH 3:17

Chapter One

*H*ey batter, batter, batter—swing!" Leah Hudson leaned over the counter of the Snack Shack at the Glenbrooke Little League ball field and yelled. "Swing, batter, swing!"

The young batter swung and missed.

"Stree-ike three!" the umpire called.

Leah checked the scoreboard. Bottom of the ninth. Score tied 7 to 7. The Edgefield Pirates took the outfield as her beloved Glenbrooke Rangers hustled up to bat.

Leah smiled. She took a sip from her can of Dr Pepper and flipped her feathery blond hair behind her ears. "It doesn't get any better than this," she murmured to herself, gazing at the lavender sky. The retiring sun had left a dozen pale pink streak marks on its way home. A flock of chattering wrens flitted overhead.

Little blond-haired Travis ran over to the Snack Shack with a golden retriever bounding behind him. Chinning himself up on the counter, the almost five-year-old asked, "Can I have a Sno-Kone, Auntie Leah?"

Leah was "auntie" to lots of children in Glenbrooke. She had lived there all of her twenty-seven years. Twenty-seven single years. Twenty-seven years of helping everyone else raise their children.

"Here you go, Travis," Leah said, handing him the rainbow Sno-Kone. He smiled and produced a fistful of money.

"Tell your mom I'm coming over early on Saturday to help with the Easter egg hunt, okay?"

"Okay," Travis said. Without looking back, he trotted to the bleachers with the retriever beside him.

That's when Leah noticed the guy in shorts. He leaned against the side of the bleachers with a large Dairy Queen shake in his hand. His black shorts and forest green knit shirt were the uniform of the Parker Delivery Service, which made almost daily deliveries to the admitting desk of Glenbrooke General Hospital where Leah worked. She knew all the delivery guys. This one had to be new. She would have remembered those legs. No one in Oregon had legs that tan this early in spring.

A cheer rose from the home crowd, and Leah realized she had missed a hit. The tallest of the Glenbrooke Rangers dashed to first base while the Pirates fumbled with the ball in the out-field. The runner made it to third base before the ball was back in the pitcher's mitt.

"Come on, Rangers!" Leah yelled, as the next batter stepped up to the plate. "You can do it! Bring him home!"

Her voice must have really traveled because the delivery guy with the bronzed legs turned halfway around and watched her instead of the game. Leah allowed her gaze to linger in his direction a little longer. She strained to make out any distinct facial features, but his baseball cap cast too much shadow for her to come to any real conclusions. She was pretty sure she had never seen him before.

Leah turned away when another young customer came up and asked for a candy bar. Just then, a cheer rose from the bleachers.

"What happened?" She didn't have to wait for an answer. The whoops and hollers from the bleachers indicated that the Rangers had just scored a run. Dozens of parents stood and cheered for their kids. Leah knew almost everyone.

She felt a familiar twinge of pain as she watched the parents' joyous outburst. It was the same ache she felt whenever she realized she was on the sidelines while all the women her age were holding babies or hugging their husbands or both.

Leah glanced again at the uniformed delivery guy. He had squatted down and was using both hands to rough up the golden retriever behind the ears.

Look away, Leah, look away! Don't do this to yourself.

A well-used recording played in her psyche right on cue. The voice was that of her oldest and least favorite sister. The words had been spoken a long time ago, yet Leah never had forgotten them: "You have neither the frame nor the frame of mind to ever attract someone stable."

Leah's three oldest sisters were willowy blonds, like their mother. They all married before they turned twenty-two. The next two sisters had inherited their father's height as well as his thick, brunette hair and milk-chocolate brown eyes. Both of them had married intelligent men and had moved to the East Coast.

Somehow Leah managed to be the only daughter who inherited what she considered the lesser qualities of both parents. She had her father's round face and candy apple cheeks and her mother's long neck. Her eyes were a cloudy gray, and she had worn glasses starting in the second grade and contacts since ninth grade. Her blond hair, which she had inherited from her mother, was the only attribute she liked. She had her mother's short stature but her father's strong, muscular frame. The years she had spent transferring her heavy father from his sickbed to his wheelchair had done her figure a favor by giving her great muscle tone. Perhaps that would be her only reward for being the daughter who stayed in Glenbrooke to care for her elderly parents, which she did faithfully until they both passed away a year ago.

Leah's Glenbrooke friends were her family now. She knew better than to be deluded about the possibility of marriage and family over some guy with tan legs. A guy who obviously loved dogs. And Dairy Queen shakes. And Little League games and gorgeous spring evenings.

Oh, stop it, will you! Leah chided, forcing herself to turn away from the delivery guy by the bleachers. She tried to focus on the price list sign behind her. One of the *r*s in "burrito" was crooked. She fixed it and brushed a spider web from the top right-hand corner of the sign.

Another blast of hurrahs echoed from the bleachers. Leah turned to see the Rangers galloping out to the field, tossing their caps and mitts into the air.

She let out a loud cheer. "Way to go, Rangers!"

The exuberant crowd came rushing in her direction, looking for post-game refreshments. Leah snapped into action, reaching for canned drinks in the ice chest and counting out Pixie Stix. The faster she worked, the louder the crowd grew— and the larger. Just when she had appeased nearly all the parents from the bleachers with their toddlers, the players on both teams joined in the mob, waving tickets from their coaches for free treats.

The side door of the Snack Shack trailer opened, and without looking to see who it was, Leah said, "Hey, we have to keep that door shut, you guys."

"I thought you could use some help," a deep voice said.

Leah looked up at the delivery guy, who was now standing beside her. She realized again the disadvantage of being only 5'4". It meant she constantly had to look up to men. That had been a problem for her more than once and in more ways than one.

"Ah, well, okay," she stammered, feeling her apple-round cheeks begin to blush. "I guess."

He had the gentlest, deep blue eyes she had ever seen. And the whitest smile. Or was it just his rich tan that made his eyes and smile stand out?

"Who's next?" he asked.

A chorus of eager sugar hounds responded with one, high-pitched note of "Me!"

"Point to them one at a time," Leah suggested. "The yellow tickets are worth a dollar each. The blue ones are fifty cents. And if you can get them to form a line, you'll do better than I have."

A shrill whistle pierced the air. Leah nearly dropped the Sno-Kone she had just finished making for her customer.

"Line up! Single file. Let me see two lines here. That's it. You guys are awesome. Now what can I get for you?" he asked, pointing to the first sweaty face in the line.

Leah looked on in amazement. "How did you do that?"

"Years of practice," he said. "Where are the drinks?"

"In the ice chest. I only have cans. The ice over there is for the Sno-Kones."

"Do you have frozen Snickers bars?" Leah's next customer asked.

"No, sorry. I'll be sure to freeze some before the next game. Do you want an unfrozen Snickers instead?"

He nodded, and she handed him the last one.

"Nope," Leah heard her partner say to his next customer above the rising noise level. "Looks like that was the last one. How about a Hershey's bar? Or what else do we have here? A Milky Way?"

Leah had orders for five Sno-Kones in a row, followed by a burrito, which she tossed in the microwave while scooping up two popcorns and passing out a few candy bars. And then the customers were all gone. In record time.

"How do these tickets work?" the guy asked, examining one of the yellow slips of paper.

"They're marked with the player's name and the coach's name. The players can pay into a snack fund when they sign up for Little League so their coins don't fall out of their pockets while they run around the field. All I have to do is sort them and give them to the coaches, who pay me back."

"'Buchanan,'" he read on one of the slips. "Would that be the same Buchanan with the golden retriever?"

"Yes, Kyle." Leah scanned the nearly empty field and spotted Kyle in the twilight. "Do you see him over there by home plate? He's the coach. How did you know?"

"I read the dog tag." He graced Leah with a gentle smile and then turned to go. "Maybe I can still catch him."

Leah felt the need to say something more. Her handsome prince was leaving, and she didn't have a clue as to his identity. His work boots definitely weren't glass slippers, and neither of them looked as if it was about to fall off.

"Hey, thanks!" she called out, as he opened the door to exit. "Sure you don't want a free Sno-Kone for your trouble?"

"No," he said with a wave over his shoulder. "Thanks!"

"Thank *you*," Leah called out. And then he was gone.

"'Sure you don't want a free Sno-Kone for your trouble?'" Leah repeated under her breath. "Oh brother, what kind of line was that?"

Leah pulled herself back into reality by sorting out blue and yellow slips and beginning her routine to close down the Snack Shack. Her gaze wandered out to the ball field twice as she cleaned up. The first time she saw her mysterious stranger talking to Kyle, but on the second glance they were both gone. She turned the crank that rolled down the front window of the Snack Shack and unplugged all the electrical appliances. Balancing her keys and the cash box on top of an ice chest containing the leftover frozen burritos, Leah locked the outside door of the Snack Shack and headed for her car.

The field appeared empty now. Only three cars remained in the dirt parking lot. A cool breeze came sweeping through as soon as the sun set, a reminder that spring wasn't here yet. Leah climbed into her Blazer but before turning the key in the ignition she looped her arms over the steering wheel and stared at the first star that had risen in the clear night sky. She knew it was probably a planet since it was so bright. Venus, most likely.

Venus. Isn't that supposed to be the planet of love? What if I make a wish upon a planet—the love planet—instead of a star? Will I have a greater chance of my wish coming true?

Leah thought of the promises she had made to herself since her parents had passed away. She had been so determined to start fresh and to build a new identity for herself. Unfortunately, all her Glenbrooke friends seemed to have a set image of her. And their expectations had remained the same making it difficult for her to change.

However, this tan-legged delivery guy with the deep blue eyes didn't know who she was. He didn't have any expectations. He didn't know she had been her father's last hope for a son.

Most of Glenbrooke had heard her father tell the story of how he chose the name Leah for his sixth daughter. The book of Genesis contained the account of Jacob's first wife, Leah. Jacob had worked seven years to earn adorable Rachel's hand in marriage, but he was tricked into marrying Rachel's less desirable sister, Leah. When Jacob woke the morning after his wedding, he turned to see that "behold, it was Leah" next to him and not his long anticipated Rachel.

Leah could hear her father's voice echoing in her imagination. *"Saddest verse in the Bible, Genesis 29:25. 'Behold, it was Leah.' Yup, after five daughters, when I saw her I felt just like Jacob, and I said, 'We'll call her Leah.'"*

Early on Leah learned that if she worked hard—as hard as a son would have worked—she could please her father. So she became his tomboy and was one of the first girls in Glenbrooke to play Little League baseball on this very field.

Leah wondered if that bit of news would impress the mysterious newcomer. Or did he prefer soft-spoken women with manicured nails? He had said he had experience getting kids to line up. Did he work with kids? He definitely appeared to like dogs. That was a good sign.

Gazing up at the bright planet, Leah whispered, "I wish…I wish…."

It was no use. She had stopped wishing a long time ago. She didn't dare permit herself to speak aloud the silent wish that had long lay nestled in her heart. The dream, the wish, for someone to love and for that someone to love her back. The unattainable dream of one day handing a Sno-Kone to her own son and at long last being the mother in the bleachers who yelled the loudest when her boy was at bat.

Leah blinked and swallowed quickly. Bright Venus was still shining down on her.

Yeah, well, for all I know, I'm looking at Pluto, not Venus. What happens if I wish on Pluto? Does a floppy-eared dog with big feet show up on my doorstep?

Leah glanced at her watch. "Yikes! What am I doing sitting here talking to myself?" She started her car and headed for home. But first she had an important stop to make at the grocery store.

Chapter Two

Dashing to the checkout stand with a cartful of groceries, Leah greeted the clerk with, "I know, I know, I'm the last one in the store, right?"

"That's okay," he said. "Looks like you were a little low on the essentials." He rang up the four cartons of a dozen eggs and looked at her over the top of his glasses.

"It's Easter," Leah said merrily. "They're for the big egg hunt at Kyle and Jessica's."

"Of course. I should have guessed. My kids are going."

"It's going to be fun," Leah said. "I hope the weather stays clear. It was beautiful today."

The clerk rang up an economy-size package of newborn diapers. "Looks like you're going to be ready for just about everything."

Leah only nodded. *Do you have to comment on everything I'm buying?*

Apparently he did because he kept going. "Great price on

the roast beef this week, isn't it?"

Leah nodded again.

"My wife likes these crackers. Are they any good?"

Leah didn't know. She had never tried them. In an effort to speed up the process and avoid further questions, she stepped to the end of the checkout stand and assisted in bagging her own groceries. She wanted to get as much as she could into two bags and keep the eggs separate in a third bag. The clerk chose to comment on that as well.

"You know what they say about putting all your eggs in one basket? You should put only two cartons in a bag. Eggs can be heavy, you know."

Leah didn't know. But she followed his instructions and left the store as quickly as she could. One of the disadvantages of living in a small town was that everybody could figure out what everyone else was doing, which made it difficult for Leah to cover her tracks. She had come to the grocery store late so she would be the only shopper. People who knew her well would have realized she would never buy a roast for herself since she rarely ate red meat.

Stashing the groceries in the back of her Blazer, Leah took off for the address she had scribbled on a sticky memo pad at work that afternoon. The dashboard of her car was freckled with notes she was forever writing to herself. Reminders of things to do, places to go, people to see.

She had a pretty good idea of where this house was located. It was one of the many homes on Glenbrooke's outskirts, tucked behind a forest of evergreens and then down a poorly marked dirt and gravel road.

Leah found it on her first try. She turned off the engine as soon as the porch light came into view. The Blazer rolled to a stop. As quietly as she could, Leah collected the two bulging bags of groceries and stepped lightly, heading for the front door.

From inside the house came the sound of a newborn's cries. As soon as Leah heard them she walked faster, feeling sure that the baby's cries would cover up any noise she made. It had only been a week since Leah had filed the papers at her hospital desk to send this newborn baby home. Four days later, the father had shown up in admitting with a mandatory hernia operation. He was teased plenty about overdoing it with the sympathy pains for his wife's recent delivery.

Leah had read the concern in the faces of the young couple. This was their first child. The husband worked construction and would now lose income during his recovery time. Their insurance had a $500 deductible.

That afternoon the hernia patient had been sent home, and Leah hoped the groceries would save the new mom from having to make a trip into town for a few days.

Leah carefully balanced the two heavy bags on the front door mat and gingerly made her way back to the car. When she was sure she was out of sight from the front door and that her car was sufficiently camouflaged down the road, she reached into the glove compartment for her cell phone. Holding a penlight between her teeth, she read the number off her sticky note and dialed the phone.

A woman's voice answered. The sound of the wailing baby came through the receiver so loud Leah had to pull the phone away from her ear.

"Hello?" the woman said a second time.

Leah lowered her voice to the basement of her range and said, "Yes, hello. I'm calling to let you know a gift is waiting on your doorstep. God bless you. Good night."

She hung up and waited. From her hiding place, she could

see the door slowly open. Her heart started to race. It always did when she thought of what her gift receivers must be thinking and feeling in that first moment of realization.

The woman stood a moment in stunned silence, holding the crying baby in her arms. She looked left and right and then tried to pick up one of the bags with her free hand. It was too heavy.

I should have put the groceries in more bags so they wouldn't be so heavy. What was I thinking? She just had a baby, and he just had hernia surgery.

It was all Leah could do to stay in the car and not hurry to the front door to help carry the groceries inside. But whenever Leah made her secret deliveries, it was incognito. That's the way she wanted it to stay. Her joy was in the giving, not in being discovered.

The woman went inside and came back with her arms free. Slowly she lifted the bags one at a time. When the front door closed, Leah waited a few minutes before starting the engine and backing down the road. It was difficult to maneuver in the dark so she went slowly. She kept thinking about the fifty eggs that were bouncing around like crazy in the back of the Blazer.

Just as her tires hit the paved street, her cell phone rang. Leah jumped. She stopped the car to answer the phone.

"Who is this?" the male voice asked.

"Who is this?" Leah retorted.

After a pause, the man said, "I got your number off my caller ID so I know that you, or someone at this number, just called us and said a gift was on our doorstep."

Leah's heart began to pound. She had never been traced this way before. She felt a rush of disappointment mixed with fear at the thought of being found out. No one had come this close to catching her after almost eight years of clandestine drop-offs.

"I just want to say thanks," the man said. "You don't know how badly we needed some of this stuff. Especially the diapers."

Leah smiled but didn't say anything. She had answered the phone in her natural voice but made the original call in a deep voice. She wasn't sure now which voice to use.

"You don't have to say anything," the man said after another pause. "We just wanted to say thank you. And God bless you, too." He hung up.

Leah drove home quickly. A sense of joy overpowered the rush of fear she had felt when she was nearly found out.

The next day at work Leah was all set to carry out another undercover mission. This time to find out the identity of the tan-legged PDS delivery guy by asking Harry, their usual PDS man.

However, by lunchtime not a single delivery had been made to the hospital. Leah had planned to run errands during her lunch break, but now she didn't want to leave the hospital in case Harry came while she was gone. She ate in the lunch-room, facing the door so she could see the admitting desk.

Harry never arrived. Leah found it hard to believe the hospital had no deliveries all day. When she left at four-thirty, still no deliveries had arrived.

Leah closed her car door and checked the sticky notes on the dashboard for her list of errands. The first note reminded her to drop off three muffin tins at Ida Dane's home on Fourth Avenue. Ida was making cupcakes for the Easter Saturday event and had left a message on Leah's phone the night before asking if she had extra tins.

Leah parked in front of the blue house and paused a moment to take in the carousel of color that surrounded the fifty-year-old A-frame home. Ida's flowers were her joy. Bright red tulips, nodding yellow daffodils, and deep purple pansies lined the steps to her front door where a clump of tall iris stalks looked as if they were getting ready to open in time for Easter Sunday. Ida's dogwood tree on the side of the house had burst into a canopy of bright pink blossoms.

Heading for the front door, Leah noticed the dainty white alyssum and abundant grape hyacinth that ran the length of the border along the front of the house. She knocked on the front door and watched as the afternoon breeze danced through the dogwood tree, causing the blossoms to flutter to the ground like confetti.

"Ida?" Leah called out, knocking again. "It's Leah."

The front door was closed. Leah guessed Ida was running errands. She was one of Glenbrooke's most active senior citizens, although in the past few years Leah had noticed Ida becoming more easily confused and keeping more to home than she used to. Leah left the muffin tins propped against the side of the screen door and told herself to call Ida later to make sure she had found them.

Leah was down the front walk and opening the door to her Blazer when she heard the deep rumbling sound of a delivery van rounding the corner onto Fourth. Something prompted her to duck inside her car and watch to see who was driving the van. It might be "him."

The brakes squealed as the van came to a stop in front of her car. She peered expectantly, waiting until the driver hopped out and headed up Ida's walkway with a clipboard and a small package.

Leah smiled. There he was, tanned legs and all. With her window rolled down, she sat back and decided to watch and listen. He obviously hadn't noticed her when he rushed up to Ida's door to make the delivery.

He was knocking on the door when thin, little Ida came

bustling around the far side of her house wearing garden gloves and waving a pair of clippers in her hand. "Yoo-hoo! I heard your truck pull up. I was hoping my package would arrive today. Oh, why, you're new, aren't you?"

He handed her the clipboard. "Yes, I am. Could you sign for me, please? Line 19."

Leah watched as Ida signed the paper and then looked him over. "Do you have time for a glass of lemonade?"

Leah thought this was the perfect setup. If he went inside for lemonade, she could go back to the front door saying she wanted to make sure Ida had found the muffin tins. Ida would invite Leah inside for lemonade, too, and voilà, Leah could meet Mr. PDS.

"No, I have a few more deliveries to make," he said. "Thank you, though."

"Oh!" Ida said, reaching over and picking up the muffin tins. "Did you leave these also?"

"No, they were there when I came up."

"Really?" Now Ida seemed intrigued. She looked around but didn't notice Leah in the car. Leah didn't know if she should wave and call out or start the car and dash away. Either choice seemed awkward so she stayed where she was, feeling relieved that neither of them seemed to have noticed her sitting there, spying on them. The lilac bushes must have hidden her from easy view.

Ida held up the muffin tins and triumphantly announced to the delivery guy, "I bet the Glenbrooke Zorro left these for me. He must have known I do lots of baking for Easter. I've always hoped I'd be visited by the Glenbrooke Zorro, and it looks like today was my day!"

Leah sank down in her seat. She couldn't drive away now. How could Ida have forgotten that she had called Leah to bring over the muffin tins?

"Well, have a nice afternoon," the delivery guy said before turning to go.

"Wait!" Ida called out. "I don't know your name, young man."

Leah thought that was a much better departing line than "Care for a Sno-Kone."

"Seth," he called to Ida from the middle of her garden walk. "Seth Edwards."

"Next time you come to my door, Seth Edwards, you make sure you have time for a nice glass of lemonade."

"I will. Thanks." He waved and hustled back to the delivery van.

Leah stayed slumped in her seat, watching and waiting for him to leave. Seth. Seth Edwards. It had a nice, stable sound to it.

Seth settled into the front seat of his van and appeared to be checking a map before pulling out. Leah waited. Seth put down the map and glanced in the rearview mirror. He was at just the right angle to look into the cab of Leah's Blazer, and when he did, their eyes met. Leah sheepishly waved. Seth smiled and waved back. He looked to the front door of Ida's house. Ida had gone in and taken the package and muffin tins with her. Seth looked back at Leah and smiled again.

Did he just deduce that I was the one who left the muffin tins? He's new in town. He can't know anything about the Glenbrooke Zorro. I hope he ignores that comment as the prattling of an old lady.

Leah expected him to start up his van and be on his way. After all, he had said he had several more deliveries to make. But to her surprise, he grabbed his map and exited the van. Before Leah knew what was happening, the bronzed, bare legs of Seth Edwards were striding toward her.

Chapter Three

*R*esting his arm on the open window of Leah's Blazer, Seth leaned in and said, "Hi there."

"Hi." Leah felt certain her round cheeks were a bright shade of tulip red.

"I wonder if you could do me a favor."

"Sure," Leah said quickly. Too quickly, she thought, so she added, "I owe you a favor after the way you helped me out last night. You really saved the day for me."

"Good. Now maybe you can save the day for me. Can you tell me how to get to Medford Court? The map shows it as being off Nineteenth, but I was just there, and Nineteenth doesn't go through."

"What's the name on the package?" Leah asked.

"I think its Jamison or Jameson."

"Oh, sure, the Jamelsons'. I know right where that is. It would be easier for me to show you than to tell you. Why don't you follow me?" Leah volunteered.

"You sure it wouldn't be too much trouble?" Seth's deep blue eyes expressed his appreciation.

"No trouble at all." Leah turned the key in the ignition, but nothing happened. She checked to make sure the key was in all the way and tried again. Still no spark. "That's odd."

"Want me to look under the hood?" Seth asked.

"Sure." Leah popped the catch on the hood. She got out, and the two of them stood next to each other, both checking the engine. Leah was aware again of how small she felt next to this man. She concentrated on the equipment under the hood, her eyes running through all the familiar connections in the engine.

"Looks okay from what I can see," he said. "Do you think it might be the battery?"

"Not likely," Leah said. "I replaced it two months ago." She decided not to mention that she had literally been the one to replace it with only the aid of the car manual.

Would he be put off if he knew I'm mechanically inclined?

"We could try to jump-start it," Seth suggested. "I might have cables in the truck."

"I have some," Leah said, going to the back of her car and reaching for the cables, which were next to her tool chest. She returned and connected them quickly and easily.

"I'll pull the van closer," Seth offered. When he did, he popped open the hood and Leah connected the cables to the battery, then she returned to her car and tried to start it up.

Nothing happened. The key turned, but the engine didn't respond. Seth got out of the delivery van and disengaged the cables.

"Could be the starter," they said in unison when Leah climbed out of her car. They both laughed.

"Can I give you a ride somewhere?" Seth offered.

"Why don't I go with you to show you how to get to the Jamelsons'. Then, if you don't mind bringing me back here, I can call for a tow truck."

"That would be great," Seth said, checking his watch. "I'm supposed to have these next two deliveries made before five o'clock, but I don't think I'm going to make it."

Leah grabbed her cell phone and her backpack. "Let's go," she said. As a last attempt to figure out what was wrong with the car, Leah tried her keypad to see if the automatic lock would respond. It didn't.

"This is really strange," she muttered, jogging to the passenger side of the delivery truck. She hopped up into the seat and moved a portable CD player. She wondered what kind of music he listened to. Settling the CD player onto the floor, she allowed herself to feel a fresh sense of delight at the adventure of all this. Maybe she was glad her car didn't start.

"Which way do I go?" Seth asked, maneuvering around Leah's stalled vehicle and rolling down Fourth Street.

"Turn right at the corner, then right again on Madison," she said.

"Have you lived here long?" Seth asked.

"All my life," Leah said.

He glanced over at her and smiled. She couldn't help but smile back.

"I'm Seth Edwards, by the way," he said.

"I'm—"

Before she could answer, he finished for her. "Leah. Leah Hudson. Right?"

Leah looked at him more carefully. "How did you know that?"

"I asked Kyle last night."

She nodded slowly, squinting her gray eyes when he

glanced at her again. "And what else did Kyle tell you about me?"

"Enough," Seth said with a tease in his voice. He came to a four-way stop and said, "This is where I turned left last time."

"You need to keep going straight," Leah told him. "We'll go about four more blocks. You're going to take a left and then another left. It's a new housing development, and I don't think it's on the maps yet."

"That would explain it," Seth said.

"How long have you been in Glenbrooke?" Leah asked. She had no way of knowing how many details of her life Kyle had divulged to Seth. It seemed only fair that Seth volunteer some information about himself.

"This is my fourth day in Glenbrooke," he said. "I started working for PDS on Monday. You can see why I still can't find my way around town."

"Don't worry," Leah said. "It's pretty small; you'll have it figured out in no time. This is where you want to turn. Right here."

He rounded the corner and then turned right again when they came to Medford Court.

"It's the beige house at the end of the court," Leah said.

"You can sure tell this is a new neighborhood," Seth said. "It seems bare without all the trees and flowers the last street we were on had."

"I don't care for the way all these houses look alike," Leah said. "On the street where I live every house is different. Some are big with gorgeous landscaping. Then there's my little cottage. I think the maple tree in the front yard is bigger than my house."

"I'd like to see it sometime," Seth said before parking the van and jumping out. He went around to the back. A moment later he wheeled a large box up the Jamelsons' driveway on a dolly.

Leah leaned back in the seat and crossed her arms, watching Seth carry the large box up to the front door. *What's going on here? Why is this guy so attentive to me? He asked Kyle about me. Why? What did he mean when he said he'd like to see "it" sometime? Did he mean the maple tree or my house? Why would he want to see either of them? Who is this guy?*

Seth returned and showed Leah the next address on his clipboard. "This is the last one. The *Glenbrooke Gazette* on Main. I know how to get there. Would you like me to drop you off first, or do you have enough time to drive around with me?"

Leah was loving this. Of course she wanted to ride around with him some more. But all her suspicions had risen to the surface, and first she felt compelled to explore them. "I have the time," Leah said slowly.

"Good," Seth said.

"But I have to ask," Leah added. "Why are you doing this? I mean, first helping me at the Snack Shack last night and now this."

Seth smiled and reached for his sunglasses as they turned left and headed into the early evening sun. "I guess this isn't exactly fair to you. You see, I'm related to one of your biggest fans."

"My biggest fan? I didn't know I had any fans."

"How about Franklin Madison?" Seth flashed her a grin.

Franklin Madison and his late wife had been close friends of Leah's grandparents and lived three doors down from them. As a child, Leah took bouquets of tulips to the Madisons' every year on May Day. She used to leave the flowers in a water-filled mayonnaise jar on their front doorstep, ring the doorbell, and run and hide behind the neighbor's lilac bush.

At ninety-two, Franklin was the last living relative of Cameron Madison, who had founded Glenbrooke in the 1870s.

"You're related to Franklin Madison?" Leah scanned Seth's profile for a resemblance. He certainly didn't have Franklin's long nose and narrow chin. Seth's chin was rounded and more masculine than Franklin's was. Seth's nose was broad, but not too broad. It fit his face and was a good balance to his deep-set, dark blue eyes, which were hidden behind his sunglasses.

"Franklin is my great-uncle." Seth grinned. "Last week was the first time I've seen him in ten years. Maybe even longer. Twenty years, maybe." Seth stopped at a red light and put on his turn signal, prepared to turn onto Main Street without any direction from Leah.

"You know what?" Leah said, studying Seth's profile another moment. "I've seen your picture. Franklin has your high school graduation picture on his mantle."

"Yes, he does. I saw it there the other day," Seth said.

"And I remember Franklin talking about you, too. You're the one who went to Europe instead of going to college, aren't you?"

"I went to college," Seth said defensively. "True, I took some time off and traveled through Europe, but I returned home to Boulder; that's where I grew up. I went to the University of Colorado there. Took me five years, but I graduated."

Leah had heard so many stories about Franklin's twenty-four grandchildren and great-nephews and -nieces that she wasn't sure which of the stories were about Seth. "He may have told me that. I don't remember."

"Did he tell you I've been in Costa Rica for the past four years?"

Leah laughed aloud as she made the connection. "So you're the one! Yes, he told me all about you. He calls you the hippie boy in the rain forest."

Seth glanced at Leah and grinned slowly. "Yep, that's me. Not exactly at the top of Franklin's list of favorite people. You are, though, you know. You're right at the top of his list."

Leah ignored the comment and asked, "So what are you doing in Glenbrooke?"

Seth parked the van on Main Street in front of the *Glenbrooke Gazette*. He pulled off his sunglasses, and raising his eyebrows, he said to Leah with a sly grin, "I'm here to obtain the favor of Uncle Franklin so that when he dies he'll leave all his riches to me." With that he hopped out of the delivery van and hurried across Main Street with a large manila mailer in his hand.

Leah sat still, her eyebrows furrowed. *Was he serious? He couldn't be serious. Franklin doesn't have any riches. He lives in that old house and eats spaghetti and canned green beans. Seth had to be joking.*

Leah leaned back in the front seat of the delivery van and tried to remember what else Franklin had told her about this "hippie boy." She knew Franklin had mentioned Seth over the years because he was the only one of the clan who had done much traveling. She remembered three postcards Franklin had kept on his coffee table for several years. One was of the Austrian Alps, one of the Seine River in Paris, and one was of Venice. That was Leah's favorite. The postcard pictured a gondola docked by a red-and-white-striped pole. The gondolier, wearing a wide-brimmed straw hat with its blue ribbon hanging down the back, stood on the dock. He leaned casually against the pole and indicated with his hand that his gondola was available for the next rider.

Seth had sent those postcards.

Every time Leah had visited Franklin, she would study the cards, especially the one from Venice. And if Franklin wasn't watching, Leah would whisper to the gondolier, "Wait for me. One day I really will come ride in your gondola."

She hadn't yet made good on that promise. For years she

had dreamed of exotic travel adventures but could never pursue any such whims because of her obligation to her ailing parents.

A wash of insecurities came over Leah. If Franklin considered Seth the hippie in the rain forest, then how had Franklin spoken of her to Seth? Did Franklin consider her the matronly nurse, destined to make house calls offering charity to all the old people of Glenbrooke until she herself was too old to leave her rocking chair?

Just as she was beginning to feel overwhelmed with self-doubts, Seth returned with a grin on his face. "Kenton says hi," he said.

Leah looked out the van's windshield. She couldn't see into the front window of the newspaper office, but she could guess that Kenton Buchanan, the owner and editor of the paper was in there, watching her in the PDS van with Seth. Leah smiled and waved at the window, which, due to the sun's angle, only reflected the image of the delivery van.

"I suppose you figured out that Kenton and Kyle are brothers," Leah said. "The Buchanan boys."

"So he just told me. News travels fast around this burg, doesn't it?" Seth started the engine but kept his foot on the brake. "I asked Kyle about his dog last night, and he told me he has three puppies at home. I'm going there now to pick one. By any chance would you like to come with me?"

Leah nodded. "Sure." As long as the whole town knew she was spending her Thursday evening driving around with the new boy in town, she might as well show up at Kyle and Jessica's with him. After all, Seth had admitted he had asked Kyle about her. Why not give her friends something to speculate about? Especially since she was the one who was starting to speculate the most.

Chapter Four

After Seth dropped off the delivery van at the PDS main terminal, he and Leah climbed into his rusted Subaru station wagon and headed for Kyle and Jessica's Victorian mansion on the top of Madison Hill. Leah had lots of questions for Seth but couldn't ask them because Seth kept talking. He told her about how he had found a place to live in Edgefield, twenty miles away, and had moved in last week. He was hired for his job with PDS after answering an ad in the paper, and the car had been sitting on a used car lot a mile from his apartment, just waiting for him.

Leah still couldn't understand why he had left Costa Rica for this. She was sure that if she ever got away from Glenbrooke, Oregon, she would stay wherever she was as long as she could. Especially if it was some place as exotically romantic as Costa Rica.

"What did you do while you were in Costa Rica?"

"I worked for Real Planet Adventures. Have you ever heard of them?"

Leah shook her head.

"They run tours for young people's groups. We usually worked with high school students."

"So that explains your experience with snack lines."

"Exactly. We would take them through a three-week course: backpacking, kayaking, sometimes orienteering. We would give them a couple of matches and a bag of granola, and they would have three days to find their way out of the rain forest."

"Are you serious?"

"Maybe it wasn't exactly that severe, but you get the idea. The program was designed to develop leadership skills. The most interesting groups were the management teams sent to us by big corporations. We would have four days to build them into what the brochure called 'a harmonious team' before sending them back to the concrete jungle. Those groups were always the biggest challenge."

Leah could believe that. She could also believe that Seth had enough leadership skills to take on any group of students or corporate managers and handily shape them into a team.

So why is he delivering packages in this insignificant corner of the planet?

"Why did you leave?"

Seth glanced at her and looked surprised. It took him a moment before he said, "I turned twenty-nine last month."

Leah wasn't sure what that was supposed to mean, although it gave her a small sense of comfort to realize he was older than she was.

The grand, two-story Victorian mansion came into full view, and Seth stopped the car to take it all in before continuing up the driveway. "Wow! They sure fixed that place up. I only saw it once, when I was in eighth grade. We came to Glenbrooke for my great-aunt's funeral."

Leah hadn't gone to that funeral, but she remembered when Franklin's wife, Naomi, had passed away. She also remembered how creepy the old Madison Estate used to look when she was a child. It had been vacant since the '50s, and when Kyle and Jessica bought it almost seven years ago, it had taken months of extensive renovations before they could move in.

The gem of Madison Hill now glistened, creamy white and inviting. New life had been breathed into the old masterpiece of a house. A wide porch wrapped around the front, complete with a porch swing on the right and a set of wicker furniture on the left. Large, moss-lined baskets of Martha Washington geraniums hung at intervals across the porch's overhang. A rounded turret ran up the side of the house and was topped by a pointed spiral and a rooster weathervane. The gingerbread trim along the roofline had been repainted recently and made the house look fresh in the glow of another gorgeous spring evening.

"These Buchanans must have some money," Seth observed. "What does Kyle do when he's not coaching Little League teams?"

Leah didn't know how much to tell Seth. The truth was, the money came from Jessica. When Jessica married Kyle, she was a millionaire. However, Jessica didn't like people to know that, and she and Kyle had done a commendable job of settling in and living a fairly normal life in Glenbrooke. The initial shock and novelty of her wealth had worn off, and over the years it had become less and less of an issue to the townspeople.

"Kyle does a lot of things," Leah said. "They have some money."

Then, in an effort to redirect the conversation, she said, "I wonder why your great-uncle never moved into this mansion. You know it was built by his grandfather, Cameron Madison."

"Funny you should mention that. I asked Franklin just a few days ago." Seth slowed down as he neared the top of the driveway. "Cameron was bankrupt when he died. He put all his fortune into building this house and was so in debt by the time he died that the place was no longer his to will to anyone. I'll be honest," Seth said, parking the car. "I'm really curious to see inside."

"It's beautiful," Leah said.

The golden retriever that had been barking at them from the front porch now bounded down the steps to greet them. Travis, the Buchanans' oldest son, held open the screen door and called out, "Hi, Auntie Leah. Did you bring the eggs?"

"No, I haven't finished them yet. Are you looking forward to the big party on Saturday?"

Travis nodded and looked shyly at Seth.

"Travis, this is Seth Edwards. He's come to look at your puppies."

Travis's cherub face lit up. "I'll show them to you. They're in the laundry room."

Seth trailed behind Leah as they followed Travis into the house. Seth seemed to be taking in the hardwood floors, the spectacular staircase, and the evening sunlight coming in through the door's beveled glass. Travis led them down the hallway into the kitchen where Jessica was clearing the dinner table.

The toddler of the family, Emma, squealed with delight when she saw Leah and hopped down from her chair to run into Leah's open arms. Leah kissed her soundly on the cheek and then proceeded to tickle her madly. As Emma tossed her curls and burst into giggles, Leah tried to introduce Seth to Jessica. Fortunately, Kyle stepped in from the back room and finished the introductions.

The Buchanans' youngest, Sara, sat in her highchair and pounded her spoon on the high chair tray, demanding some attention, too.

"I wasn't ignoring you, Sara Bunny," Leah said, going over to the high chair while Emma clung to her like a baby koala bear. Leah managed to release Sara from the high chair and scooped her up, holding a happy little girl on each hip. "Do you two want to show Seth your puppies?"

"I was going to show him," Travis said, standing in the doorway of the laundry room with his hands behind his back.

"I can hear them," Seth said. "Why don't you all show me?"

Kyle, a tall, good-looking man in his mid-thirties, stayed in the kitchen and slipped his arm around his wife, Jessica. She was a gentle-spirited woman and more of a big sister to Leah than any of her own sisters had been.

Jessica rested her fair-skinned cheek against Kyle's chest. "Let us know if you guys need any help, although I doubt you will. Travis is our resident expert on the puppies."

Leah followed Travis into the large laundry room. A separate area had been sectioned off by a board that was low enough for Lady, the young mother golden retriever, to step over. Lady lay comfortably curled up on top of what looked like a flat beanbag pillow. Leah had one, too, for her dog, Hula. The pillow was filled with cedar chips and was supposed to ward off fleas.

As Seth bent down, the three beautiful bundles of vanilla fluff yelped and tumbled over each other in an effort to climb out of their box and play with the visitors.

"They're silly puppies," little Emma said.

Sara patted Leah's cheek with a sticky hand.

"They have gotten so big since I was here last!" Leah said. "Look at that one."

The largest of the three fur balls romped toward them with

a strip of bed sheet tangled around his hind leg. He took a flying leap in an effort to jump over the board barricade. He would have made it, too, if one of his siblings hadn't been sitting on the other end of the sheet, halting his escape in midair. The confused pup hung halfway over the board with the sheet still holding him by the leg.

Seth reached for the daredevil and released his hind leg from the sheet. Lifting him up for a closer look, Seth said, "You're quite a little Bungee jumper, aren't you?"

"They never could jump that far before," Travis said with concern. "Daddy, come here."

Kyle entered, and Travis told the story of the flying puppy.

"Sounds like we better find a taller board," Kyle said.

"Or send this one home with me," Seth suggested. Then, in a tender gesture that made Leah smile, Seth squatted down to eye level with Travis and said, "What do you think? Is this puppy looking for a new home?" The pup licked Seth's chin as if right on cue.

"He likes you," Travis surmised.

"I like him," Seth said.

"They're all boys," Travis said. "The two girls already got sold."

"Do you think I should buy this one?" Seth asked.

Travis seemed to ponder the question deeply but only for a moment before saying, "I think you two are good for each other."

Leah pressed her lips together so she wouldn't break into too big of a smile. She loved all three of the Buchanan children. Whenever any of them did or said something especially endearing, Leah allowed herself to get all choked up. If she couldn't have her own children, she would funnel her motherly emotions into these three pixies every chance she had.

"It's a deal," Seth said, putting out his hand for Travis to shake. They shook vigorously, and the puppy yapped his approval.

Emma covered her ears. "Stop barking," she ordered.

Leah adjusted her precious cargo and realized how heavy Emma was getting. "I have to put you down, sweetie. Auntie Leah is getting to be an old lady, and she can't hold you as long as she used to."

As Leah bent at the knees, Emma got down and went right to her daddy, who effortlessly picked her up and slipped her around to his back so that her arms were around his neck and her legs around his middle.

"What are you going to name him?" Travis asked.

Without hesitation Seth said, "Bungee. I'm going to call him Bungee."

Travis laughed and repeated, "Bungee."

Leah doubted that Travis knew what a Bungee jumper was, although it was possible. He had surprised her more than once with his keen sense of observation. It was a fun word to say, and Travis repeated it. "Bungee."

"I better take this guy home so he can get used to his new house tonight," Seth said. Looking at Kyle he added, "Is it still okay if I write the check next week?"

"No problem," Kyle said. "Whenever it's convenient for you."

"You can give the money to me," Travis said. "It's for me to go to college."

"We'll make sure it goes into your college account, son," Kyle said. Then looking at Leah he asked, "Do you want to stay for a while? Have you had dinner yet?"

"We need to get going. My car decided to have a nervous breakdown this afternoon," Leah said. "I have to call Martin to see if he can tow it over to his station tonight."

"Do you need any help?" Kyle asked.

"I think I'm okay. Seth said he could drop me off back at my car."

"That is, after we make a stop at Dairy Queen so I can repay Leah for helping me out today," Seth said.

Kyle looked at Leah and then back at Seth. "I'll tell you what's even better than a fast-food dinner. You talk Leah into making you one of her spinach casseroles, and you'll be tempted to turn into a vegetarian."

"I am a vegetarian," Seth said. "I'm only into Dairy Queen for their shakes. I'm making up for lost time during the past four years in Costa Rica. So far I've only tried three of their flavors. I'm making my way down the list."

Leah caught Kyle's eye, and she knew what he was thinking. Leah happened to know that Kyle was a Dairy Queen Blizzard aficionado as well.

"Have you tried the Oreo yet?" Kyle asked.

"Not yet," Seth said.

"And did you know that Leah is a vegetarian, too?" Kyle added.

Seth smiled at Leah as the squirming puppy tried to crawl out of his arms. "No, I didn't know that. I think Leah and I are discovering quite a few things we have in common."

To Leah's surprise, she didn't blush at his comment. For some reason it didn't embarrass her. She felt natural standing here with Kyle and Seth and hearing Seth say such a thing. It was as if the two of them were long-lost classmates, getting caught up at an impromptu reunion. Seth was connected to Glenbrooke in a unique way: He was related to the man who had built the house they were standing in.

"If you're free on Saturday, Seth, you're welcome to come for our Easter egg hunt," Kyle said.

"And bring Bungee," Travis said, patting the puppy on the head. "He might want to visit his mommy."

"Will do," Seth said.

"We can go out the back here," Leah suggested, pointing to the screen door. It led to the back deck where Seth stopped to admire the sprawling backyard lawn bordered by ancient evergreens and cedars.

"You have a beautiful home," Seth said to Kyle. "It's really something, the way you've fixed it up."

"When you come back on Saturday we'll give you the grand tour," Kyle said, putting down Emma and taking Sara from Leah. Neither of the little girls liked being displaced, and both put up a fuss.

"I'll see you real soon," Leah said, blowing the girls a kiss. She and Seth left side by side.

"What should we do first?" Seth asked. "Eat, or take care of your car?"

"Either one. You pick." At that moment, Leah didn't care. She felt as if her wish upon Pluto or Venus was coming true. She was in the company of a charming man, and he happened to have a puppy under his arm.

Chapter Five

*I*t does your heart good to see a real family like that, doesn't it?" Seth said, as the two of them got back in his car. "Mom, Dad, 2.5 kids, and a couple of dogs, living the American dream. I noticed they even had a hammock in the backyard."

"You didn't see a lot of those in Costa Rica?" Leah asked, holding Bungee on her lap.

"What, families or hammocks?"

"Either. Both."

"I saw very few families because of the kind of organization I was with. And I spied a few hammocks here and there. But I never had one I could call my own."

"And that's what you came to Glenbrooke for? A hammock of your own?" Leah asked, still trying to obtain a clearer under-standing of why a man who had the world at his feet would give it up to move to Glenbrooke of all places.

Seth grinned as he headed down the driveway. Once again he avoided Leah's pointed question. Bungee sunk his pointed teeth into Leah's hand, and she pulled away with a cry. "Hey, no biting, Bungee."

"We can put him on the floor in the back, if you'd like," Seth suggested.

"No, he's okay," Leah said. "He's going to have to learn his manners sooner or later."

"Not necessarily at your expense." Seth stopped the car at the end of the driveway. He reached over and took Leah's hand in his, pulling it closer for an examination of the teeth marks. Leah noticed how rough and worn Seth's hands felt. She was used to holding hands with little girls and elderly friends. Compared to them, her hands always felt like the rough, dry, overworked ones. As they were cradled now in Seth's hand, she actually felt feminine. The sensation surprised her, and she pulled away.

"It's okay," she said. "Why don't we take care of my car first." She really didn't want her time with Seth to end, and she wasn't sure why she had suggested dealing with the car rather than eating.

Seth took her request to heart and drove toward Fourth Avenue. Silence nestled down between them for a full two minutes, and Leah didn't like it. She had enjoyed the way they had chatted freely. *I was too abrupt, pulling away like that. Why did I do that?*

"Or," Leah suggested tentatively, "we can swing by my place. I just happen to have a spinach casserole in the freezer. I could put it in the oven while we get my car, then we could eat at my home afterward."

"Sounds like a plan. Tell me how to get there," Seth said.

Leah directed him into one of Glenbrooke's older neighborhoods, less than half a mile from where she had left her car. They pulled up in front, and Seth said, "This is your house?"

Leah nodded and tried to evaluate her quaint bungalow from Seth's point of view. The house had a steep roof with a brick chimney that ran up the left side. The chimney was painted white, like the rest of the house. The front door was rounded at the top and had a leaded, stained glass window in the upper section. She had found the stained glass, which depicted a pale blue morning glory, at an estate sale and had it fitted into a new front door when she moved in almost six months ago. Her small front yard had been mowed recently, but she hadn't planted a lot of flowers or bedding plants yet. Two overgrown azalea bushes stood to the right of the front door like a pair of matronly sisters, heads bent close, sharing a bit of juicy gossip. They were both budding and about to cast a spray of white blossoms across their four-foot-wide bosoms.

"You're right," Seth said, eyeing the maple tree's trunk. "That tree is almost larger than your house."

"I might need to get it trimmed back one of these days."

"Great house!" Seth said.

"It needs a lot of work still." Leah thought of the long row of self-sticking notes on her refrigerator that listed all she planned to do to make her property and home look better. She had focused her efforts over the past few months inside, including installing a dishwasher, which she had managed by herself with no problem. "And it's really small inside. It wasn't as nice looking when I bought it. It was gray with a red-brick chimney, and the front door was painted red."

"Nice choice on the color and the new door. I envy your being a home owner."

"It's not all that great when you need a plumber in the middle of the night."

Seth laughed and opened his door. "Do you want me to leave Bungee in the car?"

"Of course not," Leah said, scooping him up. "He has to come in and meet my dog, Hula."

"Hula?" Seth asked as he took Bungee off Leah's hands. "Named after an exotic Hawaiian vacation?"

Leah opened her front door without a key.

"You don't lock your door?" Seth asked, stunned.

"Sometimes. I left it open today because my friend Lauren was coming over this morning to pick up some of the eggs for the Easter egg hunt Saturday. I volunteered to decorate more than I could handle."

Leah led Seth through a narrow entryway into a small kitchen. On the tile counter sat fifty hard-boiled eggs in their cartons, waiting to be decorated. Leah had left a note for Lauren on top of the first dozen.

"Looks like Lauren didn't make it over here." Leah turned to Seth, and with a cunning grin she said, "So, how do you feel about dyeing a couple dozen eggs tonight?"

Seth was examining her ceiling. "Did you put in the skylight? It looks new."

"Yes," Leah said looking up. "It was too dark in here. I put in the ceiling fan, too. It can get hot here in the summer." She reached over and stroked Bungee behind the ears. He was gnawing on Seth's thumb. "Do you want to meet Hula?"

"Of course."

Leah led Seth and Bungee only a few feet to a door off the kitchen.

"You keep her in the pantry?"

"This isn't a pantry," Leah said. "This is something I think you only find in old houses in the Northwest. It's a mudroom." She opened the door into a small room with a linoleum floor, a deep sink, and a metal baker's rack stacked with gardening pots and tools. A doggy door opened to cement steps that led to the backyard. Hula wasn't in the mudroom.

"She must be in the backyard," Leah said, opening the door and stepping outside. Hula had positioned herself comfortably at the bottom of the steps, basking in the last bit of sunlight that spilled through the gap between two large trees in the neighbor's yard.

"Hi, girl," Leah said as Hula slowly rose and came to check out the puppy in Seth's arms. "This is Bungee. What do you think?"

"Your yard isn't fenced, I see," Seth said. "I better not put Bungee down, or we might end up chasing him all over the neighborhood."

"He can stay in the mudroom, and we can put a board over the doggy door, if you want to leave him here. You don't mind, do you, Hula?"

Hula returned to her corner of sunlight as if to register her apathy.

"I'll stick the casserole in the oven and set the timer," Leah said. "I'll also call Martin to see if he can meet us at the car with his tow truck."

Leah made her call and placed the homemade spinach casserole in her not-so-clean oven while Seth situated Bungee in the mudroom.

"All set?" Leah asked, hanging up the phone.

"All set," Seth replied. He had washed his face, and a few beads of water still clung to his eyelashes.

"All I have in the mudroom are paper towels," Leah said apologetically. "Did you want a hand towel?"

"No, I'm fine. I like your house. It's really nice."

"You've just seen half of it. The clean half."

"Only one bedroom?"

"Yes," Leah said.

"I had hoped to get into a little house like this," Seth said as they made their way back to his car. "I had to settle for an apartment in Edgefield, at least for the time being."

"You're really set on the supposedly 'normal,' Middle-American lifestyle, aren't you?"

Seth closed the car door behind him and gave her a puzzled look. "Why does that keep surprising you?"

"Because," Leah spouted, shutting her door hard for emphasis. "It's so uneventful here."

"Costa Rica can be uneventful, too. So can Sweden. It's not the place; it's the people."

"Well, this is all I've ever known. I would think that someone who has been to Europe and who has camped out in a tropical rain forest would find all this pretty blasé."

"If you're seventeen, maybe," Seth said, starting the car. "That's why I left the U.S. at that ripe, know-it-all age. I spent my senior year of high school as an exchange student in Sweden. Later I backpacked through Europe as far south as Greece."

"And you saw the Alps and Paris and Venice," Leah said.

Seth turned and gave her a humored expression as if Leah's three stated locations were all good guesses. "Yes, I saw a lot of Europe. A lot of wonderful places. And I met a lot of fascinating people. But I returned to the U.S. for college. That's when I lived in Boulder. For the last four years 'home' has been a Quonset hut with a wide variety of roommates who have no idea what the terms 'privacy' and 'lights out' mean."

"Turn right at this corner," Leah said, motioning for him to keep talking.

"I've never had a place of my own, the way you do. I looked around one day and realized the incoming staff kept getting younger and younger. I was the oldest staff member except for Keegan and Marabella, who ran the program. And they're settled in for the long haul. They have their own cabin. They even have their own hammock."

Seth pulled up in front of Ida's house where Leah's car was parked.

"So you came to America in search of your own cabin and hammock," Leah surmised.

"Something like that."

"Boy, are we ever different," Leah said, leaning against her door. "Ever since I was fourteen I've dreamed of going places and seeing things. What I wouldn't give to live in a Quonset hut or hike the Alps or go dancing in the streets of a Greek fishing village."

Seth laughed. "It's not all like the movies."

Leah returned his smile. He had such a nice smile. "I know. But I always wanted to see for myself that it wasn't like the movies, you know?"

"Why didn't you?"

Leah looked down. She wanted to answer with the phrase that filled her mind at that moment and to admit to him what he obviously hadn't figured out yet. She wanted to say, "Because, behold, I'm Leah." That phrase had been enough to determine her destiny.

But Seth didn't know that. He didn't act as if her options were limited.

Leah lifted her head, and with a fresh breath of hope, she answered, "You know, maybe I will someday soon."

Chapter Six

$\mathcal{M}$artin showed up with his tow truck before Seth could comment on Leah's statement, but that didn't matter. She felt brave and strong for having said what she did. And she meant it, too. Maybe she would take off and see the world someday. The freedom the very thought gave her was exhilarating.

Leah found it hard to keep from smiling as Martin checked under the hood for possible problems. At this moment she felt she didn't need a car to take her anywhere. She had something better. She had hope. And hope could take her places she hadn't been in a long time.

How strange that hope should have returned to my life after such a long, cold season of silence.

Leah glanced at Seth. He and Martin were engrossed in examining her car's engine. When Martin said he didn't see anything obvious that could cause the problem, he hooked up her Blazer to his tow truck and promised to have a look at it first thing in the morning.

Seth drove Leah home, but before they entered her front door, they could hear Bungee barking from the mudroom. They hurried to rescue the forlorn pup and remove the board from the doggie door so Hula could get in and have her dinner. Poor Hula looked offended that Leah had locked her out but had allowed the little pip-squeak to take over her domain.

Seth comforted Bungee in his arms while Leah checked on the spinach. The oven was turned off. "Oh no, don't tell me my oven is breaking down, too."

"Hey, I think your friend came by and took some of the eggs while we were gone," Seth said, nodding at the kitchen counter.

Leah noticed that half the eggs were gone. A note from Lauren replaced the note Leah had left on the counter. It read,

Sorry it took me all day to get over here. Molly Sue had her two-year-old checkup at the doctor's this afternoon. I turned off your oven because it smelled like something was burning. Hope I didn't ruin your dinner. See you tomorrow night at the Good Friday service.

   xoxox Wren

Leah checked the frozen state of the spinach and reset the oven. "Looks like it'll take another half an hour. Can your stomach wait that long?"

"You know, I was thinking I should probably head home and get this guy settled." Seth seemed to have turned self-conscious. He looked at the clock and then at Bungee in his arms. "I need to stop by the store on the way home and buy a few necessities for him. Thanks for the offer on dinner. Maybe another time."

Leah felt as if she was being rejected even though Seth

hadn't overtly indicated that. *What happened to my burst of hope? Where did those restored dreams fly off to without me?*

She felt the old, junky emotions rise to the surface. Familiar old thoughts. It was hard to make them go away.

"Let me ask you something," Seth said, hesitating on his way to the front door.

Leah's spirits rose. "Yes?"

"Do I turn right at the end of your street to get back to Main?"

"Yes, right at the corner."

"Thanks," he said. And then he was gone.

She stood silently for a few minutes, fighting back the disappointment. She had come so close to experiencing what she had longed for, the start of a new and rather promising friendship. But he left. Right on cue.

Did I sabotage the whole thing by continually asking why he had moved here? Why did I pull away when he took my hand? Why did he leave? Would he have stayed if I hadn't been so pushy?

Leah gave up on the spinach and settled for a Little League frozen bean burrito. She leaned against the kitchen counter trying to remember what Brad, one of her friends, had told her last summer when she went to him for counseling. She had slumped into a state of depression when her parents' house wasn't selling. The house she had wanted to buy was sold before she could make an offer, and nothing seemed to be moving forward in her life.

Brad had told her, "Blocked goals lead to anger, and blocked anger leads to depression. Readjust your goals and find healthy ways to express your anger or you're going to be one depressed little chickadee."

Brad's counseling methods weren't always conventional, but his words had helped her. She readjusted her goals regarding the house, and she confided her anger and frustration to Jessica, who listened without offering any advice other than "Let's pray about this some more together." Every Monday evening for four months, Leah had met with Jessica, and they prayed together.

Now Leah could look back and see how God had worked out everything better than her original plans. Her parents' house sold for less than she had hoped, but her sisters had had a change of heart and agreed Leah should have all the profit from the house's sale. The amount had been enough to buy this house outright, which meant she had no monthly mortgage payment. The house that fell through was twice the size and twice the price. If she had ended up with that other house, she would have been paying on it for at least fifteen years.

Leah had to admit God had been good to her. That didn't mean she was ready to trust him completely, though. Over the past few years it had become safer to keep God nearby but at a bit of a distance. She was one of his children. She knew that. She also knew she wasn't one of his favorites. It was best not to bother him too much but to take care of matters herself as much as possible.

With that in mind, Leah wondered if she should readjust her goals again.

Should I plan a trip to Europe? I don't exactly have enough money at the moment. I could start a special savings account and try to put away two hundred dollars a month. In six months I'd have… No, I'd have to put away more than that!

Leah set to work dyeing her mound of Easter eggs since she did her best thinking when she was busy on a project. She knew she didn't want to take off for Europe by herself; it would be much more fun to go with a friend.

But who?

Leaning against the counter with an egg in each hand, Leah

said to herself, "Go ahead; be honest. The only friendship you're interested in developing right now is with Seth Edwards. And you have no idea if he feels the same way."

In an effort to readjust some of her goals, Leah began to formulate a plan. First she decided she would make Seth feel welcomed in Glenbrooke by throwing a party at her home in his honor. Next she would make some cookies this weekend and surprise him at work on Monday.

Before she went to bed, Leah had a long mental list of wonderful things she could do for Seth. Giving was what Leah did best. It delighted her to fall asleep thinking of all the creative ways she could give to Seth.

The next morning, Leah caught a ride to work with her coworker, Mary. Mary showed up at 7:15 with a box of donuts on the passenger's seat. "Do you mind holding those?"

"Only if I can eat one on the way," Leah said.

"Sure. They're for the lunchroom. They're left over from my son's band performance at high school last night. What's wrong with your car?"

"Who knows?"

"Have you had your review yet?" Mary asked.

"No, I think I'm scheduled for next week."

"I had mine yesterday. No raise. The wage freeze is remaining in effect for another six months. I'm so upset I could spit! How do they expect us to keep up with the cost of living?"

Leah nodded but was glad she had a bite of old-fashioned buttermilk donut in her mouth. She didn't find her salary a hardship. She knew it had to be harder for Mary, who was trying to raise three teenagers by herself.

They were a block from the hospital when Leah spotted a PDS van. She perked up and leaned forward, trying to see who was driving.

"What are you looking for?" Mary asked.

"Oh, I just wondered if that was Harry," Leah said. The van turned in front of them. It was Harry, not Seth. Leah waved, and Harry waved back. "Nice guy, that Harry," Leah said awkwardly.

Mary gave her a strange look.

When Leah reached her desk, a note was waiting for her from Martin. She called him, and he said he had no idea what the problem had been the day before. The car started up for him on the first try, and everything checked out fine.

He told her to swing by after work to pick it up, which she did. After getting her car, Leah drove out to the PDS station and asked if Seth was around. One of the guys told her he was still on his route. She waited for half an hour and then left a note on his car's windshield since she knew she had better get going. The note read:

> Hi, Seth.
> I just stopped by to say thanks for giving me a ride last night and to tell you my car is working fine now. As I see it, I still owe you dinner as a way of thanking you.
>   Leah

She stopped at home for a few minutes and then hurried on to church. It was Good Friday, and the special communion service was scheduled to begin at seven o'clock. However, Leah wasn't going to the communion service. She was working in the church nursery, as she did every Sunday. Several years ago, Leah had discovered the nursery was a safe place. She could keep going to church but didn't have to participate in the service, which only reminded her how distant she felt from God.

When Leah arrived, Jessica already was in the toddler nursery changing Sara's diaper. Leah told Jessica how the Blazer had refused to go last night but was running perfectly now.

Jessica stopped her task at hand and gave Leah a wide grin. "Do you know what I think?"

"No, what?"

"I think your guardian angel dislocated some wires just long enough for you to have to go around town with Seth."

Leah laughed. "Do you really believe that?"

"Why not? You remember Teri Allistar, don't you?"

"She used to be Teri Moreno, right?"

"Yes."

"Of course I remember her," Leah said. "She was my Spanish teacher my senior year. Is she still in Hawaii with her husband? What was his name?"

"Gordon. Yes, they're still in Hawaii. He pastors a church there."

"Oh, yes, Gordon. I liked him. He was a good match for her."

"I think so, too. She and Gordon and the boys are doing great. Teri was the first friend I made when I moved here," Jessica said. "She used to call unexplainable circumstances such as your experience with your car 'pockets of grace.' We don't control them. We just fall into them, and God catches us and directs us in ways we never imagined."

Leah had been raised with the philosophy that God helped those who helped themselves. She tended to be leery of the inexplicable being credited to angels or labeled miracles. "I think the car problem was a fluke, and it turned out okay. A loose wire or clogged something. I'm sure it was nothing more than that."

"I used to think that, too," Jessica said, finishing up with Sara and letting her crawl over to the play kitchen where Emma was making pies. "When I came to know the Lord, I started to see all those coincidences actually were his interventions. His 'pockets of grace.' I know now that he was doing those things to get me to turn to him and trust him. I remember one time, right after I moved to Glenbrooke, I came home and found groceries on my front doorstep."

Leah looked away, pretending to flick a speck of lint from her shirtsleeve. *That was my first secret delivery! I've never heard Jessica mention it before. She doesn't know I was the one who left the groceries, does she? Nah, she couldn't have known.*

"And in the bag," Jessica continued, "was a box of Dove ice cream bars. I love Dove bars. Nobody in Glenbrooke knew that."

Leah remembered how she had stood by the freezer section with the grocery cart already full with everything she thought this new teacher in town might need. Leah, who had worked as a volunteer at the hospital before being hired full-time, had been there the day Jessica was brought in after being run off the road by a logging truck. Leah still didn't know why she had progressed from May Day bouquets on Mr. Madison's porch to buying groceries. But she did know she had felt compelled to buy the Dove bars even though she didn't think she had enough money and was afraid the bars would melt. She had headed toward the checkout stand and then went back, returned the large package of peanut butter cookies, and bought the Dove bars instead. Leah remembered it all like it was yesterday.

"Teri was with me that afternoon," Jessica went on. "That's when she told me about God's pockets of grace. I know those groceries were a gift from God; his own little miracle to me because no one knew it, but I had no money and absolutely no food."

"You're kidding." Leah felt goosebumps run up her arms.

"No." Jessica shook her head and lowered her voice. "You know how I told you I left home secretly when I moved to Glenbrooke? I didn't have enough money with me, and I couldn't get any more until my first paycheck. For more than a week I lived on this giant zucchini from the garden and some noodles I found in the cupboard, left by whoever lived in the house before me."

All these years Leah had felt so foolish for taking groceries to Jessica after finding out how wealthy Jessica was. Now Leah felt as if she simply had been a delivery person for God. She leaned against the counter, stunned at the insight.

"Pride can make a person do very stupid things," Jessica said softly.

Leah could hardly move. Maybe a greater plan really was unfolding in people's lives. In *her* life. Why else would she have felt so compelled to give the groceries to Jessica and especially to go back and pick up the Dove bars? Leah wanted to blurt out that she had been the one God had used to cushion that little pocket of grace in Jessica's life. But it was better this way. Jessica didn't need to know.

A mother with two toddlers showed up at the nursery's half-door and greeted Jessica and Leah. Jessica gave Leah's arm a squeeze and rose to receive the toddlers. She said, "Trust me on this one, Leah. The car problem yesterday could have been orchestrated by God. I'm not saying that's how it was for sure, but just consider the possibility and be thankful."

"Thankful," Leah repeated under her breath.

For the next hour, Leah did what she loved to do. She played with the youngest citizens of Glenbrooke and let their innocence and whimsy fill her emotional well. Ever since Seth Edwards had walked into the Snack Shack two nights ago, Leah had felt as if her life was changing. Her routine was the same, but she wasn't the same. She was changing.

Maybe Jessica is right. Maybe I've just fallen into a pocket of God's grace. If I have, I don't think I want to get out.

Chapter Seven

The Good Friday service lasted an hour, and the parents came for their toddlers right away. Leah was almost finished cleaning up when she heard a voice at the open door say, "So here you are."

She turned to see Seth standing there in khaki slacks and a light blue oxford shirt with a button-down collar. He smiled at her, and she smiled back. Leah felt as if everything else around her blurred like the pastel background of a Monet painting. All that stayed in focus was Seth's clean-shaven face and his steady smile.

"I thought that was your car I saw in the parking lot," Seth said. "What was the problem with it?"

Leah couldn't stop smiling, thinking of Jessica's explanation. "Apparently it's a little miracle. It's running fine now."

"That's good," Seth said. "I got your note. You don't have to thank me. I was glad to help out. Anytime. Really."

Leah put down the basket of toys and walked over to Seth.

"I had an idea last night. I thought it would be fun to throw a welcome party for you. Nothing fancy. Just a little get-together at my house so you can meet other people from Glenbrooke."

"I don't know," Seth said. "I'm not big on social events. I appreciate the thought, but no thanks."

"Oh," Leah said, feeling a surge of rejection rising inside.

Seth leaned closer and said, "Actually, I was going to ask you something. This may be short notice, but do you have any plans for Easter Sunday?"

"I'll be here," Leah said. "I'm watching the toddlers."

"I mean early Easter Sunday. Sunrise, to be exact. The last few years in Costa Rica I went on a sunrise hike to the top of this hill behind our camp. I thought I'd try to keep up the tradition."

"Sounds great," Leah said. "I love to hike. When and where?"

"I was hoping you could help me figure out where."

Leah thought. "Only two hills are around here. Madison Hill, where Kyle and Jessica live. And a hill at the end of Camp Heather Brook. No one ever goes there, but I would guess some old logging roads lead at least partway up."

"Sounds like exactly what I was looking for. I knew you would know where to go."

"I could fix a picnic breakfast," Leah suggested. "Do you have any preference of what you like to eat?"

"You don't have to bring anything."

"You sure?"

"Yes. I'll pick you up nice and early. How does four sound?"

"Early," Leah said.

"I'll find a map, and we'll figure out how to get up that hill."

"We can ask Shelly and Jonathan," Leah said, gathering up a basket of plastic toys. She planned to take them home to wash and then bring them back Sunday. "The hill overlooks their camp property."

"Okay." Then with a grin he added, "I knew you would be interested in an adventure like this."

"Why do you say that?" She stopped and looked at him.

He came closer. "My great-uncle told me you have the makings of an Amelia Earhart."

"He said that?"

Seth nodded.

Leah turned out the lights and closed the door. Seth walked with her to her car.

"Amelia, huh? That's interesting. What else did Franklin tell you?"

"He said you visit him about once a month and that you've been doing that for years."

Leah unlocked the back and shoved in the basket of toys. "I like Franklin. He has the spirit of a twenty-year-old."

Seth leaned against the Blazer and looked at her curiously. "So what's in it for you?"

"What do you mean?"

"Why are you in Glenbrooke serving Sno-Kones and visiting old people and running the church nursery? Why aren't you flying off to parts unknown?"

Leah looked down at her hands. Her weathered, always busy, giving hands that never had experienced a manicure. "It's kind of a long story, Seth." This was the first time she had said his name aloud to him, and it warmed her to hear the way it sounded coming from her lips.

"I'm not doing anything the rest of the evening," Seth said. "Do you still need help to decorate those eggs?"

"No, the eggs are finished. But you're welcome to come over, if you would like."

"Yes, I'd like that."

"Do you want to follow me? Or do you remember how to get there?"

"I'd better follow just to be sure."

Leah climbed into her Blazer and subtly checked her reflection in the rearview mirror. Her cheeks weren't flushed red. She looked calm. She felt calm. This all seemed so natural. Did it really matter that Seth had left in a rush the night before? He was back. She didn't have to throw parties or bake cookies for him. Seth Edwards was pursuing her. This was nice. No, more than nice. It was amazing.

When they reached her house, Seth asked, "Are you a tea drinker or a coffee drinker?"

"It depends," Leah said. "If I make the coffee, I'm a coffee drinker. I usually don't care for other people's coffee. I like it darker and stronger than most people."

"It's never too strong for me. In Costa Rica, we used to brew true java—I don't know where we got those coffee beans, but they were the best. Where do you keep your coffee? I'll make you a cup 'Rica' style."

Leah opened the cupboard next to the oven and displayed her collection of coffee paraphernalia.

"Grinder, natural unbleached filters, perfect," Seth said, taking inventory. "Are these your bags of beans here? You look like you're running low."

"I don't drink that much coffee. It seems pointless to buy a lot that will sit for months. I'd rather buy the beans fresh every few weeks. You'll find a bag of decaf and a bag of regular in there. Which do you want?"

"Leaded, of course," Seth said. "I want to hear your whole story."

Leah smiled. "I don't think it's going drag on into the middle of the night."

"I'll be ready, just in case." Seth went to work preparing his gourmet coffee while Leah checked on Hula in the mudroom. She contentedly wagged her tail when Leah entered.

"You need some more water, girl," Leah said, filling the bowl. Then she went out the back door to her car and brought in the basket of toys so she could soak them in the basin sink.

Returning to the kitchen, she found Seth loading her dishwasher. "You don't have to do that. Come on, let's sit down in the other room. Is the coffee ready?"

The coffee was not only ready, but it also was the best Leah had tasted in a long time. "What did you do to make this so good?"

"Nothing special," he said. "You had good beans to work with."

At first Leah thought he said "good genes," and her sister's comment about her having "neither the frame nor frame of mind to attract a stable man" sprang to her mind. If she had good genes, then she would have inherited the "right frames," the ones her sisters had all inherited. Despite all that, she seemed to have attracted someone. A very appealing someone. He didn't have to be here, making coffee for her, loading her dishwasher, and inviting her to accompany him on sunrise hikes. She had done nothing to coerce or lure him.

Leah leaned back as Seth made himself comfortable on her denim blue loveseat. Actually, it was her parents' old avocado green loveseat, which had sat in the upstairs guestroom of their house and had very few visitors. Since it was such a sturdy piece of furniture, Leah had covered it with a denim slipcover that matched the blue in her recliner. It was the only furniture she had room for in her small sitting area, but it was all she needed. Instead of a coffee table, she had stacked two old brown suitcases she had found at a garage sale. The one on top still had the original antique travel stickers affixed and in good condition.

"Cairo," Seth said, reading the sticker nearest him before placing his coffee cup on a coaster on top of the suitcase. "Now there's a place I'd like to go someday."

"Me, too," Leah said.

"Where else would you like to go?"

"Anywhere."

"Tell me why you never took off with your Amelia spirit and left Glenbrooke behind."

Briefly, Leah told him about being the youngest of six daughters and how she ended up being the one to stay home and care for her parents.

"How did you finish college?" Seth asked.

"It took me seven years. All part-time. Driving back and forth to Edgefield. But that's the only place I went. Edgefield. Not Paris. Not…what is that one?" she said, tilting her head and reading the stickers. "Roma."

"Your parents have been gone a year, right?"

Leah nodded and sipped her coffee.

"Why don't you go to Rome now?"

"I don't know," she said after a pause. "I might go. Later. Not right away. I bought this house, and I have all kinds of commitments and obligations here. I don't think it's my turn to leave Glenbrooke."

"Or do you mean it's not your turn to leave Bedford Falls?"

Leah gave him a quizzical look. "Bedford Falls?"

"You know, in *It's a Wonderful Life.* Jimmy Stewart. Donna Reed. You sound to me like the female version of George Bailey."

It took Leah a moment to make the connection. When she did, she laughed. "You think I sound like George Bailey?"

"A little."

Leah shook her head. "I'm not that discouraged about my life in this small town. Just don't try telling me you're really my guardian angel, and I'm your ticket to a pair of wings."

Seth laughed. "I don't hear any bells ringing, do you?"

Leah laughed with him and felt captivated by the man sitting on her couch. Did he have any idea that *he* was the reason she wanted to stick around Glenbrooke?

Seth reached for his coffee cup and said, "I have a question for you."

"Yes?" Leah felt open and unguarded.

"Tell me about the Glenbrooke Zorro."

Chapter Eight

"The Glenbrooke Zorro?'" Leah repeated. "What about the Glenbrooke Zorro? I mean, what have you heard?"

"I've heard someone in town loves to give. And that some-one is generous and random and—" he leaned forward for emphasis—"has managed to keep his or her identity a secret for many years."

"That's what I've heard, too," Leah said, pulling her coffee cup to her lips. She downed the last sip and stood up. "Is there more coffee?"

"Let me get it for you," Seth offered. "Would you like me to fix it the same as the first cup?"

"Yes," Leah said, fidgeting in her chair. All her happy, secure feelings had flown.

What is this man doing in my house? What does he want? It's one thing for me to entertain the thought of an innocent little crush on him. But it's something else for him to pry into my personal life.

Leah couldn't sit still. Hopping up, she joined Seth in the

kitchen. "I feel funny having you serve me. Why don't I get that?"

Seth was pouring the thick, dark brew into her cup. "Is it hard for you to let other people serve you?" he asked without looking at her.

"No," she answered immediately. "It's just that you're my guest. I should be serving you."

"All done," he said, holding a mug in each hand and heading back into the other room. "Come on."

"Would you like to watch a movie?" Leah asked, trying to sound casual.

"I'd rather talk. I want to hear your take on the Glenbrooke Zorro."

Leah sat down on the loveseat this time, thinking Seth would take the recliner. Instead he sat on the loveseat with her. She didn't know how she could feel so at ease with Seth one minute and so uncomfortable the next.

Sipping the fragrant brew and drawing up her courage, Leah decided she had no reason to be nervous. This was her house, her couch, her good coffee beans. This was her life he had stepped into, uninvited. She didn't have to make room for him. She could, should, and would stand her ground.

"Look," Leah said, "you obviously have a point you want to make. Go ahead and make it."

Seth looked surprised. But not too surprised. "Okay, here's my point. I think you are the Glenbrooke Zorro."

Leah looked at her coffee cup and ran her finger around the white ceramic mug's rim. She had met her match when it came to standing her ground. Lifting her eyes to meet his, she said, "Why do you say that?"

"Oh, no. Uh-uh. No," he said, shaking his head and giving her a subdued smile. "If I can't be coy with you, you can't be coy with me. Come on, George. Level with me."

"George?" she repeated. As soon as she said it, she realized he was making reference to their George Bailey-Wonderful Life conversation. *Did he just give me a nickname?*

The small gesture warmed Leah in an unexpected way. While she was growing up, she always wanted her dad to give her a nickname to prove his affection. She thought a boy's name would be the best because then she would know he had come to consider her equal to the son she should have been. But her father only called her Leah. Everyone only called her Leah. She didn't even have a middle name.

"You're the Glenbrooke Zorro, aren't you?" Seth pressed her again.

Leah impulsively decided to risk everything for the sake of being honest with this man. "Yes, I am."

Seth slapped his knee. "I thought so! I was almost positive."

"Why?" Leah asked. "Why do you even need to know? What does it matter?" It struck her that she had just confessed to him something she had never told anyone. Was this level of vulnerability the price she had to pay for a relationship with someone "stable"?

I don't know if I'm ready for this.

"Some guys were talking about it at work today. One of them said his sister just had a baby, and her husband had surgery a few days later. He said someone left groceries for them on their doorstep and that the Glenbrooke Zorro was back. That's when they gave me the history on this invisible superhero. Or should I say superheroine?"

Leah felt as if Seth, who was practically a stranger, had just run in and stolen something vital to the core of her identity. Her secret deliveries all these years had been her one private, silent source of delight. The secrecy allowed her to feel that even though she was only a "Leah" she could do noble things.

This is my secret. What is he doing sharing my secret?

"You probably feel pretty proud of yourself, don't you?" Leah said, pulling back and crossing her legs in the other direction to put a definite distance between them.

"Why?"

"Because no one else has figured it out. You come to town, and three days later," she snapped her fingers for emphasis, "you solve the mystery." Leah crossed her arms and gave him an angry look, which was not completely in jest.

"Oh, come on," Seth said, playfully tagging her shoulder. "Do you mean to tell me that no one has ever challenged the identity of this anonymous gift-giver?"

Leah shrugged. "I don't know."

Seth sat back and in a more serious tone said, "You know what? Your secret is safe with me. I promise I won't tell anyone."

Leah tried to relax. This was what she wanted: a close friendship with someone she could trust, someone with whom she could be open and honest. If self-disclosure and vulnerability were the price she had to pay, maybe it was a fair price.

"About a year ago," Leah began, leaning back, "Kenton at the *Glenbrooke Gazette* wrote an editorial. He was the one who used the term, 'Glenbrooke Zorro.'"

"Is that right?"

Leah nodded.

"And how did people react?"

"Everyone was talking about it and coming up with all these ridiculous speculations as to whom the Glenbrooke Zorro could be. I felt like telling some of the people at work that it was me, just so they would stop with the dumb guesses. I don't know if they would have believed me. Your great-uncle was one of the candidates. They said Franklin inherited a fortune from Cameron Madison and used his riches to help others."

"Was that in the paper?" Seth said, leaning forward.

"No, it was just what people said at work and at the grocery store. You and I both know your great-uncle is far from wealthy."

"Right," Seth said quickly.

"It was terrible around work and church for a couple of weeks," Leah continued. "Everyone assumed the phantom was a male. And then people started writing letters to the editor. You wouldn't have believed it. Actually, I kept some of the letters." Leah rose and went over to a bookshelf in the corner and picked up a photo box. She pulled out a few pictures and some newspaper clippings.

"Look at this one."

Seth read it aloud. "Dear Glenbrooke Zorro, Please bring me $447 so I can have my terrible leaking kitchen sink fixed. It keeps me awake at night."

He looked up. "Did you give her the $447?"

"No, I didn't do anything. I found out later that a guy from our church went over and fixed it for her for free."

"Cool," Seth said with a smile. "What's this one?" He read another newspaper clipping. "Dear Glenbrooke Zorro, I am a fifty-two-year-old gentleman through and through. I'm hoping you can send me a new wife." Seth burst out laughing.

Leah pointed to the clipping. "Read the rest of it."

"She must be a nonsmoker who likes to cook and do crossword puzzles. My preferences on height are over 5'6"; weight, under 130 pounds; brown hair and green eyes. No visible scars and no pets. Please have her contact me at the P.O. box number listed below. With appreciation, Mr. X."

Seth shook his head. "Mr. X. Now there's a real clever guy for you. Did he get his ideal wife?"

"Who knows!" Leah said. "I had nothing to do with it. I'm not Santa Claus. Or the Tooth Fairy. I'm not even Zorro! Wasn't Zorro a sword fighter? What does that have to do with giving?"

"What happened with all these letters?" Seth asked.

"I guess when none of their expectations from the Glenbrooke Zorro were fulfilled, they gave up. The letters to the editor dropped off after about two weeks."

"But you went back to giving."

"Eventually."

"May I make an observation here?" Seth asked.

Leah laughed. "As opposed to keeping your opinion to yourself as you've been doing the rest of this evening?"

Seth gave an open-armed shrug. "What can I say? I tend to be opinionated."

"Oh, really?"

"And it's my opinion that you have the gift of giving. Or maybe the gift of service. It's definitely a spiritual gift when you feel compelled to continue even though it isn't as easy or as uncomplicated as when you started."

Leah asked Seth what his spiritual gift was and that prompted a discussion on their spiritual journeys for the next hour. Leah found that she and Seth had similar backgrounds. Both of them were raised going to church and made decisions to ask Jesus into their hearts when they were in grade school. Seth described himself as being in a growing season in his relationship with the Lord. He paused, looking at Leah gently, as if waiting for her to express her view of her current walk with Christ.

"For me, everything with God has been the same for a long time," Leah said. "He's there, I'm here. I don't ask much of him. He doesn't seem to be asking too much of me. I think everything is okay." She didn't elaborate. She didn't need to. Seth was, in every way, right there with her.

"I'll tell you something," Seth said. "We all go through different seasons in relationships. Including our relationship with God. Things are rarely what we imagine them to be; our understanding is too limited."

Leah nodded.

"I say that because you definitely weren't what I imagined."

Leah waited for an explanation.

"When I was at my great-uncle's last weekend, he said I should meet you because I'd find you 'delightful.' That was his word. Delightful. He said, 'For twenty years she's been bringing me flowers on May Day.' With all those clues, I thought for sure this delightful woman he adored must be at least sixty, maybe seventy years old. Especially when he said your name was 'Leah.'"

Leah felt herself drawing inward.

"Hey, I'm trying to compliment you here. I'm saying you weren't an old lady like I thought you would be. Why did you pull back?"

Leah waved her hand for him to disregard her actions. "It was nothing."

"You're not a very good liar, you know. Obviously it was something. What did I say?"

Leah was beginning to learn that if this man wanted to drag the truth out of her, he could be rather convincing. She saw little point in trying to cover up what she felt.

"It wasn't anything you said. I mean, it was, but you didn't say anything wrong. It's just my name. I've never liked my name. And when you said that Leah sounded like the name of someone who was sixty, well, that's what I was reacting to."

Seth sat back and didn't say anything for a moment. He sipped his coffee and seemed to be considering Leah. She felt as if he were looking at her the way a painter sizes up his subject before attempting to tackle the task of transposing one reality into another form.

"The name Leah comes from the Bible, doesn't it?" Seth asked.

"Yes," Leah said sharply.

"So does my name."

"But Seth was a Bible hero, wasn't he?" Leah said.

"I suppose. He was Adam and Eve's third son. The blessing of God was on Seth and not on Cain. And of course, Abel was murdered. That left Seth to carry on the godly heritage. What do you know about the Leah in the Bible?"

"Enough," Leah said flatly.

"Tell me. I don't remember."

"Her father tricked Jacob into marrying her first, instead of Rachel, the one Jacob really loved."

"Is that all?"

"That's all I know about her." Leah didn't want to quote the verse that prompted her name, but it was fresh in her mind. The pain from it must have shown on her face because Seth reached over and took her hand. The gesture surprised her yet she didn't pull away as she had when he had taken her hand to check for doggy teeth marks.

The tender look on his tanned face reflected sincerity. "If you don't like the name Leah, then how about if I just call you George?"

Something inside Leah broke, and she burst into tears.

Chapter Nine

*A*nd then what happened?" Jessica asked Leah. The two of them were in the far corner of Jessica's huge backyard the next morning, tucking Easter eggs into the tufts of grass.

"I bawled like a baby for two minutes straight, and then I somehow turned off the tears. He said he should get going, and I apologized for falling apart. Of course he told me not to worry about it. Then he left, and I sat up half the night worrying about it."

Leah bent down, leaving a blue-and-green-striped egg next to a clump of wild daffodils. "I'm telling you, I was scared. I can't remember ever crying like that. And never in front of someone I hardly knew, all because he held my hand and called me, 'George.' Do you think I need counseling, Jess?"

Jessica left the last of her eggs and plucked several fresh, yellow daffodils. She linked her arm through Leah's, and the two women headed toward the house across the newly mowed, spring grass.

"I think the same thing I told you at church last night," Jessica said after a pause. "God has scooped you up and plopped you into a pocket of grace. You can't exactly control what happens."

"That's for sure," Leah said, gazing at the pastel streamers and balloons that adorned the back deck of Kyle and Jessica's Victorian home. Tall, canvas umbrellas were opened above the two patio tables. Curls of smoke rose from the covered barbecue where Kyle was cooking the first group of the two hundred shish kebabs Leah had helped him assemble earlier that morning.

"It's not as if I had control of my life before, but now I can't predict how I'm going to react!" Leah let go of Jessica's arm so she could pick up the tennis ball at her feet and toss it to one of the golden retriever puppies. Travis was keeping them corralled in the sandy play area under the jungle gym. Jessica and Leah hung back from the house and play area to finish their conversation.

"At least before in my life," Leah continued, "I knew what was expected of me, and I always did my best to fulfill those expectations. For years my life was on a controlled, tight schedule. Now, everything is tumbled around. I can't depend on myself for anything!"

Jessica chuckled. "You know that verse in Joel about how God says he will restore to you the years that the locusts have eaten?"

Leah didn't know that verse. "Are you trying to say my parents were locusts, and they ate up my best years?"

"Not exactly," Jessica said gently. "I was wondering if in some way God was restoring to you the feelings and experiences you might have had over the last decade, but those years were taken up in your giving and caring for others. Maybe some of those feelings had to be placed on hold. You had to act older than you were. You can be younger now."

Leah looked at Jessica, trying to absorb what she was say-ing. "Could be," Leah said with a sigh. "I don't know."

She paused to admire her friend in the shimmering bril-liance of the late morning sunshine. Jessica wore a long, flowing, pastel pink-and-gray skirt with a matching pink sweater set. Her honeyblond hair was a darker shade than Leah's was and longer. It billowed from beneath the wide-brimmed straw hat Jessica wore every year for the Easter egg hunt. The hat had a circle of silk flowers around the band, and pink satin ribbons raced down the back, almost to Jessica's waist. It was the kind of hat that per-fectly suited an Easter egg hunt, and it distinctly marked Jessica as the hostess of this grand event. Leah had on overalls and a plain white T-shirt because she knew she would be running in the grass with the little kids today. Leah didn't even own any-thing as soft and feminine as the outfit Jessica had on.

"I can't say I know exactly what God is doing in your life," Jessica said.

"That makes two of us," Leah muttered.

"But you know I'm always here for you, and I'm praying my little heart out."

"I know," Leah said. "And if you guys ever need anything, you know I'm here for you, too."

"We know that. You have given so much to us and to oth-ers, Leah. I know God is going to give abundantly back to you. You can't out-give God, you know. Maybe he's giving you back some of your emotions."

"And what exactly would someone like me do with more emotions?"

Jessica looked past Leah to the deck where Kyle had been stringing tiny white lights on the insides of the two patio umbrellas. Jessica stood there holding her fresh daffodils and smiling past Leah in a way that highlighted the half-moon scar on her upper lip. "Oh, I can think of one direction you might want to toss some of those emotions."

Leah turned and followed Jessica's line of sight. There on the deck, next to Kyle, stood Seth, holding Bungee under his arm. He had on shorts and a white, knit shirt, which accentuated his bronzed skin.

Leaning closer to Jessica, Leah murmured, "Does that man have any idea how good he looks in shorts?"

Jessica laughed. "No, but I think you and your revived emotions might find a way to tell him!"

Leah worked hard not to burst out laughing. Instead, she waved at the guys, and they both waved back.

Just then a loud wail came from the upstairs open nursery window.

"Sounds like Sara woke up," Jessica said.

"I'll get her," Leah volunteered.

"No, not this time. You have a guest to entertain."

Before Jessica and Leah made it to the deck, Kyle had gone inside to answer his daughter's cries. He had left Seth to turn the shish kebabs on the barbecue. Seth tied Bungee to the leg of a patio chair, and Jessica went to the play area to check on Travis, leaving Leah alone to greet Seth.

"How are you doing?" he asked before she was all the way up on the deck.

"Well. I'd like to apologize again for last night."

"You know, I have a philosophy about tears," Seth said. "Tears wash the windows of our souls, and afterward we can see ourselves more clearly."

"That's poetic," Leah said, smiling at him.

He smiled back. "You like it? I just made it up. It's yours."

The back door opened, and two-year-old Emma paraded out in a white Easter dress with pink sash, white shoes, and lacy anklets. On her head was a white straw Easter bonnet with an elastic string that tucked under her chin. She walked toward Leah as if she were the Princess of Just About Everything.

"Oh, look at you!" Leah said, putting her hands to her face with an exaggerated expression of amazement. "Who is this absolutely gorgeous little princess?"

Emma played right along, and with her chin in the air she said, "It's me!"

The backdoor opened again, and Kyle's brother, Kenton, and his wife, Lauren, appeared with their two-year-old, Molly Sue. Lauren wore her short hair tucked behind her ears. She recently had colored it a shade of cinnamon brown that was close to her daughter's hair color. Molly Sue wore a frilly Easter frock with a big pink bow in her hair.

"And look at you!" Leah said, making over Molly Sue with equal enthusiasm.

Lauren said hello to Leah and told her the eggs she had decorated were on the kitchen counter. Kenton introduced Lauren to Seth.

The four of them chatted a few minutes before Kenton asked if he should start to hide the eggs they had brought.

"I can do it," Leah said.

"Actually, I was kind of looking forward to it," Kenton said. "I have a few favorite spots where I hid them last year." Kenton resembled his brother with his strong jaw and dark hair, but he was a little heavier than Kyle and not quite as tall.

"Then I wouldn't want to spoil your fun," Leah said. "Jessica and I already hid a lot in the back section of the yard. You might want to put some around the sides of the house."

"Okay, got it," Kenton said, going inside for the eggs.

Lauren called over to Jessica, "Did you see your daughter here? We came early to help, but we've been inside the last fifteen minutes. I'm afraid we created a little peer pressure. When

Emma saw Molly Sue all dressed up, she wanted to wear her Easter dress, too. I hope it's okay that I let her change into her Easter outfit."

Jessica smiled at her little charmer. "You look beautiful, Miss Emma."

"You probably didn't want her to wear all this cute stuff until church tomorrow, did you?" Lauren asked.

"No, it's okay," Jessica said, joining them on the porch.

Lauren fussed with the ruffles on her daughter's dress. "I decided this morning that I'd put so much money into Molly's outfit I wanted her to get as much wear out of it as she could before she outgrows it."

"I agree," Jessica said. "As long as we have them in their finest, let's go out front and get a picture of these two cousins on the porch swing."

They all left, and Leah stood there with a big rip in her heart. She had never been anyone's little princess. She couldn't remember an Easter or any holiday when she had been dressed up and made a fuss over. It never had bothered her before. Why did it hurt so much now?

Seth was looking at her. Leah blinked and tried to sniff quietly. It didn't work.

"Do the windows of your soul need another cleaning today?" His voice was kind but also carried a pinch of teasing. That was enough to convince Leah to buck up and put her exasperating emotions back inside, somewhere deep, where they couldn't get out again and make her look foolish.

"No, I'm okay. Must be the smoke from the barbecue. It messes up my contacts." Leah quickly wiped her right eye. "Do you need any help there?"

"I think these are about done. Kyle told me to load them up in that tray and then put on another round."

"I'll get the next round. They're in the refrigerator."

When Leah entered the kitchen, Kyle was holding baby Sara and talking to his brother, Kenton, about the Little League game coming up on Tuesday.

"Is Seth ready for more kebabs?" Kyle asked when he saw Leah opening the refrigerator.

"I can get them," Leah said.

"Tell him I'll be right there after I change Sara. Jess wants her in her Easter dress, too, so she can take pictures on the porch."

"I'll trade you," Leah said to Kyle. "You can take the shish kebabs out, and I'll change Sara."

Kyle handed Sara over a little too willingly. "Jess wants the little bows in her hair," he said, admitting that wasn't his area of expertise. "I think Jess had to use Scotch tape the last time."

"I'll figure it out," Leah said, balancing the sleepy-eyed girl on her hip.

"And I better get these eggs hidden," Kenton said.

Leah talked softly to nine-month-old Sara all the way up the stairs. The nursery smelled like baby powder and lilacs mixed with a twinge of barbecue smoke. From below the open window came Kyle and Seth's voices with an occasional yap from Bungee.

Leah looked out the window, still holding Sara close. Sara nestled her head in the curve of Leah's neck and breathed with the calm, steady rhythm of a heart secure and at rest.

For several minutes Leah took in the closeness of her little Sara Bunny and the view out the nursery window, which consisted of rich grass bordered by deep woodlands and the fair, blue sky with a handful of fluffy clouds frolicking over the tops of the giant cedars like spring lambs at play. It all was beautiful.

Leah had lived in Glenbrooke all her life but never had the sky, the trees, or the birds' songs seemed as magnificent as they did this moment. If she ever did pack up her Amelia Earhart spirit and fly to the ends of the Earth, this was where she would want to come home. And these were the people she wanted to greet her when she returned.

This is where I belong.

Brad's counseling advice from last summer made even more sense now. For so long she had thought her parents were blocking her goal to see the world. Then, for years, she stuffed her anger inside and fought depression. Yet the truth was, when she no longer was bound by her obligations to her parents, what did she do? She had enough money to pay for a memorable trip. Instead, she bought a house and settled into Glenbrooke even more firmly.

This must really be where I belong.

Chapter Ten

"Do you remember what Shelly said at the party yesterday?" Leah asked Seth, as his car bumped along the dirt logging road in the dark on Easter morning. "Didn't she say keep to the left off the side road at the end of the camp property?"

"I thought she said right," Seth said.

He had arrived punctually at four that morning to pick up Leah for their sunrise adventure. She had been ready twenty minutes early and had made a thermos of coffee, which they had given up on drinking as soon as the road turned bumpy. They also gave up trying to listen to the CD in Seth's portable player since it kept skipping. At the moment, drizzle covered the windshield. The wipers' steady swish filled the strained silence between Seth and Leah. Things weren't going the way she had thought they would.

The day before, at Kyle and Jessica's Easter party, the only time Seth and Leah had really talked to each other was their brief exchange right after he had arrived. Once she had dressed

Sara, other guests began to show up, and Leah ran around at her usual pace, doing everything she could to help with the event.

Seth left right after the egg hunt. He came up to Leah while she and Shelly were lacing the kids together for the three-legged race. "Four o'clock tomorrow okay for you?" he asked.

"Sure," she said. "Have you asked yet about the logging roads?"

"No."

"Well, Shelly here is the one to ask. Do you remember I told you she and her husband, Jonathan, run Camp Heather Brook? Shelly," Leah called to her recreation partner, "can you tell us how to get to the top of that hill behind the camp? Seth and I want to go there for an Easter sunrise view of the valley."

Shelly, who had been a flight attendant for many years before marrying her childhood sweetheart and moving to Glenbrooke, gave Seth directions. She pointed with two fingers the way a flight attendant indicates where the emergency exits are located on a plane.

Leah wished Shelly and her two efficient fingers were with them now in Seth's Subaru so she could point out the emergency exit on this dark, bumpy road.

"I'm almost positive Shelly said to turn this way," Leah said, holding on to her shoulder safety strap so it wouldn't press against the side of her neck with each bounce. "This road is really bad."

"Are you kidding? This would practically be a super highway in Costa Rica," Seth said, bringing the car to an abrupt halt. "Look, there's the cedar tree she told us about and the fork in the trail."

"You're right," Leah said, squinting into the light of his high beams at the obvious division in the trail.

"At this fork we go right," Seth said.

"Right," Leah agreed, and on they went, bouncing like crazy.

The road curved and led up a steep incline. Seth punched his way to the top and stopped with a jerk when the road suddenly ended.

"Looks like a moderate hike, from what I can see," Seth said, getting out of the car.

Leah was glad the rain had stopped as they began to hike. She had to hoof it fast to keep up with Seth. He held a large flashlight high to spread light for both of them. The earth beneath their feet was soft but not so muddy it slowed them down.

They hiked in silence for ten minutes before Seth said, "This looks like a worthy spot." He swung the light to the right and left. Leah could make out that they were standing on the knoll of the hill. Half a dozen sawed-off tree stumps revealed that this area had been the victim of a clear-cut decades ago. What lay beyond them and in the valley below remained to be seen.

"I'd put a bench right here, if I owned this mountain," Seth declared.

"It's not exactly a mountain," Leah stated, brushing off the top of mossy log before sitting down and removing her left boot. She shook it, and a tiny pebble fell out.

"Was that in there the whole time?" Seth asked.

"Yes, but I didn't want to stop." They were speaking in hushed voices, as if the rest of the world was still in a deep sleep. Their whispers carried far on the top of this windless hill. The moist scent of earth and decayed leaves filled the air.

Seth sat on the stump closest to hers. "You're the kind of camper we loved to have on our tours. The ones who didn't complain and could take a bit of inconvenience."

"That's me," Leah said. "The original happy camper."

"You know, it took us a lot less time to get to this lookout point than I thought it would," Seth said. "Are you cold? Do you want to walk around some? It's going to be awhile before we see the sun."

"I'm fine."

The low-hanging clouds served as a canopy, covering the stars and keeping the earth warmer than it would have been if the sky were wide open above them.

Seth flashed the light around. "It is pretty dark, isn't it? Not much chance of being mauled by a mountain lion here in the clear-cut, is there?"

"Oh, now, that's a nice thought," Leah said. She noticed for the first time that she could see her breath. Crossing her arms, she tucked her hands under her armpits to warm them.

"Tell me about your family," she suggested as an alternative to concocting spooky images in the darkness.

"My family?" Seth turned toward her. He placed the flash-light on the ground between them. The light shot upwards like a beacon. Its brilliance dispersed in the fine mist of the clouds.

"You said you grew up in Colorado, right?"

"Yes, the Boulder area. My parents are mild, law-abiding citizens. My dad is a financial consultant. I have one older sister, who lives in Canada with her husband and three kids. That's about it." Seth gazed into the vast night, preoccupied with his own thoughts.

It disappointed Leah that he wasn't acting more attentive to her. The closeness and warmth that had overpowered her on Friday night when he had called her George didn't seem to be with them in the damp chill of this early morning. She wanted that feeling back. She wanted him to say something tender and poetic like he had said yesterday about her tears washing the window of her soul.

Seth's thoughts obviously were elsewhere because he said, "Do you know an elderly woman named Ida?"

"Yes." Leah looked at Seth in the light of the flashlight beam. "Ida Dane. You met her. You delivered a package to her last week. My car stalled in front of her house."

"That's why she acted as if she knew me. The lemonade. She invited me to come back for lemonade the day I delivered a package to her."

"You should take her up on it," Leah said. "Ida makes terrific lemonade. She uses local summer berries and makes it in the blender."

"I did try some. She gave it to me at the Easter party yesterday."

"That's right," Leah said, "Ida did bring some yesterday, didn't she? My favorite is her marionberry lemonade."

"I think that's the one I had. It was great. Although when she started to talk to me, I didn't realize I'd already met her. Do you think Ida knows what she's talking about?"

"Most of the time. She gets fuzzy every now and then. Why?"

Seth stretched out his legs in front of him and stomped his right heel in the damp earth, dislodging a mud clod from the bottom of his boot. "When Ida found out I was Franklin's relative, she had all kinds of trivia to tell me. For instance, she said this hill and the surrounding 150 acres belonged to Cameron Madison, as well as another 50 acres on and around Madison Hill."

"That sounds about right," Leah said.

"Ida also said that Franklin inherited all two hundred acres."

"How could that be?"

"I don't know, but that's what she said."

"It doesn't make any sense." Leah paused. "I always heard

that Cameron was bankrupt when he died. How could he leave anything to Franklin? Or, if he did, then Franklin must have sold it all long before I was born."

"That's what I thought, too. But Ida got me curious. I went to the library when I left the party yesterday, and I tried to look up information on the area. I didn't get very far. It's quite a research project. I was thinking of asking Kenton if the newspaper has a reference system I could use to look up notices of land sales."

"Why don't you just ask Franklin?" Leah asked.

"Do you think he would tell me?"

"Why not? He's your great-uncle."

"Has he ever said anything to you about owning lots of land?"

Leah thought a moment before shaking her head. She was beginning to feel chilled. "No, the subject never has come up. And why would he discuss it with me, anyway?"

"Because..." Seth paused before finishing his answer. "I have a feeling you're in his will."

"Me? Why on earth would you say that?"

"He likes you a lot. He said something the other day about planning to reward you for all your decades of kindness to him. That's when I still thought you were his sixty-year-old girlfriend."

Leah shook her head. She felt like telling Seth he didn't know what he was talking about. "I'm sure Franklin's idea of rewarding me would be with a candy bar or tickets to the movies. He did that once when I was in high school. He called the theater in Edgefield and arranged for the manager to send me two passes."

"Do you think that's it?" Seth said. "A candy bar or a movie?"

Leah tried to make out Seth's expression in the hazy light.

"What? You think he's going to leave me his house when he dies? No thank you. It took me months to clean out my parents' house and get it ready to put on the market. I don't ever want to go through that again."

"Did you hear that?" Seth said, looking behind them. "We woke up the birds."

Leah listened to the melodic twittering and felt as if this chilly, barren hill had just warmed. With a lighter tone to her voice, she said, "Let me know if you find out anything interesting about this area and what Cameron Madison actually owned. I'd be curious to know."

Seth nodded.

She could see him more clearly now in the approaching light of the dawn. Leah wished she could read his thoughts.

What does Seth think of me? Am I merely a "happy camper" to him? Someone to keep him company? Or is he attracted to me the way I'm attracted to him?

Leah thought about how she had freely given Seth her secrets a few nights ago. Now Seth insinuated that Franklin also had secrets. Seth seemed to have an exceptional ability to uncover information. If Franklin had money, Seth would find out. And then what would happen?

Leah shivered, even though the morning sun was breaking through the clouds and pouring out a pale, golden glow across the valley.

I hope with all my heart that I can trust you, Seth Edwards.

Chapter Eleven

"Very early on the first day of the week, they came to the tomb when the sun had risen,'" Seth read to Leah from his thin, leather-bound Bible that he had pulled from his coat's inside pocket.

He looked up and surveyed the valley before them, which was now flooded with light. "When the Son of God had risen," Seth said more to himself than to Leah. "The light of the world."

Snapping out of his private thoughts, Seth returned his attention to the passage in the Gospel of Mark and read the rest of the resurrection account.

Leah thought his voice was easy to listen to, and she enjoyed hearing the recounting of the first Easter and how the women went to the garden tomb early in the morning to seek Jesus. But Jesus wasn't in the grave. He was alive. Christ was resurrected and walking among them without their knowing it.

By the time Seth had finished reading, the world around

them was filled with a soft, diffused light. Thin clouds hung over their heads, making the golden sun on the horizon even more spectacular.

"Amen," Seth pronounced when he had finished reading. "Amen and amen! He is risen!" Seth stood and declared.

"He is risen indeed," Leah echoed, rising to her feet. She remembered answering with that phrase on Easter morning when she was a child. The children of Glenbrooke Community Church used to be invited to sit through the Easter morning service. When the pastor ended his short sermon with, "He is risen," all the children took their cue to jump to their feet and at the top of their voices answer, "He is risen indeed!" The opportunity to yell in church after sitting under the intoxicating influence of a hundred pungent Easter lilies always gave Leah a rush.

This morning the memory gave Leah the idea of bringing in a few Easter lilies for her toddlers class. The church no longer included the little ones in the service, which now ran an hour and a half instead of an hour. Her young friends would enjoy the chance to jump up and shout.

Leah noticed that Seth had set his face toward the valley below. They stood in silence, both taking in the vastness of the lush green spread before them. She stood close enough to him that he could have put his arm around her shoulders if he chose to, but he didn't.

"Can you imagine what old Cameron must have thought when he first gazed on this?" Seth asked.

"I can't imagine," Leah said. She was thinking how dearly she needed Seth to put his arm around her. Then she would know he was thinking of her as fondly as she was thinking of him. She would be able to trust him again.

"Look at that perfect blue ribbon," Seth said, lost in a world beyond the one where he and Leah now stood.

Leah drew in her vulnerable feelings and said, "That's Heather Creek. It's full this year because we had a wet winter. Over to the left, do you see that forest? A gorgeous waterfall lies just on the other side of those trees."

"Really? A waterfall?"

"Yes. You would never guess the land drops off enough for a large waterfall. And the meadow there in the middle is behind the main lodge of Camp Heather Brook. It's too far away to see the lodge, but it's there."

"What about the woodlands on the right?" Seth asked.

"That's a beautiful area," Leah said. "I've only been there once. The camp doesn't own it, but they want to buy it. Shelly told me they have plans to add a junior camp. What they want to do is make it a tree house camp. Isn't that a fun idea? I would have loved to spend the night in a tree house when I was in grade school."

"Who owns it?"

"I don't know. I'm not sure Jonathan and Shelly know. Actually, Kyle is the one who is handling buying the property. He and Jessica bought the land for Camp Heather Brook about five years ago."

"Really," Seth said, stroking his chin. "Interesting."

They lingered on the knoll only a few more minutes. Seth remained distant, preoccupied in a world of thoughts to which Leah didn't have a passport to enter.

She knew her emotions were too far out in front of reality. They needed to go away. And quickly. But in the same way that she had done nothing to bid them to take center stage in her life, she felt powerless to make them leave.

If Seth isn't going to reciprocate or indicate that he's interested in me, I should pull back. Now, before I get hurt.

"We probably should get going," Seth said, picking up the flashlight and bending to tie his boot laces.

"Right," Leah agreed.

They drove home with Seth lost in his thoughts and Leah struggling with her feelings. She noticed he held the steering wheel with his right arm fully extended. His knuckles were large, and his fingers were thick and rugged.

She wanted Seth to say something when he dropped her off at her house. Something promising like "When can I see you again?" or "I loved being with you this morning." But all he said was, "Don't forget your thermos."

In a way, it was a good thing she didn't linger to talk with Seth because Leah had just enough time to change for church, gather up the clean nursery toys, and dash out the door. When she arrived at the nursery, the first, dressed-up toddler already was there with his parents. He was clutching the head of a chocolate Easter bunny in his fist.

She had to forgo the fragrant Easter lilies, but she did get the fourteen children going with a rousing, "He is risen, indeed!" yelling session.

All her friends wished her a happy Easter, and she received three invitations for Easter dinner. But she turned each one down, waiting in the classroom until the church halls were empty. She kept hoping Seth would show up as he had Friday night.

When he didn't come sauntering down the hall, Leah closed up her room and went to the parking lot. Her car was the last one.

She ended up going to Kyle and Jessica's since she knew they wouldn't mind if she reconsidered their earlier invitation. She spent the afternoon, along with nine other guests, dining on ham, scalloped potatoes, green beans, and gourmet chocolate Easter eggs in the Buchanans' formal dining room. They all lingered at the table, telling stories, bouncing children on their knees, and laughing at Jessica every time she scolded Kyle for slipping table scraps to Lady and her last, unspoken-for puppy.

Travis called the puppy "Skipper." He was supposed to stay in the laundry room, but he kept mysteriously "skipping" into the dining room behind Lady, who knew that Kyle would be the soft touch when it came to table scraps.

Little Sara settled herself on Leah's lap and nodded off as the conversation continued around the table. The afternoon sunshine danced through the lace curtains, sprinkling Sara's back and Leah's legs with a delicate pattern of fairy light. Leah kissed the top of Sara's head and thought how perfect all this was. The only element missing was Seth. He would have enjoyed this. A real family. A big, holiday dinner. Where was he? With Franklin? By any chance was Seth thinking of her? She was mad at herself for not taking the initiative to invite him to Kyle and Jessica's. They gladly would have welcomed him. Why didn't she think of it sooner?

From Sunday afternoon until Leah saw Seth again on Tuesday, she went through a gigantic loopty-loop of emotions. She wanted to see Seth. Did he want to see her? Why hadn't he called? Should she call him?

On Monday she decided to make cookies for him. That would give her an excuse to stop by his work on Tuesday and see him. She didn't know exactly what she would say, but it would come to her. What guy didn't like receiving a batch of homemade cookies?

All the ingredients were lined up on her kitchen counter when Leah felt overwhelmed with feelings of rejection. If Seth wanted to see her again, he would have called her. How could she have been so foolish as to think he had been captivated by her the way she was captivated by him? She knew she had frivo-lously allowed herself to dream about Seth in the first place.

She was only setting herself up for defeat.

Leah bent over the sink and began to cry. She knew this feeling. It was anger. Anger at having her goals blocked. Her wishes would never come true nor would her prayers ever be answered. A man like Seth would never be interested in someone like her. She was mad that he had come into her house and sat on her couch and called her George. She was angry with herself for admitting her secret about being the Glenbrooke Zorro.

Hula padded into the kitchen and stood beside Leah, comforting her as her tears fell. "Why did I do it, Hula? Why did I let myself open up like that? Why?"

Leah didn't trust herself to make cookies in her emotional state. She didn't trust herself to do anything. She hated the power of her feelings. The only way to gain control over them was to shut them down, to allow the old tapes to play themselves over in her mind, reminding her that she "had neither the frame nor frame of mind to attract anyone stable." "Behold, it was Leah."

By the time Leah saw Seth again Tuesday night at the Little League game, she successfully had shut down all her feelings. The evening was cool and drizzly, and the bleachers were dotted with umbrellas. Definitely a smaller crowd had gathered for this game than had been there the week before. Seth showed up at the Snack Shack during the second inning and bought a hot chocolate.

"I guess you're not doing much of a Sno-Kone business tonight, are you?" Seth asked.

"No. You're my tenth hot chocolate order," Leah said.

"Is this pretty typical spring weather for this area?" he asked, while he stood there with his hands in his jeans pockets.

"Yes, sometimes the rain hangs on through June."

"What you're trying to tell me is that my first week here

was just a tease. It's usually not that sunny and nice."

You got that right, Leah thought, as she turned her back on him to stir the cocoa mix in the boiling water. *Your first week was just a tease for both of us.*

She handed him the cocoa and matter-of-factly said, "Be careful; it's hot. We don't print a warning on our cups, so I have to make sure you hear me say it's hot."

"Got it."

Leah thought he would turn to go, but he stood there under the metal awning, sipping his cocoa and not saying anything. Several other customers came up in search of something warm, and Leah made more hot chocolate and a few burritos.

"I spent Easter Sunday with Franklin," Seth offered after Leah had passed a cup of cocoa on to the last waiting customer. "We had a nice time. He wanted me to ask if you would come by to see him sometime this week."

"Is he okay?"

"He seems okay to me. He said he wanted to talk with you about something that couldn't wait until May Day when you came by with your annual bouquet."

"Did he say what it was about?"

"No. I didn't ask."

"Thanks for relaying the message," Leah said. "I'll check in on him this week." She went back to inventorying the candy bars, which is what she had been doing when Seth walked up.

"I guess you're not going to need help with the crowd after the game this week."

"No. Thanks anyway." Leah knew she sounded curt. Mild indifference was the only safe route for her. She refused to let her feelings rise to the surface.

"I guess I'll be on my way," Seth said. "I'll see you around."

"See you around."

As soon as Seth was gone, she felt depressed.

What did you think he was going to do? Ask you out to dinner? Invite you to sail off into the sunset on his private yacht? See what happens when you let your emotions get all gushy, and you start wishing on planets and opening yourself up? You set yourself up for failure, Leah. You set your course on a road that eventually will become a dead end. Why do that to yourself?

Leah suddenly realized the words playing in her head weren't her words. The phrases about setting herself up for failure and setting a course on a dead-end road were her father's words. He had used them in a lecture to her years ago when she first announced she wanted to go to college.

But look, Leah prompted herself, *I did go to college. And I finished! It wasn't a dead-end road for me. I didn't set myself up for failure.*

If she had a place to sit in the tiny Snack Shack, Leah would have let herself down with a thud. This was earth-shaking news. Not all of her father's predictions about her life were necessarily true. Perhaps the predictions her sister had made of her weren't true either. Could it be she wasn't destined to fulfill everyone else's expectations of her?

Leah stood still and whispered, "Could that be true?" Her question was directed at God, the heavenly Father with whom she had maintained a cordial distance.

Chapter Twelve

$\mathcal{L}$eah didn't receive any thundering answers from the heavens about whether her family's prophecies regarding her destiny were all true. She didn't expect any thunder. But Glenbrooke did receive a sudden downpour of rain that caused the game to be called. She closed up the Snack Shack and ran to her car.

The rain continued through the night and was still coming down when she left for work the next morning. She didn't know if it was the darkness of the skies or the overpowering revelation she had discovered last night, but she felt sapped of energy. The week had been emotionally draining.

Leah sat at the front admissions desk, forcing herself to catch up on phone calls to fill out insurance forms. She dialed the number listed for a patient and was checking her notes on what missing information she needed, when a robust male voice on the other end of the line said, "WPZQ, where the hits just keep on coming. And your name?"

"Ah, this is Leah Hudson from Glenbrooke General Hos—"

Before she could explain for whom she was calling, the booming voice said, "Well, congratulations, Leah Hudson! You are caller number nine, and you have just won the WPZQ bonus jackpot!"

A chorus of chipmunk voices sang into her ear, "You won! You won! You really, really won!"

"That's right!" The enthusiastic radio announcer said. "Leah Hudson, you have just won an exciting cruise for yourself and a friend to—are you ready for this?—Alaska!"

The chipmunk voices sang out again. "You won! You won! You really, really won!"

"What do you have to say, Leah Hudson?"

Leah was speechless.

The announcer jumped in. "You're on the air, so go ahead and tell all the listeners what you think of the hottest station in the nation playing all the hits all the time."

"Um, I, ah, the number I dialed…it's…"

The announcer broke in with deep laughter. "I think our winner is in shock, folks. Winning the WPZQ jackpot can have that effect on a person. Nevertheless…"

The chorus chirped in with, "You won! You won! You really, really won!"

"But, you see—" Leah tried to explain.

"Now you just stay on the line," the announcer said, "and Tina will tell you all about the fabulous cruise you've won."

After two clicks, a female voice said, "May I have your name and phone number, please?"

"Actually…Tina, is it?"

"Yes."

"Tina, I was trying to call a patient from our hospital who left this as his phone number. But I think I misdialed the number."

After a pause Tina said, "What number did you think you dialed?"

Leah repeated the number she was trying to reach, and Tina verified that was the number for the radio station.

"What area code did you dial?" Tina asked. "This is 203."

Leah began to laugh. "Well, that explains it. I meant to dial 503 for Portland, Oregon. Sorry to have troubled you."

"No, wait!" Tina said. "Don't hang up. You won the cruise."

"But how could I? I don't even live...where is your station located, anyhow?"

"New Haven."

"New Haven what?" Leah asked.

"Connecticut," Tina said.

Mary, who had just returned from lunch, slid her purse in the bottom drawer of the desk, giving Leah a curious look as Leah echoed, "Connecticut?"

"Look, you won the cruise," Tina said. "We just announced you live on the air. We can't go back and say the last winner was a hoax. Nothing in our rules says you have to know you're entering the contest to win. Or that you have to be in Connecticut when you call. You were caller number nine. You won the cruise, whether you want it or not."

"I can't believe this," Leah said.

"Would you be so kind as to give me your name, phone number, and a fax number for your travel agent? We deal directly with travel agents for all our arrangements."

Leah figured she might as well give Tina the information. Reaching for the telephone book, Leah looked up the number for A Wing and a Prayer, the only travel agency in Glenbrooke.

Mary stepped closer to Leah's desk and mouthed the word "What?"

"Thank you," Tina said. Then sounding as if she was reading

from a card, Tina continued, "Congratulations, Leah Hudson, on winning the WPZQ jackpot. All prizes are for promotional consideration only and cannot be exchanged for cash value. We hope you will keep on listening to the hottest station in the nation, playing all the hits all the time. Enjoy your cruise."

Leah hung up the phone and turned to Mary, who asked, "What was all that?"

"I just won a cruise to Alaska. Via Connecticut."

Word of Leah's trip spread quickly at work, and everyone agreed Leah "deserved" the cruise. She didn't know how she "deserved" anything. She had dialed a wrong number. It was all pretty crazy in her opinion.

One of the ER nurses had been to Alaska, and she was eager to tell Leah all about it. The woman even went home on her lunch break and brought back four travel books on Alaska, a large photo album, and two home videos of her trip, which she told Leah to watch that night at home.

Leah left work at 4:30, as usual, and drove directly to the travel agency for her 4:45 appointment.

Alissa, the owner and only travel agent at A Wing and a Prayer, was on the phone when Leah entered. In Leah's opinion, Alissa was beautiful enough to be a model. She carried herself with a bit of a swish when she walked and always looked fresh, as if she had been born with naturally gorgeous hair, skin, and nails. Alissa and Brad had moved up from Southern California, and whenever the weather warmed, Alissa wore the classiest outfits in town. Today, however, Alissa was wearing gray, just like the sky.

Taking a seat on the couch by the window, Leah flipped through a travel magazine and gazed at pictures of the Bahamas.

Is it wrong for me to wish I'd won a cruise to the Bahamas instead of Alaska? I mean, I should be happy to go anywhere. But after seeing all those pictures of that frozen land, this picture of warm blue water sure looks appealing.

Alissa hung up the phone and turned to greet Leah. "Sorry to keep you waiting. I received the fax from the radio station this afternoon. This is pretty exciting, Leah!"

Leah rose and went to one of the chairs in front of Alissa's desk. "I have a question. Do you know if this cruise is transferable?"

Alissa looked down, carefully reading the fax paper in her hand. "The only conditions they list are that you can't work for the radio station or be related to anyone who does."

"No problem there. I don't even know anyone in Connecticut!"

Alissa smiled. "And you're limited on when you can go. It looks like you have to take the cruise offered from May 15 through 19."

"This year?" Leah asked.

Alissa nodded. "These limited promotional packages often tie into the lowest priced season, which I'd guess is the case here. But, no, it doesn't say anything about transferring to another person. I can call them to make sure. Did you want to try to sell the ticket?"

"No. No, I didn't mean transferring it to another person. I meant transferring the destination." She pointed to a poster behind Alissa of the Grand Canal in Venice. It showed a man and a woman lounging on a mound of pillows in a gondola. Behind them stood a dashing gondolier, who was doing all the work while they cuddled. "Now that's my idea of a real vacation. If I had my choice, I'd like to go someplace warm."

Alissa shook her head. "No, sorry. It's valid only for the Alaskan cruise."

Leah kept staring at the poster. The way the gondolier was positioned, he seemed to be singing. For some reason the thought of being sung to made her feel like crying. She tried hard to hold back the tears, but they welled up in her eyes and tumbled down her cheeks before she could stop them.

"I'm sorry," she said to Alissa, who was offering Leah a tissue and looking startled. "I've been like this a lot lately." Leah continued to stare at the poster.

Alissa turned around to see what Leah was fixated on.

"Jessica says my emotions are being released after being pent up for too long, or something like that. I think I'm slowly going crazy."

Alissa reached across her desk and gave Leah's hand a squeeze. "Maybe this cruise is exactly what you need. You've had an intense year, Leah. I've heard Brad say that sometimes people don't start to grieve until months or years after a shocking loss. It might do you a world of good to get away and completely relax."

Leah nodded.

"And you do know, don't you, that if you ever feel like talking to someone, my husband has a way of helping make sense of all the pieces. Brad would be happy to talk with you."

"Thanks," Leah said quietly. She took another tissue and wiped the last tear. "I appreciate it, but I'm okay. Really."

Leah rose to leave when Alissa said, "By the way, do you know anyone who needs a couch? It's in good shape. Brad had it in his duplex in Pasadena, and I've never liked it. We finally found a new one we could both agree on, but now I have to haul the old one to a donation center—unless you know someone who wants it."

Leah immediately thought of Seth. "I know someone who just moved into the area, but I don't know what his furniture situation is."

"If you talk to him, could you tell him it's available? And it's free," Alissa said.

"Thanks," Leah said. "And thanks for the Kleenex."

"Remember what I said about talking with Brad."

Leah nodded. "I will. Thanks again."

Leah left the travel agency and sat in her car a few minutes, trying to decide what to do. She was planning to visit Franklin next. She could ask him for Seth's phone number, and then she could call Seth, the way she would call any one of her friends and tell him about the couch. It didn't have to be awkward. Just because she had let her feelings get the better of her the first few days she was around him, that didn't mean they couldn't settle into a nice, everyday relationship like she had with so many other men in Glenbrooke.

Leah wondered what Brad, who had provided wise counsel for her in the past, would say about that. Was she repressing her true emotions? Maybe. But that had to be better than dreaming up some one-sided romance in which she was the only one doing the dreaming.

She closed her eyes, but all she could see was the poster of the gondola and the singing gondolier. She wished she was nestled in those cushions right now, floating down a canal instead of sitting in the middle of Main Street, hugging the steering wheel, alone in her car.

It's just so hard to admit to anyone that I have a problem. How could I tell Brad I'm confused by my feelings for Seth? Or that I've realized for the first time that my father's predictions of me weren't true? Or that I'm wondering if maybe I do have the right frame and frame of mind to attract someone stable after all? Would Brad tell me to grow up and start to act my age?

Leah drew in a deep breath.

No, Brad wouldn't do that. Brad would listen carefully, and he would have sound, caring advice. But then he would know the deep thoughts of my heart. I'd have to trust him to keep my thoughts and feelings private. It was hard enough opening my heart to Seth and

*telling him my secrets without any guarantee that he was trustwor-
thy.*

Leah wasn't in the habit of trusting anyone but herself. And
now that she realized she couldn't trust herself to settle her
own emotions and to make sense of the tumble of recent
events in her life, she felt completely lost.

Opening her eyes, Leah turned the key in the ignition.
That's when she noticed a note on her windshield, wrapped in
what looked like a used plastic sandwich bag. Apparently it
was supposed to keep the note dry. Leah retrieved the note,
which was damp despite the plastic bag. The name at the bottom of the scrawled lines was "Seth."

Chapter Thirteen

*H*er heart began to pound as she read Seth's simple words on the note he must have left while she was in the travel agency.

> *I thought of you this morning when I read this verse: Song of Songs 6:11.*
>
> *Seth*

Leah's spirits instantly rose. *He thought of me? But what does the verse say?*

Since Leah didn't have a Bible handy, she laid the note flat on the passenger's seat so Seth's words could dry out. Then she drove to the grocery story for a quick purchase and on to Franklin's house, as she originally had planned.

Seth thought of me.

Leah arrived with a smile on her face and found Franklin napping in his favorite recliner. The spry old man always left the door unlocked. He said it was so the "Cleaning House" people would know to come on in if he didn't hear them knock. Leah tried to tell him once, years ago, that the contest was run by the Publishers Clearing House. But Franklin still called them the "Cleaning House" people.

As far as Leah knew, Franklin sent in his entry form every time one came in the mail. He only subscribed to two magazines but that didn't stop those "Cleaning House" people from inviting him to enter every contest they had.

Leah called out from the entryway, "Franklin? Hello, it's Leah. I brought you a little something."

Franklin stirred in his old, brown recliner and immediately perked up. "Well, look at you! And with flowers to boot."

"Flowers and candy." Leah waved the bag of peppermint patties for him to see. She knew they were his favorite candies. Or at least they were the easiest candies for him to eat.

"It's not even my birthday," Franklin said, struggling to stand up with the help of his cane.

"Don't get up." She went over and gave the old gentleman a kiss on the cheek.

He settled comfortably back into the recliner.

"What have you been doing?" she asked.

"Making plans," Franklin said with a twinkle in his eyes. His glasses were so dirty Leah didn't know how he could see her.

"Here, let me clean your glasses, Franklin. I'm going into the kitchen to put these flowers in water. I'll be right back."

"Leave the candy here with me," he said, reaching for the bag.

"Yes, sir," she teased. "Don't eat them all before I come back."

"Just watch me try," Franklin quipped.

Mavis, the day nurse who cared for Franklin, was in the kitchen fixing chicken for dinner. She had a small television on the counter and was engrossed in an afternoon talk show. Leah helped herself to a vase for the daffodils and then washed and dried Franklin's glasses.

When she returned to the living room, Franklin had opened the bag of candy and was letting one of the mint patties melt in his mouth. She handed him his glasses.

"Oh, much better," Franklin said, adjusting them a bit. "You are much too kind to me, Leah darlin'. And that's why I've been making plans."

Leah slid over to the couch, where she sat down, wondering if Seth had been right about the will. Was Franklin going to announce he had left her his house? His old recliner? Or was Franklin going to declare he had bought her tickets to the movies?

"You know I enjoy visiting you and bringing you treats," Leah said. "You don't have to make any plans to do anything for me, Franklin. And you certainly don't have to give me anything."

"Who said I'm doing anything for you?" Franklin spouted. "I've been making plans for you to do something nice for me."

"Oh!" Leah felt her cheeks turn red. "What do you want me to do for you?"

"I want you to take me to Hamilton Lodge."

"Do you mean at Hamilton Hot Springs? That's more than four hours away. Why do you want me to take you there?"

"I haven't been there since Naomi passed on." He leaned back, and a tender look crossed his face the way it always did when he spoke of Naomi. "That used to be our favorite place. We were among the first customers to stay in their new facility. That was on our twenty-fifth wedding anniversary. After that, we went every other year. Like clockwork. It was our special place."

Leah quickly calculated and deduced that the new facility must have gone up in the sixties. This brought her an instant vision of a resort done up in harvest golds and avocado greens, just like the house she had grown up in.

"I'd like you to take me there," Franklin said. "You name the weekend."

"I—I don't know."

"You don't know what? You don't know if you want to take me, or you don't know which weekend?"

How could she say that the last place she wanted to go was a sixties-style hot springs resort? She knew she shouldn't be so picky, after complaining for years about never going anywhere. But this all seemed so strange. First the cruise to Alaska and now the hot springs. And both of them on tight time schedules so she had to make decisions right away.

That wasn't the only reason Leah hesitated. She didn't know how to tell Franklin she didn't want to be responsible to care for him for a weekend away. Visiting at his home and occasionally taking him out for a drive was one thing. Going all the way to Hamilton Hot Springs and caring for him for a weekend was asking a lot.

"Wouldn't you be more comfortable with someone else like Mavis?"

"Mavis deserves some time off," he said.

Leah knew the next obvious choice would be Seth. She had a funny feeling Franklin was waiting for her to ask about his nephew. "What about Seth?"

The glimmer was back in Franklin's eyes. "I have his picture right up there on the mantle."

"Yes." Leah noticed the photo of Seth was now front and center. The picture showed a much younger, less tan version of Seth with hair longer and darker than his current shade of sun-kissed blond. The smile was the same. Leah tried not to let her feelings show. Seth had such a nice smile.

"He turned out all right, didn't he? You know he had that crazy spell when he lived with the monkeys in the jungle. You know that, don't you?" Franklin paused, waiting for Leah's reaction.

"Wasn't it the rain forest in Costa Rica?"

Franklin feebly waved his hand as if to dismiss all the details he couldn't keep straight. "Point is, he turned out all right in the end, don't you think?"

Leah hesitated.

Franklin sat up a little straighter and answered for her. "Yes, he did. He turned out all right. And so did you. Now answer my question, Leah. Will you take me to the hot springs this weekend?"

"I can't go this weekend."

"Then how about the next weekend?"

"I don't think so." She was starting to feel bad about saying no.

"Why not?" Franklin persisted.

"It's May Day weekend, and I'm helping Shelly with the May Day event at the camp."

"Oh," Franklin looked down at his thin hands. "Then it was nice of you to bring me the May Day flowers early this year. I 'spect you'll be too busy on May Day to stop by. I understand." He lifted his gaze. "You've been good to me, Leah, honey. I wouldn't want to take you away from all your other friends."

Franklin was a sly one. Did he sound more frail than usual? Was he making his voice weak so she would take pity on him? Leah knew she would miss him when he was gone. It made her realize that once Franklin died, the last piece of her childhood would be gone. She didn't have parents or grandparents left to connect her with her early years. Only Franklin.

"Oh, all right, you ruthless trickster, you," Leah said, picking up a throw pillow and pretending she was going to toss it at Franklin.

"Good. Which weekend?" His voice seemed to have improved.

"The last weekend in May. Is that okay for you?"

"That's just fine. I'll make the reservations tomorrow."

"I don't know how you talked me into this," Leah said, sauntering over and snatching one of the candies from his bag. She also didn't know how she could go on the cruise and fit in a trip to the hot springs with Franklin.

"We'll have a grand time," Franklin said. "All three of us."

Leah stuck the candy in her mouth and froze before letting her teeth sink into the thin layer of chocolate. "And who would the third person be, Franklin?" she finally asked after swallowing the mint.

Franklin smiled smugly but said nothing. He just sat there smiling and chuckling to himself.

Chapter Fourteen

$\mathcal{I}$nstead of driving home from Franklin's house, Leah drove straight to Kyle and Jessica's. Too much had been happening too fast for Leah. She needed perspective, and Jessica often had provided her with just that.

Travis answered the doorbell and said his mommy was upstairs with Sara. Leah asked, "Could you tell her I'm here and see if she needs any help?"

Travis took off up the stairs, and Leah called after him, "And ask her if she has a Bible nearby."

Leah thought she remembered seeing a Bible on the living room bookshelf so she meandered in and pulled the leather Bible off the shelf. Turning to Song of Songs 6:11, Leah eagerly read the special message Seth had left for her. "I went down into the garden of nuts to see the fruits of the valley, and to see whether the vine flourished, and the pomegranates budded."

She stared blankly at the wall. *"Garden of nuts"? "Fruits of the valley"? This verse reminded Seth of me?*

Jessica appeared holding Sara, who was bathed and in her pajamas. "Congratulations!" Jessica said.

"For what?"

"Alissa told me you won a cruise to Alaska. That's fantastic! When are you going?"

"May 15. Would you like to go with me?"

Jessica hesitated.

"I'm only kidding. You have your hands full." Leah put down the Bible and stood, reaching out for Sara. "Come here, my little Sara Bunny."

Sara went right to Leah and cuddled up.

"She's really tired," Jessica said. "We had an early dinner. All my kids need to get to bed early tonight. I think the weekend of parties and sugar took a toll on them."

"It has been a wild week," Leah said.

"Do you want to put Sara to bed, and I'll get the other two settled? Then we can talk. I want to hear all about this cruise. Kyle won't be home for a couple of hours so you and I can have a good, long visit."

Leah felt relieved. That was exactly what she needed to hear. Jessica had time to listen and hopefully to help Leah figure out what was going on in her life.

Just then Travis padded into the room with a heavy Bible in his hands. "Here you go, Auntie Leah. You can use my dad's Bible."

"Thank you," Leah said, taking the Bible from him. "You are such a great helper, Travis. How about if you and I help your mom tuck your sisters into bed?"

Travis slipped his hand in Leah's, and they followed Jessica up the stairs. It took almost an hour to settle all three of the kids into bed. Leah helped herself to some cheese and crackers and poured a large glass of orange juice. She and Jessica sat in the living room facing each other in comfy chairs by the window that looked out over the driveway.

"You know this pocket of grace you said I fell into?" Leah began their conversation. "Well, I don't think I want to be there any longer. It's way too crazy."

Jessica smiled. "Why do you say that? Don't you want to go on the cruise? I think it's another one of God's gifts to you. Do you remember what I said before? You can't outgive God."

"It's not the cruise," Leah said. "It's everything. A week ago Seth Edwards walked into my corner of the world—my little Snack Shack—and nothing has been the same since."

"You two seemed so comfortable around each other last week when you came to pick out a puppy. Have your feelings changed?"

"Changed?" Leah said. "Ever since I fell into this 'pocket of grace,' my feelings have changed every hour on the hour. Who knows how I feel about anything? I don't think I trust myself to answer any questions until I get my emotional equilibrium back."

Jessica laughed softly. "I have a funny feeling that might not happen for a while, my friend."

"Look at the note he left on my car today." Leah handed Jessica the note and then retrieved the Bible so she could read the crazy verse to Jessica. "Are you ready for this? This is what it says, 'I went down into the garden of nuts to see the fruits of the valley—'"

Jessica interrupted Leah's reading with a giggle. Then Jessica covered her lips with her fingers and said, "I'm sorry. Go ahead."

"The rest of it is, 'and to see whether the vine flourished, and the pomegranates budded.'"

Jessica raised her eyebrows and kept her fingers over her

smiling lips. "What is that supposed to mean?"

"That's exactly what I'd like to know." Leah couldn't help it; she had to laugh. Jessica's initial reaction was correct. This was laughable.

"'I went down into the garden of nuts to see the fruits of the valley,'" Leah repeated, laughing. "Do you think he's trying to tell me I'm one of the nuts or one of the fruits in this valley?"

Jessica released a ripple of laughter. "Oh, Leah, that is so funny!"

"To you, maybe, but I'm feeling desperate here. You know how on Saturday I told you I burst out crying when he called me 'George'? And you told me I was getting back all the emotions the locusts had eaten?"

"That was sort of what I said, yes."

"Well, right after that, I took Sara up to her room, and I decided I didn't want to see the world like I thought I did. I wanted to stay right here in Glenbrooke. I wanted to pursue a relationship with Seth. Then we went hiking Sunday, up that hill behind Camp Heather Brook. Seth barely noticed I was there. So I told myself my whacked-out feelings had gotten out of control. I could never hope for a relationship with someone like Seth, and I completely shut down."

Jessica's expression changed from mirth to concern.

"I know. It's not good when I swallow my feelings and hold them in. Don't worry, I've been crying like crazy. Last night I had this huge revelation at the Little League game that some of the things my father said about me years ago weren't true. It never occurred to me before. I started to wonder if all those other messages I've believed about myself are false, too."

The phone rang, but Jessica sat quietly, waiting for Leah to continue.

"Do you need to get that?"

"No, this is more important. If it's Kyle, he'll call back

immediately. Otherwise I can let our machine pick it up. Go on, you were saying you realized you had believed some things that weren't true."

The phone stopped on the fourth ring. Leah picked up her train of thought. "I gave up my old wish of wanting to travel and then, bing! I won this cruise. I gave up on Seth, and then I stopped by Franklin's today and bing! Franklin wants me to take him to Hamilton Lodge for the weekend, and he's invited another guest to go with us."

"Seth?" Jessica ventured.

Leah nodded. "It's all happened in a week, Jess! I don't know what I'm supposed to think or feel anymore. I hope this 'pocket of grace' is well padded because I feel as if I'm about to start bouncing off the walls!"

Jessica smiled.

Leah pointed at Seth's note Jessica still held in her hand. "See? Even Seth agrees. Fruits and nuts! Further proof I'm going wacky, and everyone else recognizes it."

Jessica chuckled and looked more closely at the paper. "Are you sure this is chapter 6 verse 11? This number looks like a two to me."

"Let me see," Leah took the paper and examined it more closely. The rain had smeared the letters so that all she saw was the loop of the number. She had assumed it was a six. Possibly Seth made loopy twos. Leah turned to Song of Songs 2:11. Jessica turned there as well in Kyle's Bible that Travis had brought downstairs for them.

"Oh, yes, I think this verse is the one he had in mind," Jessica said before Leah could read the whole verse herself. Jessica read aloud, "'See! The winter is past; the rains are over and gone. Flowers appear on the earth; the season of singing has come.'"

Leah looked up at her, feeling humbled. "That's a little different than the fruits and nuts verse."

"Yes, it is." Jessica smiled. "Much more fitting. I think Seth was trying to encourage you, Leah, by saying you're entering into a new season in your life. That's what I was saying on Saturday when I told you the verse about God restoring the years the locusts had eaten. You need to feel free to move on in your life."

"Move on to what?" Leah asked.

Jessica smiled and then hopped up from her chair. "It just so happens that now I'm the one who has a verse for you."

Leah knew where Jessica was going. She kept a stack of three-by-five-inch cards at the desk in her kitchen with various verses written on them. Those cards often ended up taped to bathroom mirrors or framed and placed above the kitchen sink. Jessica carried verses in her purse, she had them in the car, and Leah had even found them in Sara's diaper bag. Kyle referred to the verses as his wife's "spiritual snacks."

Jessica hadn't grown up going to church, and she didn't know a lot about the Bible when she and Kyle married. In an effort to get to know God's Word in the midst of her busy days, Jessica had written out dozens of these verse cards. More than once she had passed a card on to Leah. Leah usually stuck them in her Bible and didn't bother to really look at them.

Jessica returned with a card for Leah and handed it to her as it if were the key to a treasure chest. "This is it," she said, reciting the three verses from Psalm 37 from memory. "'Trust in the LORD and do good; dwell in the land and cultivate faithfulness. Delight yourself in the LORD; and He will give you the desires of your heart. Commit your way to the LORD, trust also in Him, and He will do it.'"

Leah looked at the card, hoping the words would instantly work some special blessing on her as they obviously had on Jessica, judging by the expression on Jessica's face.

"It's that middle verse you need to concentrate on right

now," Jessica said. "'Delight yourself in the LORD; and He will give you the desires of your heart.' Don't concentrate on figuring out what your heart's desires are. Concentrate on delighting yourself in the Lord. Then the rest will fall into place."

"You promise?" Leah asked.

"I don't have to promise. God is the one who made that promise."

When Leah looked skeptical, Jessica added, "He hasn't broken a single one of his promises yet, you know. I doubt he would start now."

Chapter Fifteen

$\mathcal{A}$t five the next morning Leah lay awake, unable to fall back asleep. She felt as if she had gone riding through the night on the tattered edges of midnight's dark, velvet cape. She knew emotionally she was going somewhere—and fast. But where?

When Leah realized she wasn't going to fall back to sleep, she reluctantly rose and shuffled into the kitchen for a drink of water. The stillness comforted her. The rain had stopped, and it was quiet outside. She stood at the window, sipping her glass of water and trying to see the sky, but it was still too dark.

On a whim, Leah reached for a blanket in the living room and went through the mudroom out to the back steps. Hula rose and padded after her, not fully awake but ever faithful. For a long while Leah sat on the cold, cement steps, wrapped in the blanket and with her arm around Hula. Leah stared into the deep, quiet darkness, waiting for the morning light to come.

Her thoughts were of God and trying to understand who

he was and what he expected of her in light of the conversation she had had with Jessica the night before. For so long Leah had pictured God as a cosmic motorcycle cop, hiding behind a billboard and pointing a radar gun at her. That's why she always followed the rules. As long as God couldn't catch her doing anything wrong, he wouldn't be mad at her. And if he wasn't mad at her, maybe he wouldn't mess up her life.

Until this point, that image of God had made sense to her. She never had mentioned it to anyone, but she was sure if she had it would have seemed right and not at all twisted. Now, just as she was recognizing other lies she had believed for years, Leah realized how inaccurate that image of God was.

God, you're not standing there, pointing a radar gun at my heart, are you? The inaccurate image immediately dissolved. *What do you want, God? What do you expect from me? How am I supposed to respond to you?*

For the first time since high school, Leah felt a hunger in her spirit. She wanted to know God. To hear how others viewed him and responded to him. Leah thought of Jessica as someone who had a deeper relationship with God than she did. Seth had seemed so much more connected with God when he read aloud the Easter account on their morning hike. It was all so real to him. Leah felt she was missing something. She had felt it for some time.

In the quiet of her intense contemplation, the morning came softly, a blessed contrast to the frenzy of the past few days. A chorus of birds greeted her from the treetops. Hula barked at a squirrel as it scampered across the lawn. Leah held Hula back from running after the intruder. The scent of the rain-soaked earth rose and circled Leah, inviting her to come into the garden.

Leah reached for a hoe in the mudroom and slipped her

bare feet into an old pair of wooden clogs she kept by the door. In the pristine morning light, she trotted into the yard in her flannel pajama bottoms and T-shirt with the blanket tied around her shoulders like a cape. She grinned at her impulsiveness. What did it matter? No one was up to see her, digging the hoe into the damp earth.

The previous owner had sectioned off a plot for a small vegetable garden, but Leah hadn't had a chance to do anything with it. Now, as she turned over each clod of dirt, she made plans for peas, carrots, tomatoes, and some sort of melon. Cantaloupe sounded good.

The rain-kissed earth turned for her like soft butter. She could have dug this garden with a spoon. Bending to grasp a handful of the mink-brown dirt, Leah rubbed it between her fingers and breathed in deeply its dark, spicy fragrance.

Gently, the words from Seth's verse came back to her. Not the verse about the fruits and nuts, but the verse about the rains being over and the flowers appearing. The season for singing had come.

Leah didn't sing. She barely breathed. Standing still in her blanket cape and flannel pj's, with her hand full of moist earth, she prayed. It had been a long time since she had really prayed.

"Lord God," she whispered, "You're here, aren't you? I mean, you're really, truly right here. And you're here in my heart, even though it's been so long since I've talked openly and intimately with you. You never left. I was the one who ignored you."

Leah let the dirt fall through her fingers. "The winter is over. The storms have ceased in my heart. You're trying to plow things up, aren't you? You want to plant something new." A gentle breeze lifted the feathery strands of her hair from her neck.

"I'm sorry I've been so resistant to you. Please forgive me. I want to learn how to delight myself in you because I honestly don't know how to do that."

The longer Leah stood in the morning chill, the more she shivered. She didn't want to move. One doesn't step away from holy ground too quickly. This place, this simple earth, this garden, had become holy to Leah. God had met her here. And she had responded.

"You want me to trust you, don't you?" Leah curled and uncurled her toes inside her wooden clogs. "You know how hard that is for me."

Feeling compelled to kneel in the moist earth, Leah went down slowly. First on her right knee and then on her left. "Okay," she whispered. "I promise. I'll trust you."

A full five minutes later, Leah returned to the house with Hula beside her. Kicking off the muddy clogs, Leah scampered barefooted into the bathroom where she jumped into a warm shower. The soothing water washed over her, refreshing her. Her spirit had never felt so clean.

Leah wrote on a yellow sticky note to buy some three-by-five cards. She wanted to start writing down verses the way Jessica did. It was time to plant some new seeds in her life.

It was also time to plant seeds in her vegetable garden, now that the earth was ready. She began a list of the vegetables she had decided on while she was hoeing. She could go buy the seeds on her lunch break and then plant them as soon as she got home from work. The thought made Leah smile. This was her home. Her garden. It was a small blessing, one she hadn't fully appreciated until now.

Leah entered the hospital with a light step and greeted everyone she saw on her way in. On her desk sat another tour book of Alaska.

"Did you see the memo on vacation time yet?" Mary asked

as Leah settled in her chair. "I'm taking off the third week of May because my sister's coming to visit."

"That should be fun," Leah said.

Mary shook her head. "I don't know about that. We're not going anywhere. It's her fiftieth birthday, and she's pretty depressed about it. I'm not sure what I can do to cheer her up."

Leah turned and looked at Mary. "Why don't you take her on a cruise?"

"Yeah, right."

"Take her on the cruise to Alaska," Leah said. "The two of you can use the free tickets. It's the week she's coming, and I don't know who I would go with."

Mary stopped and stared. "Are you serious?"

"Yes, I'm completely serious. This would be good for you and for your sister. You haven't been on a vacation in years, Mary."

"Neither have you, Leah. You're the one who always wants to go somewhere exciting. This is your trip."

Leah laughed. "It was my fluke. My goofed-up dialing. I didn't do anything to win the trip."

"But it's your trip," Mary protested.

"Okay, it's my trip, and I can do what I want with it. And what I choose to do is give it to you and your sister." Leah began to dial the phone number for A Wing and a Prayer.

Mary sat down on the edge of the desk. "Are you sure?"

Leah smiled. "Very sure. Hi, Alissa? This is Leah. Hey, you know how you said those tickets were transferable to another person? Well, I'd like to transfer them. Here's Mary. She'll give you all the information."

Mary took the phone and relayed the details to Alissa and agreed to go by the travel agency at lunch to pick up the papers. When Mary finished the call, she leaned over and hugged Leah.

"You have no idea how much I appreciate this." Mary began to cry. Leah guessed those tears had come often, quick and silent like that, during the last five years since her husband had left with a woman who worked at the gas station on the outskirts of town. Mary had worked hard to rebuild her life with her three kids. This would be a nice break for her.

Leah handed the Alaska tour book to Mary. "Here, you're the one who needs to read this. And I have a couple of home videos of Alaska in my car you can watch, too."

They both chuckled, and Mary dried her tears. Settling in with the stack of patient folders before her, Leah felt good. Very good. Better than she had felt in a long time. The anxiety of the day before, when she had gone to Jessica's, had subsided. Leah's heart was more at peace with God than it had been in years.

One of her coworkers handed Leah a bunch of papers and said, "Are you ready to be impressed? This is the list of day surgeries for tomorrow and all of next week. Are we getting organized around here or what?"

"I'm impressed," Leah said, flipping through the pages. Tuesday was the lightest schedule. Friday of next week was the fullest. A name on the list for Friday caught her eye and caused Leah's heart to skip a beat.

The name on the list was Seth Edwards. And the description of the procedure was underlined in red, which meant one thing to all hospital employees: cancer.

Chapter Sixteen

"Hi, Jack, this is Leah Hudson. Could you please leave a message for Seth? Ask him to call me when he returns from his route. Let me give you all my numbers." Leah gave Jack, the clerk at the PDS station, her work number, home number, and cell phone number.

"Did you try him on his cell phone?" Jack asked.

"No, I don't know the number."

"Well, we're not supposed to give them out, but since it's you, Leah, I'll tell you what it is."

Leah was using her cell phone as she drove to the hardware store on her lunch break. She was determined to buy her garden seeds so she could get right to work when she arrived at home. Punching in the numbers for Seth's cell phone, she felt relieved when he answered after the second ring.

"Hi, it's Leah."

"How did you get this number?"

"Jack at the PDS office. He used to go out with one of my sisters."

"Oh. So what's up?"

"Yesterday Alissa told me she and Brad have a couch they would like to give away. I didn't know if you needed a couch, but I thought I'd let you know."

"I do need a couch. Thanks for telling me. Do you have a number for them?"

"Alissa runs the travel agency on Main Street. It's A Wing and a Prayer. You can't miss it. It's next door to the Wallflower Cafe and across the street from the *Glenbrooke Gazette*."

"I'm about three blocks from there now. I'll stop in and talk to Alissa about it. Thanks."

"Sure." Leah knew she could end the call then, but she didn't want to. The last time she had talked to Seth, at the rained-out Little League game, she had been cool and reserved. That was before her spirit had been plowed up. Everything in her life was fresh now. That was also before she had read Seth's name on the day surgery form next to the procedure listed as "L5-S1: removal of melanoma and surrounding lymph nodes."

"I'm headed downtown, too," Leah said. "Any chance you would like to meet for some lunch?"

Seth hesitated only a moment before saying, "Sure. Where do you suggest?"

"The Wallflower Cafe is close and easy."

"Okay. I'll see you there in a few minutes."

Leah hung up and turned left on Main, parking four doors down from the Wallflower Cafe. The vegetable seeds could wait until after work.

The small diner had once been a charming, favorite spot to stop for a sandwich or cup of soup on a rainy day. Today the sun was shining, which made the many flaws of the Wallflower stand out. The real flowers in the planters on the walls above the booths had been replaced years ago with plastic red and orange ones. The vinyl seats had too many lumps to be comfortable to sit on for long, and the menu had decreased in variety. Last year the café owners had put a for sale sign in the window, but after receiving no offers in two months, they took down the sign and compromised by trimming their menu and shop hours.

Leah greeted Hazel, the waitress at the counter, and decided to sit at the window seat so she could watch for Seth.

"Coffee?" Hazel asked, walking toward Leah with the coffeepot in her hand.

"No, thanks. What's your soup today?"

"Vegetable barley," Hazel said.

"I'd like some soup and a large orange juice."

"Coming right up," Hazel said. She shuffled past the four customers who sat at a table in the center of the cafe and filled their coffee mugs.

One of the customers was Collin Radcliffe. He was ignoring Leah, which was typical of him since their days growing up together in Glenbrooke. Collin had gone off to college and become a lawyer. He had been in California until the first of this year when rumor had it that he had returned to Glenbrooke to take over his father's law practice. Radcliffe Sr. had announced his retirement at the end of this year.

Leah looked down and noticed that her hands were shaking. She refused to think that being around Collin made her nervous. So what if he was a big, important, successful classmate who had gone out into the world and had made something of himself? He still ignored her. Leah was certain that the nervousness was because of Seth.

What am I going to say to him when he walks in? Do I tell him I know about the surgery right away or do I wait to see if he tells me?

She knew better than to make assumptions about the severity of the cancer until after the test results from the surgery. But she had been around enough to know melanoma could be life-threatening.

Does Seth understand how serious this is? Is this the real reason he came back to the States, but he hasn't told anyone? I wonder if Franklin knows?

Seth drove past the window just then. When he spotted Leah, he waved to her. She guessed he would have to drive around the block to find a place to park the delivery truck. While she waited, she tried to calm herself. It wouldn't do any good for her newly discovered emotions to overwhelm her again.

Her soup and orange juice arrived before Seth did. When he did enter the café with his casual grin lighting up his tan face, Leah saw his tan differently than before. *Didn't he realize how damaging the sun could be? Sunscreen is no guarantee against skin cancer. How could he not realize that?*

"Hope I didn't keep you waiting long. I checked in with Alissa next door, and it looks like I'm going to take their couch. Thanks for letting me know about it."

"I'm glad it worked out," Leah said. It seemed to her that Seth was saying all the right words, but he was acting reserved. It was the same way she had treated him last time she had seen him.

Hazel walked over with the coffeepot and asked if Seth wanted any.

"No, thanks. I'd like the same thing she's having. Soup and orange juice. And do you have any bread?"

Hazel nodded and returned to the counter. Seth looked at Leah and said, "I understand you went to see Franklin the other day."

"Yes, I did."

"He said you agreed to take him to some hot springs for the last weekend of May."

"Yes, I did."

"I don't know if it's such a good idea for him to make a trip like that. He told me it's been more than a year since he broke his hip, but he's still not very strong. Doesn't he seem frail to you?"

"He's an elderly man," Leah said, feeling her defenses rising. "I agree that he is frail, but this trip seems important to him."

Seth leaned back. "I just don't think it's a great idea."

"Did Franklin ask you to go on the trip, too?"

"Yes, of course. And I told him I didn't think May was the best time for him to go. So the old fox turns around and asks you."

Hazel placed a soup bowl in front of Seth as well as a breadbasket and a glass of orange juice. "Are you Franklin Madison's grandson?" she asked him.

"No, I'm a great-nephew."

Leah couldn't help but take advantage of Seth's line. "Well, if you really were a 'great' nephew, you would see how important this is to Franklin. And you would give the elderly gentleman a chance to do what he wants to do." She knew her emotions were unraveling again, and the frayed edges were showing.

Seth looked down at his soup bowl. She couldn't tell if he was praying or trying to control himself so he wouldn't snap back with an answer.

"Can I get you two anything else?" Hazel asked.

"No, thanks. Just the check," Leah said.

Seth looked up. He appeared calm. "I don't think I can go along with this. In my opinion, Franklin isn't strong enough to make such a long trip."

"What about you?" Leah asked. "Would you be strong

enough to make the trip in a few weeks?"

"Of course," Seth said. He definitely looked offended now. "Why would you ask that?"

Leah swished the last bit of orange juice around in the bottom of her glass. "I work at the hospital, you know. I see all the paperwork. I know you're scheduled for surgery next Friday."

Seth looked at her steadily but didn't say anything.

"I think I know what you're feeling right now," Leah said, lowering her voice and leaning closer. "I felt the same way when you asked me about being the…" She looked over her shoulder to make sure no one was listening. Then in a whisper she said, "the Glenbrooke Zorro. You told me I could trust you to keep my secret. I'm inviting you to trust me in the same way."

Seth drew his soupspoon to his mouth and took his time before speaking. "I had a mole removed in Costa Rica. When the results came back positive for melanoma, I decided to move back to the States. A guy I knew in Costa Rica recommended a specialist in skin cancer who retired and moved to Glenbrooke. Only this specialist didn't completely retire. He still sees occasional patients at Glenbrooke General."

"Dr. Norton," Leah said. "He and his wife moved here five months ago from Palm Springs."

Seth nodded. "I knew my great-uncle was here in Glenbrooke so I had a convenient connection. A reason to move here. I haven't told anyone since there's nothing specific to tell."

"The doctor in Costa Rica might have gotten it all," Leah said. "It's best when they find and remove it early."

"Yes, but Dr. Norton said the results from the Costa Rican lab weren't as specific as what he sees on reports from U.S. hospitals. He told me to be prepared for a lengthy surgery on Friday. He'll remove some of the surrounding tissue. If they find any cancer cells, he plans to remove a large section that day and go all the way to the bone. They'll do a skin graft if necessary."

"That's pretty standard," Leah said. "And Dr. Norton is the best. He's very thorough. I'm surprised he listed you as day surgery. It's more likely you'll be staying overnight."

Seth pushed away his soup. "If the area tests out clean after the surrounding samples are examined, then I can go home."

"And a lot of people do," Leah said, trying to be encouraging. "I see this often. We had two patients last month who came from out of state to see Dr. Norton. He tends to paint the worst case scenario just to prepare patients for what could happen. With both of those patients it was treatable."

"Let's hope that will be true in my situation," Seth said quietly. He looked as if it had taken a lot out of him to confide in Leah.

As she would with any friend, Leah reached across the table and took Seth's hand in hers and gave it an encouraging squeeze. She realized he had made the same gesture toward her twice before, and both times she had pulled away. Now Seth was the one who pulled away.

"I should get back on my route. I have a lot of deliveries today." He took some money from his pocket and left it on the table. "I'll see you later."

"Okay," Leah said, trying to sound cheerful, even though she felt as if she had been rejected. "Let me know if you need any help with the couch."

"No, I have it covered." Seth headed for the door. Then he turned and walked back to the table. "I still don't think it's a good idea for Franklin to go anywhere. Will you at least reconsider your answer to him before he makes a lot of plans?"

"Okay, I'll think about it." She waited until Seth was gone before she pulled out the remaining amount due and placed it on top of the bill along with Seth's contribution. She slid across the seat and was about to rise when Collin Radcliffe came across the room and stopped by her table.

"Leah?" he asked.

"Yes."

"Leah Hudson, right?"

"Yes."

"So good to see you," Collin said in a professional tone. He stuck out his hand to shake Leah's. With his other hand he pulled a business card from the pocket of his expensive-looking jacket. "You probably don't remember me. Collin Radcliffe. We went to school together."

How could I forget you? Leah thought. Collin was her first gradeschool crush and a disastrous disappointment. She found this attention from Collin almost humorous. In third grade she had saved her best valentine for him and bravely wrote the word "love" on the back. He had somehow managed to return it to her valentine box before the school day was over. Only, instead of a mutual, secret message of admiration, Collin had torn the valentine into two pieces and x-ed out the word "love." That was Leah's most vivid memory of Collin Radcliffe. This polite, professional version was a surprise to her.

"I was sorry to hear about your parents."

"Thank you, Collin."

"Perhaps you've heard that I'll be taking over my father's practice. If you have need of any legal advice, you feel free to call me."

Leah took his business card and then looked up at his face, just to make sure this was the same Collin she knew so many years ago. He was a nice-looking man, with rich, dark hair and dark eyebrows. He was also tall, which meant Leah had to look up to him, in the literal and figurative sense. And that was something Leah didn't do well with men.

"I'll be sure to call you if the need ever arises," Leah said politely. "But I doubt it will. Thanks anyway."

She left before Marcus Shelton, the insurance agent dining with Collin, could corner her and ask about her current life insurance policy. She had enough challenges on her plate at the moment.

Chapter Seventeen

As Leah planted her garden that evening, she thought about Seth and how life offers no guarantees. Before going to bed, she wrote out her verses on three-by-five cards, first the verses from Seth about the winter being over and the flowers appearing. Then she wrote out the three verses from Jessica about trusting in the Lord and delighting in Him.

Leah crawled into bed tired and sore from her gardening. She prayed aloud into the stillness of her room, "Lord, I don't know how to delight myself in you, and I don't know how to trust you. I think Jessica's right. These are important steps for me to take. So please teach me how to trust in you and delight in you. Plant these new seeds in my heart."

Not until she was on her way to Camp Heather Brook the next morning did Leah realize how easily she had been talking to God ever since her early morning rendezvous with him in the garden. Everything in her life felt fresh, just like the clear, spring morning that greeted her as she drove along the country road to Glenbrooke's outskirts.

I hope the weather is this nice next weekend for the May Day event.

All the other women on the May Day planning committee were saying the same thing when Leah arrived at Camp Heather Brook. Jessica and Lauren already were seated next to Shelly in the lounge area of the camp's main meeting hall. Shelly had the chairs and leather couch pulled close in a circle by the window where the morning sun poured in and troupes of dust ballerinas danced on the sunbeams.

On a thick wooden coffee table sat trays of muffins and a carafe of coffee. Hot water stood ready in a teapot covered by a quilted white cozy, and stuffed in several small baskets were tea bags, sugar, and powdered coffee creamer. The party napkins, decorated with sleek, white swans, were fanned across the front of the table. Teacups and saucers were stacked two high across the back. It looked like a picture from a magazine.

"You sure have a knack for this sort of thing," Leah told Shelly as she reached carefully for a teacup.

"I wasn't sure about sitting in the direct sun," Shelly said, surveying the room.

"It's so inviting." Lauren opened an Irish Breakfast tea bag and dipped it in her cup of hot water. "I'm ready for some more sun after all the rain we had last week."

"If we get too warm, we can move to the center of the room," Shelly suggested.

The ladies settled in with their beverages and muffins, and Shelly said, "I have a handout of the schedule." She was efficient and organized but not bossy. Leah enjoyed working on projects with Shelly.

The May Day event was Shelly's idea two years ago. At the

time, Mother's Day was approaching, and she was going through fertility tests at the hospital. She and Jonathan had been married for four years and had hoped to have children right away, but Shelly was having difficulty conceiving. That made Mother's Day a painful event for her so she decided to host a celebration that would encompass all the women of Glenbrooke, whether they were mothers or not. Leah liked the idea right away since it included her as a single woman.

"We need two greeters at the main door," Shelly was saying now.

Jessica and Lauren simultaneously signaled that they would volunteer.

"Okay, good." Shelly held up a packet of seeds. "This year I thought it would be fun if we used these for name tags. The permanent markers work well on the front and that way the women can take the seeds home and plant them. I got a great deal on the packets. They're mostly flowers, but I have some vegetables as well."

"I love it!" Lauren said, taking the sample packet from Shelly and examining it more closely. "How many women are we expecting this year?"

"Around two hundred."

"And only the four of us to run it?" Lauren asked.

"My mom and my sister Meredith are coming for the weekend. I know they'll pitch in and help us."

"How's Meredith feeling?" Jessica asked.

"Better. She thinks she's over the morning sickness now that she's out of the first trimester."

Leah wondered if Shelly found it hard to talk about her younger sister's pregnancy—especially since Meredith had gotten pregnant only a few months after she and Jake were married. Leah tried to imagine how Shelly must feel about not having children when all her married friends and sisters seemed to have no problem getting pregnant. Considering Shelly's situation made Leah realize everyone has her unique challenge in life.

"Is that okay with you, Leah?" Shelly asked, drawing Leah back to the meeting.

"I'm sorry. What did you say?"

"I asked if you would be willing to oversee the maypole event like you have the past two years."

"Sure," Leah said. "Is Jonathan going to have it up the day before?"

"We'll have it up at least the day before," Shelly said.

"Good, because I think some of the vinyl streamers tore last year when those kids were hanging on them. I'll check it out and see if we need to replace any of them."

"That would be great," Shelly said. She continued through to the end of the list and asked if anyone had questions.

"The food?" Leah asked, noticing there was no list like last year's of what everyone was supposed to bring.

"We were able to have the event catered this year," Shelly said. "Some of you may have met Genevieve Ahrens and her daughters at church on Easter. They just moved here, and Genevieve is starting up a catering business from her home. She's going to take care of all the food for us."

Leah guessed that Genevieve's daughters weren't toddlers, otherwise Leah would have had them in her Sunday school group.

"That's a huge relief," Lauren said. "Remember all those egg salad sandwiches we made last year?"

"And the fruit cups?" Jessica added. "I think Kyle and I were up until midnight filling those little pastry shells with pudding and fruit cocktail."

"Those were a big hit," Lauren said. "Are we having those again?"

"I don't know," Shelly said. "I'm leaving it all in Genevieve's capable hands. Her talent in the kitchen is surpassed only by her talent in the garden."

"That reminds me," Lauren said. "Do you want us to bring in cut flowers like we did last year?"

Shelly went over the instructions for the cut flowers, the craft table that offered a glue-it-together birdhouse or a clay pot for each guest to paint and to plant the seeds from inside her name tag. That brought them to the end of the list.

"Are you sure you don't need to delegate anything else to the rest of us?" Leah asked.

"I believe that's it," Shelly said, checking her list one last time. "Why don't we pray together about all this before you go?"

Shelly led them in a heartfelt prayer, thanking God for the opportunity to have a day they could celebrate together. She asked for his blessing on the event and asked that the time would encourage many of the Glenbrooke women.

As Leah listened to Shelly's prayer, she felt as if she were praying every word with her. Leah was no longer an outsider, listening and observing while others communicated with God. She felt connected. The sensation was overwhelming, and she found uninvited tears tumbling down her cheeks as Shelly said amen.

"Are you okay?" Jessica asked, reaching over and giving Leah's arm a squeeze.

"You guys," Leah said, encompassing Lauren and Shelly in her answer to Jessica, "I have something I want to tell you."

The three women waited in a united silence.

"Jessica knows part of this, but I wanted to tell all three of you what's been happening in my life lately." The tears kept coming, but Leah didn't care. They were like a gentle spring rain and seemed necessary to water the fresh seeds God had been planting in her heart.

She let out a breathy laugh and wiped her cheeks with her

fingers. "Seth told me that tears wash the windows of our souls, helping us to see ourselves more clearly. I think the windows of my soul must have needed a lot of cleaning because I've been crying more these past few weeks than I've cried in years."

Her three friends all looked at her with understanding smiles.

"The thing is," Leah continued, "I don't know if I'm seeing myself more clearly, but I'm definitely seeing God more clearly. Is it possible to be a Christian for a long time and then suddenly have this breakthrough, and you feel as if it's all brand new, and all you want is to know God more deeply and completely?"

All three women nodded with shared understanding.

"I experienced a huge change in my life about five years ago," Shelly said. "I was supposed to be helping with food service at a woman's retreat, but my sister tricked me into going to the chapel and listening to the speaker. I think Meri knew I needed to get my heart set back on the Lord. Do you feel as if God is pursuing you?"

"Yes," Leah said, straightening up in her chair. "That's exactly what I feel."

"Your soul is mingling with God's," Lauren said. "Don't hold back. Let your heart echo back to him all the messages of love he's sending you."

"Okay," Leah said, absorbing Lauren's advice.

"God is the relentless lover," Shelly said with a knowing smile. "You're his first love. He will never stop pursuing you because he wants you back."

Leah nodded.

"'Delight yourself in the Lord.'" Jessica quoted the Scripture softly. "'See! The winter is past…the season of singing has come.'"

Chapter Eighteen

Leah didn't sing a lot during the next week. But she found herself humming. And praying. She prayed more often and more openly than she remembered ever praying before.

At work every day that week Mary talked about the cruise and thanked Leah for giving her the tickets. She kept telling Leah how excited her sister was about going.

On Wednesday night, the Glenbrooke Rangers won their game, and even though Seth wasn't there to help her out in the Snack Shack, Leah felt content. She had posted several of her three-by-five cards inside the small building, and in between customers she was absorbing verses from 1 Corinthians 13 and 1 John. Any and all passages she could find on God's love seemed to feed her soul.

She ran into Seth on Thursday afternoon when she went past Ida's house to pick up her muffin tins. He was standing on Ida's front steps, politely sipping a glass of her lemonade while the delivery van was double-parked with the motor running.

When Ida ducked back into her house to get Leah's muffin tins, Leah told Seth, "I've been praying for you every day this week. I wanted you to know that. I've been praying that God would give you strength and that he would be merciful and heal you."

Seth smiled appreciatively at Leah. "Thank you. Ida was just telling me that you won a cruise to Alaska and that you gave the trip away to a friend at work." He tilted his head and looked at her closely. "What happened to the Amelia I met two weeks ago who was going to take off to see the world?"

Before Leah could answer, Ida appeared with the muffin tins and a glass of iced lemonade for Leah. Ida was chuckling to herself as she said, "And here I thought the Glenbrooke Zorro had left these muffin tins for me."

Seth and Leah exchanged a quick look and then both began to speak at the same time.

"I need to get going," Seth said.

"Thanks for the lemonade," Leah said. She took a gulp as Seth nodded his good-bye to both the women and hurried to his truck.

"Such a fine young man," Ida said. "I'm not surprised Franklin changed his will last week."

Leah lowered her lemonade glass and turned to Ida.

"Mavis told me," Ida said. "She's been a might concerned about him lately. Seems Franklin has it in his mind to go to Hamilton Hot Springs for some reason."

"It was a special place for him and Naomi," Leah said, defending her old friend. "He probably wants to relive some of the memories."

Ida shook her head. "He's a crazy old man. With his poor health, he has no business traveling. I told Seth that, and he agrees with me. He said he wouldn't be taking Franklin to the hot springs and that was that."

"I might take him," Leah said. "He asked me to. If Seth won't, then maybe I will. If I were ninety-two and wanted to go somewhere, I'd like to think I had a friend who would take me."

Ida blinked, showing her surprise. "Why, Leah Hudson! I'd never expect such brashness from you. Mavis said that Franklin called a lawyer last week, and he came to the house and charged Franklin a good deal of money to change his will." Ida stood her ground as if she had just made a bold declaration, and Leah should be shocked by the news.

Leah finished her lemonade and said, "I'm sure Franklin has the right to change his will whenever he wants."

Ida squinted at Leah and said, "Doesn't it make you a tad suspicious that he changed it right after that amiable young nephew came to town?"

Leah knew it wasn't her place to tell Ida that Seth had another reason for coming to Glenbrooke besides finding a way to appear in his great-uncle's will, not that Ida knew any of the specifics of how the will had been changed. Ida, of all people, didn't need to know about Seth's scheduled surgery with Dr. Norton.

Handing Ida the emptied glass, Leah said, "You certainly make the best lemonade in town, Ida. One of these days you'll have to tell me your secret ingredient."

"It's the fresh fruit, of course," Ida said with a snap in her voice. "I told you that before. Six fresh lemons and just a squeeze of fresh lime. Not too much sugar."

"It sure is good. Thanks. I need to be going," Leah said before Ida realized that she had been sidetracked from the conversation about the lawyer and Franklin's will.

"Your irises are beautiful this year," Leah said, as she headed down the front steps.

"I'm overrun with them in the backyard. Why don't you cut some and take them home with you?" Ida said.

"We could sure use them for the May Day event," Leah said. "Would you mind if I came over early Saturday morning? That way the flowers would be fresh."

"Heavens, no, I don't mind! Cut all you want. And help yourself to tulips by the back door. They need to be thinned out something awful. I don't seem to be getting all my gardening done as quickly as I should this year."

"I'll come by around 7:30 Saturday morning. If you would like a ride to Camp Heather Brook, I'd be glad to take you."

"That would be wonderful."

Leah hurried to her car, glad that she had successfully diverted Ida's attention off Franklin's will. It occurred to Leah that she was the only one who thought Franklin should take his trip. She hadn't been in favor of it when he first asked her, but now she felt as if she was his only advocate.

Instead of turning right on Pine and heading for her house, Leah turned left and drove to Franklin's. She let herself in and called out her usual greeting, but Franklin wasn't in his recliner. Mavis met Leah in the entryway and said Franklin was lying down in his bedroom.

"Is he feeling okay?" Leah asked.

"He's running a slight fever," Mavis said. "I think he's been overdoing it the last few days. He's had company nearly every day this week, and it takes a lot out of him."

"Do you think I should pop my head in or let him rest?" Leah asked.

"It's up to you. You always cheer him up. Might be just what he needs today."

Leah followed Mavis into Franklin's bedroom. He was

sound asleep on top of the bedspread with a patchwork quilt pulled up over him. Leah slipped into the chair beside his bed and held his frail, wrinkled hand. "Hi, Franklin. It's Leah. I stopped by to see you for a few minutes."

The old man's eyelids fluttered, but he didn't perk up the way he usually did when she caught him napping in his recliner. He smiled when he saw her and said in a clear voice, "I've made all the plans, Leah."

"Good," she said, giving his hand a gentle squeeze. "Mavis told me you've had a busy week. Why don't you sleep, and we'll talk another time."

Franklin didn't let go of her hand. "You know," he said in a weakened voice, "it's the blessing of the Lord." His eyelids fluttered closed, and he said, "That's all it is."

Leah wasn't sure what he meant. "You rest up, Franklin. I'll come see you later." She leaned over and kissed his warm cheek. A smile came to Franklin's thin lips, and the steady sound of his deep breathing returned.

"He said the same thing after the lawyer left the other day," Mavis told Leah on her way out. "He said, 'The blessing of the Lord makes you rich.' Now what do you suppose he means by that?"

"Maybe it's a verse," Leah ventured.

"That's not a verse I've ever heard preached about," Mavis said.

Leah opened the front door and said, "Let me know if he needs anything or if his fever goes higher. I'd be glad to help out if you need me."

"I'll let you know," Mavis said, sounding as if she had everything under control as usual.

Leah thought about Franklin all evening as she was doing laundry and cleaning up her neglected kitchen. The bottom of her oven was sprinkled with charred pizza dough crumbs.

That explained why Lauren had turned off the oven the night Leah was trying to bake the spinach for Seth and herself.

As she scrubbed, Leah thought about Seth. She wondered how he was feeling about his surgery tomorrow. Her emotional response to that man had changed so much in the past two weeks. But one thing remained the same from the start: She felt drawn to him. Connected with him. He held her secret, she held his. Leah wondered if she would feel the same way about a brother going in for cancer surgery. Since she didn't have a brother, she didn't know. It felt different from how she had handled concern for sisters and friends, young and old, who had gone in for some type of surgery. And Leah had seen them all. This time, with Seth, she wanted to be there for him in anyway she could. She didn't know exactly what that meant, but she knew she could pray, and she did.

Chapter Nineteen

On Friday Seth arrived at the hospital at ten o'clock for his surgery. Leah treated him as she would any other patient she admitted for day surgery. Seth responded as any other patient would. A little nervous. A little self-conscious.

Leah didn't leave the hospital for lunch. She wanted to hear the results as soon as they were available, and she let Shirley, the nurse in charge of day surgeries, know that she was waiting for news. By one o'clock there hadn't been any news. Dr. Norton had been with Seth for almost two hours. It didn't look like a good sign.

At 1:15, Shirley called Leah's desk to tell her Dr. Norton had completed the diagnostic check of Seth's back where the previous procedure had been performed. Those samples had been sent to the lab. Three other areas, however, appeared suspicious, and Dr. Norton was testing them as well.

Her heart racing, Leah said thanks to Shirley and hung up.

Leah sat at her desk numbly staring at the phone. This was not good. She knew that, if Dr. Norton had found so many suspicious areas, the chances of the melanoma spreading were greater than Seth may have suspected.

After trying unsuccessfully for almost an hour to catch up on her paperwork, Leah finally told Mary, "I'm going upstairs to day surgery. I need to check on something. Call me up there if you need me."

"Sure," Mary said. "Could you take this file up to Shirley? She called about it a little while ago, and I told her I didn't have it, but it was buried on my desk."

Leah took the file and went to the elevator where a number of people already were waiting. She decided to take the stairs and dashed up them as if she needed to beat the elevator. The urge to do something to help felt overpowering and yet there was so little she could do.

Shirley gave Leah a curious look after she breathlessly handed Shirley the file. "You didn't have to bring it up," Shirley said.

"I wanted to check on Seth Edwards. You said Dr. Norton was exploring several suspicious areas."

"Yes. The lab results won't be back for awhile. Did you need to check with the patient on something? He's still heavily sedated. I don't think he'll be able to answer any questions."

"I'll check back," Leah said. "Could you let me know when the lab results come in?"

"Sure," Shirley said. "I'll call you right away."

"Thanks." Leah returned to the elevator and pushed the button three times. The brutal inevitability of disease and death angered Leah. She thought of how she dealt with death every day. She filed the papers for death certificates and directed grieving family members to the hospital chapel. When her own parents had passed away, Leah was so immune to the sting of death and so conditioned to handling it as a step-by-step paperwork procedure that she had made all the arrangements for her parents with barely a tear.

The tears seemed to have been catching up with her the past few weeks and now they came again, rushing up her throat and fleeing her system through her eyes. Covering her face with her hand as she stood in the elevator, Leah tried to make it appear as if she had something in her contact. Which she did. Tears. An ocean of them.

When the elevator door opened, all the other people left the elevator, but Leah stayed inside. She pushed the button for the fourth floor and quietly made her way to the chapel where she grabbed a handful of tissues from the box by the door and then went straight to the front pew.

The chapel was empty. She sat down and prayed for Seth. "Please be merciful to him, Father. Spare his life. Don't take him yet. Let him live so he can serve you."

Leah opened her eyes and realized she had jumped way ahead in her conclusions regarding Seth's condition. Much could be done to treat cancer. Even if his melanoma had advanced, he had plenty of chances to survive and make a full recovery.

Her tears subsided. The sense of panic dissipated. She rode the elevator back to the first floor where she returned to her desk.

Mary had the phone to her ear and motioned for Leah to pick up line two.

"This is Leah," she said.

"Leah, we just received the results back on Seth Edwards," Shirley said. "Dr. Norton is right here. Would you like him to go over the specifics with you?"

"Could you ask him to wait?" Leah asked. "I'm coming

right up." She dashed up the stairs and, out of breath, met Dr. Norton at the desk.

"That was fast," Dr. Norton said, appearing amused. "Shirley said you needed information on Seth Edwards."

Leah nodded, still catching her breath. She motioned to an empty couch in the waiting area. "Mind if we sit down?"

"Not at all." Dr. Norton followed Leah to the couch.

"What are the lab results?" Leah asked, trying hard to appear professional.

"Good news," Dr. Norton said firmly. "The original area was clean, and all other areas were benign. No further melanoma."

"Does Seth know yet?"

"No. He's still sedated. We sent him to recovery. It will be a while before he's fully cognizant. I'd like to do a recheck in six months." Dr. Norton stood, tucking his skilled hands into the pockets of his white coat. "This is the kind of case I like to see. Always best when it's caught early. He'll be relieved."

"Yes, he will," Leah said. "Thanks, Dr. Norton."

"Why don't you go check on him? And let whoever is driving him home know he's ready to go."

Leah's relieved smile expressed everything that was on her heart when she stood next to Seth in the recovery room. He appeared to be awake since his eyes were open, but Leah could tell he was still floating from the sedatives.

"Good news," Leah told him, giving his arm a squeeze. "The tests all came back negative."

Seth gave her a dazed look, as if he wasn't sure what that meant.

"There's no more evidence of cancer in the original area or the other areas the doctor checked. It's great news, Seth! You can relax now."

"Okay," he answered compliantly. "I'll relax now." Seth closed his eyes.

"Wait! Before you fall asleep," Leah said, gently patting his hand, "did you make arrangements for anyone to drive you home?"

"No," Seth answered without opening his eyes. "I thought I was staying overnight."

"No, you can go home now. I'm sure you'll sleep better there. Would you like me to drive you, since you didn't make other arrangements?"

"Okay."

"I'll be back in a few minutes."

"Okay."

Leah hurried downstairs to her workstation and told Mary she needed to leave early.

"What's going on with you today?" Mary asked. "You've hardly been here when you've been here."

"I'm taking a patient home who doesn't have a ride." Leah didn't expect Mary to question that. Leah had done the same favor for other patients in the past.

"It's Seth Edwards, isn't it?" Mary asked.

"Yes, why?"

"Shirley told me you were asking about him. Did you know his insurance isn't up-to-date?"

"What do you mean?"

"I have his complete file here, and his insurance from his current employer doesn't go into effect yet because he hasn't worked there long enough."

"Okay," Leah said, not sure why that should concern her.

"It looks like we'll have to file this with his previous insurance, if it's still in effect, since it appears to be a preexisting condition."

"Right," Leah agreed. "It sounds like standard procedure to me."

"Well, there is part of it that's not standard." Mary turned

Seth's file in Leah's direction so she could see the paperwork Mary seemed so concerned about. "Look at this. There's no way to even tell if he had prior insurance."

Leah took one look and understood why Mary was worried. The paperwork was all in Spanish. "We've had those before," Leah said.

"We have?"

"It was before you started in this department. We had some medical forms in French. Or maybe it was Dutch. I don't remember. We have an agency that translates it and negotiates for us. It's not a problem."

"Oh, well, if you say it's not a problem then I guess it's not a problem."

Leah felt relieved that Mary's concern over Seth hadn't been something serious, such a mistake on the diagnosis of all clear.

"I'll take care of it tomorrow," Leah said, grabbing her purse. "You can leave the file on my desk." She copied down Seth's address in case he was too woozy to remember. Hurrying back up to the day surgery unit, Leah found that Shirley had Seth in a wheelchair, ready to go.

When Seth saw Leah, his face lit up, as if she were the only one in the room.

"Hi," Leah said, giving Seth a smile that equaled his in warmth. "Are you ready to go home?"

"That depends."

"On what?"

"Am I driving?"

Leah's smile broadened. "No, I'm driving."

"Good." Seth leaned back in the wheelchair.

Shirley said, "Remember, Leah, he's still under the influence of the Versed, and we gave him Vicoden for the pain. He'll be able to move fine and respond to you, but he may not remember the ride home after the medication wears off. He had a little more than normal since the procedure went longer than expected."

Shirley handed Leah a list of post-op instructions. "Make sure he eats something. Vicoden can be pretty rough on an empty stomach."

Leah nodded. She knew all that. She also knew that Shirley was just doing her job in relaying the information to Leah.

"Don't worry. I've done this a few times," Leah told Shirley, as she wheeled Seth to the elevator. What she didn't tell Shirley was that never before had she wanted to care for a patient as much as she wanted to care for this one.

Chapter Twenty

You know, I'm sure I can walk," Seth said when the elevator landed on the first floor. His voice sounded higher than normal, and his expression was much peppier than Leah had seen before.

"Hospital policy," Leah told him. "All patients must leave in wheelchairs."

As soon as she had Seth wheeled out front and settled in her Blazer, he became more talkative.

"I have to say that this is so very, very extra kind of you." He sounded normal but with more of an enthusiastic twist than the situation called for.

"I'm glad to do it. Would you like something to eat now? Or when we get to Edgefield?"

"You mean I get to eat? Oh, good! I haven't had anything since last night because they make you fast after midnight, you know. How about a jumbo shake. Doesn't that sound good? A nice, big, jumbo milkshake. I could really go for a shake."

Leah pressed her lips together so Seth wouldn't see her smiling at his energetic dialogue. The medication obviously had made him loopy.

"Okay, I'll stop at Dairy Queen," Leah said.

"Oh, perfect! Dairy Queen! How did you know? You're amazing. Absolutely amazing. Did I ever tell you you're amazing?"

Leah didn't answer. She pulled into the small parking area in front of the Dairy Queen and said, "You can wait here, if you like. I'll get your shake."

"Oh, I don't want to wait," Seth said, opening his door. "I think it would do me good to stretch my legs."

Leah hopped out and ran around to the passenger's side just in case his legs turned to jelly. Seth slowly climbed out of the car.

"Whoa!" he said. "It feels like a big bubble is all around my head."

"You're doing fine." She held out her hand in case he needed it to steady himself.

Seth took a few steps without assistance and then stopped and swayed slightly. "Whoa! Did you feel that? We're having an earthquake."

"No, it's okay," Leah said quietly. "It's not an earthquake."

Several people were watching Seth, including a group of teenagers at one of the picnic tables. His voice was louder than it needed to be, and his actions were drawing attention to him.

"Maybe you should wait in the car," Leah suggested.

"No, it's okay. I'm okay. We're okay. You're okay." Seth took a few more steps with improved balance. "See? I've got it. I've got it. I've got it." Then he sang the words. "I've got it. Oh, yeah, I've got it."

Leah didn't recognize the tune. She doubted it was an actual song. But that didn't stop Seth from singing as if it were a catchy commercial jingle. "I've got it. I've got it. Oh, yeah, I've got it. Baby, you know I've got it."

They stepped up to the order window, and all eyes were on Seth.

"May I help you?" the waitress asked, looking dubiously at Leah.

"A large shake to go, please," Leah said.

"What flavor?" the waitress asked.

"What flavors do you have?" Seth asked in a singsong voice with a wide grin.

"Um, they're all listed on that sign," the waitress said.

Seth looked over her head and began to read each flavor listed. After "strawberry" he slipped into singing the flavors.

The teenaged waitress leaned over and asked Leah, "Is he drunk? Because if he is, we're supposed to ask him to leave, and if he doesn't leave, then we have to call the police."

"No," Leah said, "he's not drunk."

Seth kept singing. He was merrily going through the list of burgers now.

"He's just on drugs."

The waitress's eyes widened.

"No!" Leah spouted. "That wasn't what I meant to say. He's on medication. He's just come from the hospital, and the anesthesia and painkillers haven't worn off yet. He needs something to eat."

Seth was beginning to sing the shop hours and the posted policy on bounced checks.

Leah gave the waitress a desperate look. "Please, just give him a large vanilla shake. I don't think he'll know the difference."

"One large vanilla shake," the waitress called over her shoulder. Another employee jumped right on the task of preparing the order.

Seth suddenly stopped singing and turned to Leah. "Hey, what do you know? That's exactly just the same thing as what I'm having. And what are you having?"

"I already ate," Leah said. "The shake is for you." She pulled some money from her pocket and paid for it.

"Did you just pay for my shake?"

"Yes."

"Does that mean we're on a date?"

"No, I'm taking you home," Leah said, loud enough for those around to hear. "Do you remember you had surgery today? You need to get home and sleep off the effects of the anesthesia."

"We don't have to go right home, do we?" Seth asked, leaning against the counter as if his knees were turning wobbly on him. "I mean, if you're paying, then why don't we make an evening of it? We could go to the movies. I wouldn't mind seeing a movie right now. How about it?"

"I think we better get you home," Leah said, taking the shake and motioning with her other hand for the waitress to keep the change as a tip. "How are your legs feeling? Could you use a little help getting back to the car?"

"I think I've got it," Seth said. But as soon as he leaned away from the counter, he wobbled way too far to the left.

"Here," Leah said, quickly slipping her strong shoulder under his right arm. "Lean on me."

It was the wrong phrase to use because those three words sparked Seth on to another song. He sang it with wild abandon as Leah helped him to the car, with his arm around her shoulder and her arm around his waist.

Several teenagers, who had been watching the whole fiasco,

joined Seth in singing. Two of the girls who had been sitting on top of the picnic table stood with their arms around each other and, in between their playful laughter, matched Seth's lounge lizard voice note for note.

I can't believe this is happening! I've been transported into the middle of a Muppet movie.

Yanking open the passenger's door, Leah all but shoved Seth into the cab. But he wouldn't get in all the way. Instead, he hoisted himself up on the running board and held on to the top of the open door. He faced the teen girls and held out the last note with his right arm lifted high. Then, with a conductor-like swish of his hand, he directed the concluding note, and the girls stopped right on cue.

A burst of laughter, whistling, and applause followed from the Dairy Queen audience.

"Thank you. Thank you. Thank you very much," Seth obliged them with an Elvis accent. "You've been a great audience."

"Seth!" Leah said, pulling on his arm. "Come on! You need to get in the car."

"I gotta go," he told his laughing fans. Pointing his finger at them with his thumb up, he said, "Stay sweet, girls."

Lowering himself with a controlled tumble, Seth landed in the seat, and Leah closed the door. She went around the back of the car to get in her side.

"Here," Leah said, holding the shake out for him to take. "This is for you."

He didn't take the shake. Seth sat perfectly still with a larger than necessary grin on his face.

"Are you okay?" Leah asked.

Without a flinch or any change to his life-of-the-party expression, Seth said, "You know what? I think I'm gonna hurl."

Chapter Twenty-one

Leah squealed the car's back tires, as she pulled out of the Dairy Queen parking area. She knew it wouldn't do Seth any good to lose his cookies in front of his fan club. She didn't take the time to look for a plastic bag for him or to drive slowly to avoid motion sickness. She knew that Seth wouldn't remember any of this in the morning, but those high schoolers would never forget it.

A block away from the Dairy Queen, Leah pulled to the side of the road where tall grass rose from an irrigation ditch in front of an automotive store. "Do you need to get out?"

Seth had broken into a sweat and had closed his eyes. "No," he said after a moment. "I think I'm okay. Could you put on the air? It seems pretty hot all of a sudden."

Leah turned on the air conditioner and left the window down on his side, just in case. "Do you want to try drinking any of this?" She handed him the shake that she had jammed into the cup holder before her maniac exit from the Dairy Queen.

"Sure. It might help." He took the shake and drank slowly, turning his face to the stream of cool, blowing air. "Oh, yeah," he said a moment later. "This is much better."

"Good. Do you think it's okay if I drive now? Or would it help to sit for a few more minutes?"

"I'm fine," Seth said. "We can go." He drank some more of his shake. "Boy, this is a good shake. It tastes really, really good."

Leah pulled back onto the road and drove slowly toward Edgefield.

"So where are we going?" Seth asked.

"I'm taking you home. You need to rest."

"I feel much better now. This is a really good shake."

"So you said."

"I was pretty hungry."

"I can imagine."

"This is awful nice of you to take me home."

"No problem."

"You know what I think?"

"No, what do you think?"

"I think you're beautiful."

Leah wasn't ready for that statement. She glanced at him and then turned her attention back to the road. His expression was sincere. He was no longer perspiring. He looked normal.

"I mean it," Seth said. "I thought you were beautiful from the very first time I saw you. You were in that little hot dog shack, and you were cheering your heart out for those guys on the…" he paused. "What's the name of their team?"

"The Rangers."

"Yeah, that's right. The Rangers. You were in there cheering for those Rangers, and the sun was coming through the side of that hot dog shack, and it was shining on your face and making your hair look like the flame on a candle. All glowy and warm. And I looked at you, and I said to myself, 'Now, there is one beautiful woman.'"

Leah could barely breathe. The tears rushed to her eyes, and she blinked quickly to hold them back.

"Oh," Seth said tenderly, touching her shoulder. "Are you okay? You look like you're crying."

Leah blinked and wiped her cheek under her right eye. "Just washing the windows of my soul. I seem to be doing that a lot lately." She glanced at Seth. His expression remained one of concern, and he didn't seem to recognize his own line about washing the windows of the soul.

"You know what?" Leah said. "You're not going to remember this conversation tomorrow so I'm going to tell you something. The reason I'm crying is because no one ever," she drew in a breath and repeated the word with emphasis, "ever, has told me I was beautiful. You're the first one. And it doesn't really matter if you mean it or not. I'm going to take your compliment and hold it in my heart always."

"But I do mean it," Seth said, reaching over and fingering the ends of her wispy, blond hair. "Your hair is like honey. Like fine strands of pure honey spun into gold. And your face is open and honest and clean."

Leah found herself laughing nervously at his description. "Clean?" she repeated, as he touched her round, blushing cheek with his work-worn fingers.

"Yeah, clean. It's like you look the same up close as you do from a distance. There are no surprises."

Seth withdrew his hand and went back to drinking more of his shake, as if he were caught up in serious contemplation.

Leah took the moment to calm herself and to banish any more of her relentless tears. She was glad she had driven this route to Edgefield so many times. Because she could drive it in her sleep, she had the freedom to process what was happening with Seth.

The guy is on drugs, she reminded herself. *He doesn't know what he's saying.*

"I wanted something to work out between us, but I guess that's not how you felt." Seth sounded as if he were talking to himself. He was looking straight ahead. The breeze from the air conditioner ruffled his hair in the front. "Could you turn this down?" he asked. "It's getting cold in here."

Leah adjusted the temperature and went back to his previous statement. "Why did you say that's not how I felt?"

"Hmm?" Seth asked, looking at her with the shake straw in his mouth.

"You said you wanted something to work out between us. What did you mean by that?"

Seth put down the shake. "I thought it was obvious. I'm attracted to you. I feel connected somehow. I like you. I want to spend time with you. My great-uncle Franklin…oh, yeah, you know him. Franklin. Franklin said you were the key to what I was looking for. But you obviously don't feel the same way about me, and I can't do anything to change that, I don't think."

"What do you mean I don't feel the same way? I do! I was attracted to you from the beginning, too. I just didn't think you could ever be interested in me."

Seth stared at her with his eyebrows pushed together in an expression of disbelief. "How did you ever get that idea?"

"I don't know," Leah said in an effort to drop the subject. This conversation was becoming painful. If she let herself believe what Seth was saying, it would change her whole life.

But how could she be sure he would remember any of it? She felt sneaky. It was as if unsuspecting Seth had been injected with truth serum, and she was extracting as much information as she could before the effects wore off. It didn't seem fair to either of them. He wouldn't remember what he had said in the morning, and she wouldn't be able to forget.

"I'm serious, here!" Seth said, raising his voice. "You are essential to my future happiness."

Leah smiled at his flowery words and the depth of his sincerity. Yet something in her cautioned her to pull back. She couldn't tell if it was the old recordings, reminding her that she wasn't worthy of such a man. Or if it was the new, gentle persistence of her heavenly Father who had been making it clear that he wanted Leah to delight herself in him, not in the tantalizing possibilities of a romance.

All she knew was that she couldn't continue this conversation. "Can we put this topic on hold? If it comes up another time, I think it would be better." She didn't want to mention that he was euphoric and vulnerable at the moment and that it had been too easy for her to plunder the feelings of his heart.

Seth pressed his head against the headrest and closed his eyes. "That's okay. We can talk another time. I'd like to talk another time. I think it would be good to talk with each other sometime. You and me." His voice trailed off, and he seemed to drop off to sleep—or at least to shut down his amped-up system—for the last ten minutes of the ride to Edgefield.

Leah found the apartment using the address she had written down. She parked the car, and as soon as the motor stopped, Seth looked up. "Are we here?"

"Yes, we're at your apartment."

"Good, because I am really fried."

"Your legs might feel wobbly so let me know if I can help you up the stairs."

Seth slowly climbed out of the Blazer. The vim and vigor from half an hour ago at the Dairy Queen had dissipated. Leah went to his side and helped him up the stairs.

"My legs feel so heavy," was all he said, as Leah propped him up by the front door and went through his plastic bag of personal belongings Shirley had turned over to Leah. She found the keys at the bottom, and as soon as she turned the doorknob, she could hear Bungee yelping with delight.

"Someone is glad you're home," Leah said.

"That's Bungee. My Bungee. He's my dog."

"Yes, I know," Leah said, helping Seth through the front door. She shouldn't have been surprised by the sparseness of Seth's apartment, but she was. If he hadn't gotten the couch from Brad and Alissa, which now filled the wall on the right, the only piece of furniture in the living room would have been a folding beach chair.

"Do you want to go to the couch or to your bed?" Leah asked.

"The couch," Seth said, lowering himself with a grimace.

Leah guessed the painkillers were wearing off.

"Why don't you make yourself comfortable?" Leah suggested. "What can I get you? A blanket? Some water?" She pulled the list of instructions from the bag along with the prescription painkillers. "It says here every four hours on the medicine. Shirley wrote down the time she gave you the first one and," Leah checked her watch. "Yep, you're ready for another one."

Seth stretched out on the couch and called to Bungee, who was barricaded in the kitchen where Leah noticed he had had an accident on the linoleum floor.

"I'll take care of Bungee," Leah said. "You settle yourself on the couch, okay?"

With her usual flare for jumping in and organizing things, Leah took care of Bungee and Seth. She found only one blanket in the whole apartment and that was on Seth's "bed," which was an inflatable air mattress. He had one brightly colored beach towel in the bathroom and no sheets. Now she understood why Seth had thought her house was pretty special. It made even more sense that he had been overwhelmed with Kyle and Jessica's mansion. The guy had been living with bare minimum for a long time. No wonder he was enamored with the idea of owning a house and a hammock at the same time.

"I'm going to go now," Leah said after she had fixed him a mug of soup from the meager supply of cans she found in the kitchen cupboard. She found more food to choose from in the refrigerator but only brought him juice and water. The phone was on the floor in front of the couch, and she pulled the kitchen trashcan near, just in case he felt sick.

"Thanks so much for doing all this," Seth said with a woozy slur to his words.

Bungee kept barking sharp, staccato yelps. Leah couldn't imagine how Seth could get any sleep.

"How about if I take Bungee home with me? He needs some attention, and you need some rest."

"Okay," Seth said, without opening his eyes.

Leah had to smile. For the first time, she saw a slight resemblance between Seth and Franklin when they had their eyes closed and were about to fall asleep. They both maintained beguiling little grins, even when they were nearly unconscious.

She couldn't help it; she had to lean over and kiss Seth good-bye the way she kissed Franklin. Seth didn't stir.

"Bye," she whispered, tiptoeing over to the kitchen where she reached down and picked up the hyper ball of fluff. "Come on, Bungee. You're coming with me."

To show his appreciation, Bungee lunged toward her and slobbered a big kiss on her cheek.

"Oh, you little Romeo, you. You know the way to a girl's heart, don't you?" she murmured.

Just as Leah was about to close the apartment door behind her, she heard Seth call out, "Good night, Bungee. Good night, George."

Chapter Twenty-two

$\mathcal{A}$nd then he called me 'George,'" Leah told Jessica when they saw each other the next morning before the May Day event began. They were working quickly to arrange all the cut flowers in vases for the tables in Camp Heather Brook's dining room.

"How did you react to that?" Jessica asked, snipping the end of the deep purple iris that Leah had cut at Ida's earlier that morning.

"I didn't say anything. I left." If they had had more time, Leah would have liked to keep the conversation going. But just then Shelly entered the dining room with her mom and sister. Leah and Jessica greeted them, and Leah thought pretty, energetic Meredith didn't look as if she were pregnant. The three new arrivals had their arms full of food trays, and Shelly and Meredith's mom was fussing at Meredith about carrying too much.

"I can help carry stuff in," Leah said. "Jess and I were almost finished with the flowers."

"Good," Shelly said. "Genevieve needs all kinds of help bringing in the food. She's running behind because her electricity went out this morning. If you can carry the rest in, I'll fire up the ovens."

Leah hurried out to help Genevieve unload the food, and from that moment on, she ran all morning doing what she did best—helping. Despite Genevieve's electricity failure, the food was ready right on time, and it was a big hit with the 237 women and girls who showed up for the event.

As usual, the maypole dance was a favorite with the little girls. Shelly had arranged for Christian praise music to play while each girl took a vinyl ribbon and danced around the maypole in the meadow outside the camp dining room. The clouds that had covered the sky earlier that morning blew away. The gentle breeze, which had cleared the way for the sun to attend this gala event, decided to stick around as well, creating an afternoon of perfect weather.

Leah and Ida stayed to help clean up. As they were clearing the tables, Leah decided to gather the flowers into several big buckets. She had planned to stop at Franklin's on her way home with a bouquet of May Day flowers from the grocery store, but a bucket of flowers was better. Two buckets on his doorstep would be grand!

It was nearly three o'clock when Leah and Ida pulled out of the conference grounds with their flower wagon. "Would you like me to take you home first?" Leah asked.

"Oh, no! I'd like to see the look on Franklin's face when he discovers what you're bringing him this year," Ida said with a cluck of her tongue. "And just where is that poor man supposed to put all these flowers?"

"All over!" Leah said. "Aren't they wonderful? Take a deep breath."

Ida rolled down her window halfway. "It's overwhelming. And overdoing it, if you ask me. Why must you lavish so much attention on Franklin?"

"I don't know. I like to. Nobody else seems to." Leah pulled up in front of Franklin's house and opened the back of the Blazer. She carried a bucket in each arm up to the front door while Ida waited in the car. Placing them on the doormat, Leah rang the doorbell and dashed around to the side of the house just as she used to when she was a kid. She expected Mavis to come tottering to the door, but she didn't.

Leah went back to the door and rang the doorbell again. This time she waited. When Mavis didn't answer, Leah tried the doorknob, planning to let herself in. But the door was locked.

This is a first. Leah knocked and called out. Still no answer. She peered in the front window. Franklin's recliner was in clear view, but no one was in the room.

Returning to her car, Leah reached inside for her cell phone.

"No one home?" Ida asked.

"I'm not sure. No one came to the door, and it's locked." Leah dialed Franklin's phone number and let it ring ten times before she hung up.

"Where do you suppose he is?" Ida asked.

Leah paused before answering. She had a sick feeling in the pit of her stomach. With a hesitant finger, Leah punched in the number to the hospital emergency desk.

"Annie? Hi, it's Leah. By any chance was Franklin Madison admitted today?"

"He arrived about an hour ago," Annie told her. "I don't

know the status. Would you like me to check?"

"No, I'm coming right over." Leah hung up and jumped in the car, leaving the flowers on the doorstep.

"The hospital?" Ida asked, as Leah's car lurched onto the street and sped toward downtown.

"Yes. About an hour ago. Do you mind going with me, Ida?"

"Of course not. Watch how you're driving, Leah!" Ida was clutching the door and seat with her thin hands. "It won't do to get us in a wreck on the way there!"

Leah slowed down, but inside her heart was still racing. She was blaming herself for not taking her May Day bouquet to Franklin that morning before picking up Ida and going to Camp Heather Brook. That meant she would have been ringing his doorbell before 7:30 that morning, but at least he would have been there.

When Leah pulled into the emergency parking lot, Ida had her seatbelt unbuckled and her door open before Leah did. But Leah had to slow her steps so Ida could keep up with her. The two approached the emergency desk with flushed faces.

"How is he?" Leah asked Annie.

Annie glanced at Ida and then back at Leah as if she weren't sure what to say. "You can go on back, Leah. Dr. Schlipperd is on duty. Ida, perhaps you should wait here."

"I have a right to see Franklin," Ida spouted.

Patting wiry Ida on the shoulder, Leah said calmly, "I'll come right back after I've checked on him. Then we'll see about letting you visit him as well, okay?"

Ida looked worried. "You come right back, now."

"I will," Leah said, leading Ida to a chair in the nearly vacant emergency waiting room. "You wait right here for me."

"I'm not going anywhere," Ida said.

Leah headed for the back emergency area, and Annie rose

to follow her. When they were out of Ida's view and hearing, Annie reached over and laid her hand on Leah's arm.

Leah froze and forced herself to look at Annie and to read the message in Annie's expression.

"I'm sorry," Annie said. "He was dead on arrival, but I didn't know that when you called. I wasn't sure what to tell you with Ida standing there. You can talk with Dr. Schlipperd if you want, but the cause of death was cardiac arrest."

"Do you know anything else?" Leah asked, trying to remain calm as she always had in the past when bad news came her way. She refused to let herself feel anything.

"Mavis left only a few minutes ago. She called the ambulance. She said he didn't respond when she brought him his lunch. He wasn't in any pain. She said he was sitting in his recliner and appeared to be napping."

"And he slipped into heaven on a dream cloud," Leah said, quoting a line from an old poem her mother used to say.

"He was an old man," Annie said in a comforting voice. "His heart simply stopped."

Leah drew in a deep breath. "He was a very special old man." To her surprise, no tears came. "Has anyone notified his relatives?"

"Mavis probably will. I don't know. She was going back to his house."

"Okay," Leah said, her mind beginning to line up all the details. "I'll tell Ida and take her home. She can make some calls around town. I'll check on Mavis, and then I'll call Seth." As soon as she said his name, Leah slapped her forehead, remembering that Seth didn't have his car with him. It was still in the hospital parking lot since she had driven him home last night.

"Thanks, Annie," she said, giving the attendant a quick hug.

"Are you okay?"

"Sure."

Leah sat down next to Ida and spoke to her the way she had spoken with dozens of people in the hospital waiting room. She calmly explained the situation and immediately gave a direction so the stunned recipient of the news would have something to do while the news sunk in.

"I'll take you home first," Leah told Ida. "And then would you mind making a few calls? Let Pastor Mike know and Kyle and Jessica."

"All right. Yes, I can do that." Ida rose and started toward the parking lot. "It shouldn't be a surprise, you know. He was an elderly man."

"Yes," Leah agreed, offering Ida her arm as they stepped down from the emergency room entrance curb into the parking lot. "He was a very special elderly man."

They were quiet on the drive to Ida's. Right before Leah pulled up in front of the house, Ida said, "You know, when I go, I think that's the way I'd like to go. In my sleep."

Leah nodded. As soon as Ida was safely in her front door, Leah called Mavis on her cell phone and heard the details Annie had told her repeated. Right before Leah hung up, Mavis said, "He would have liked all the flowers. This morning he asked if you had come yet."

Leah felt her throat tighten. "I should have come before the event out at Camp Heather Brook."

"No, no," Mavis said gently. "I told him you were coming after the May Day party, and he said he would wait in his recliner. He knew you were coming. But bless his soul, he just couldn't wait."

Leah drove the few blocks to her house. She was eager to burst through the front door and let her tears have a private place to fall before she went out to Seth's apartment and drove him back to pick up his car. That is, if he was well enough to drive.

Unlocking her front door and stepping in, with the tears clinging to the edge of her eyelids, Leah stopped short at the sight that greeted her. One frolicking ball of vanilla fluff with an eager yelp came bounding up to her. Somehow Bungee had managed to knock down the barricade she had put up to keep him in the mudroom with Hula. Bungee had shredded a stack of magazines and dragged the pieces all through the living room. He had knocked the trash can over, and garbage trailed across the kitchen floor. Half a bag of flour that she had thrown in the trash last night when she spotted little bugs in it was now torn open. A white trail of buggy flour dust streaked across the floor in loops, as if Bungee had sunk his teeth into the bag and turned around in half a dozen prancing circles, trying to make as big a mess as possible.

And the little scoot had succeeded right down to the flour on his nose and the barbecue sauce on his front paws. Evidence of where he had romped after he stepped in the nearly empty trash led through the house to Leah's bedroom. There she found one of her slippers gnawed to a slimy pulp. The matching slipper appeared to be MIA.

With a filthy Bungee under her arm, Leah marched to the mudroom. Poor Hula hunkered back in the corner on her beanbag bed. She lifted her head when she saw Leah and looked at her with pleading eyes as if to say, "Please, take that rabble rouser away from here and leave me in peace!"

"I really didn't need this today, Bungee," Leah said, placing the culprit in the deep basin sink. "You're getting a bath, and then you're going home!"

Hula thumped her tail against the wall.

"I know, Hula. It's been a trying day for both of us. But you didn't just lose one of your oldest and dearest friends." Leah's quick tears tumbled into the sink, mixing with Bungee's bath water. Hula rose and came to Leah's side, pressing against her leg.

"Franklin is gone, Hula. And I'm going to miss him."

Chapter Twenty-three

$\mathcal{L}$eah decided it was pointless to start cleaning up her destroyed house until after the pesky Bungee was far, far away.

After she had washed him and allowed her tears to dry up, she found a large box in her side garage and planted Bungee in the box on the car's backseat. She returned to the house to pick up a few items to take to Seth's and decided to grab the frozen spinach. With an apologetic pat on the head for Hula, who refused to move from her bed, Leah hurried to the car only to find Bungee had tipped over the box. He was on the floor, gnawing on the backside of the passenger's seat.

"You are amazing!" she said scooping up the rambunctious boy. "Come on. Let's try this again—with you in the front seat where I can keep an eye on you."

Leah moved the passenger's seat all the way back, wedged the box in between the seat and the dashboard, and settled Bungee in his cell. He yelped at first. Then the car's motion on the open highway and the soft jazz radio station lulled him to sleep.

The lack of distraction from Bungee allowed Leah to make several phone calls to locate a number for Seth's apartment. When she finally reached him, he answered on the first ring.

"Oh, good, Leah, it's you. Did you get my messages?"

"No, I didn't listen to my machine. I was only home for a few minutes." She decided not to mention the disaster that had met her at her house.

"Mavis called about forty minutes ago," Seth said. "Where are you now?"

"I'm on my way to your place with your little pal. I thought you might want a ride back to the hospital to pick up your car. By the way, how are you?"

"I think I'm in shock. How are you?"

"I'm okay. How's your shoulder and back feeling?"

"They're not bad. I'm taking the painkillers so it might be worse than I think. I don't know. The doctor did say everything checked out clear, didn't he? I'm a little fuzzy on what actually happened yesterday after they took me into the operating room."

"Yes, it's all good news for you. The original spot was clean so he didn't have to go all the way to the bone. He found several other suspicious places, which he removed and tested, and they were all negative as well."

"I thought that's what I remembered. I wanted to make sure."

"I'll be there in about twenty minutes."

"Good. I'll be ready when you get here."

Bungee slept the whole way like an adorable angel. When Leah stopped the car, she had to lift him out of the box and carry him to Seth's apartment while he was still conked out.

"Oh, sure, you're a tired fellow, aren't you? Well, you just wait until I clean up my house tonight. I'm going to be more tired than you!"

Leah knocked on the door, and Seth met her with his hair still wet from the shower. "Come in. I need to grab my shoes." He scratched Bungee under his chin and said, "Boy, I wish he'd sleep like that for me!"

Leah bit her tongue and shook her head.

While Seth went to put on his shoes, Leah settled Bungee in his bed in the barricaded kitchen. She remembered the spinach and told Seth she would be right back. When she returned, Seth was ready to go, and Bungee was wide awake and ready to play.

"I brought you a spinach casserole," she said. "Should I leave it in your freezer, or do you want it to thaw out in the refrigerator?"

Seth looked surprised. "You didn't have to do that. Thanks. Here. I'll put it in the refrigerator."

Leah noticed that the living room was all picked up, not that there was much to straighten. The kitchen was clean as well. She remembered how Seth had automatically begun doing her dishes when he was at her house. Tidiness was a trait she admired.

Maybe you can teach Bungee a few tips!

"You're feeling okay, then?" Leah asked once they were in her car and on the way back to Glenbrooke.

"Yes, I'm doing okay. I'm supposed to take another pain pill in half an hour, but I don't think I should since I'll be driving."

"Wise choice."

They traveled in silence for awhile before Seth said, "I can't believe he's gone. I only knew him for these few short weeks. He was quite a character, wasn't he?"

"He was." Leah swallowed. With Franklin's passing she had lost a major connection to her childhood. Since she was already in the midst of an identity crisis these past few weeks, this loss added to her awareness that she was on her own. Not all alone, since God had made his presence so evident in her life, but fewer and fewer people were defining who she was and how others perceived her.

Seth reached over and began to massage Leah's neck with his left hand. "You sure you're doing okay? You were much closer to Franklin than I was."

"I'm going to miss him."

Seth pulled away his hand. She glanced at him and realized that the motion of stretching his arm out like that must have made him aware of how sore he was.

"What would be easiest for you?" Leah asked. "Would you like to go to Franklin's house or to the hospital to pick up your car?"

"To be honest, I'm not sure what I should do. I've never gone through this before."

Leah explained that Mavis was making phone calls. Arrangements needed to be decided on, and people needed to be met with, such as the funeral home director and the pastor. She offered to help in any way she could.

"If you have the time, could you stick with me and walk me through all this?" Seth asked.

"Of course." The last thing she wanted to do was go home to her domestic disaster, and besides, this would help her to grapple with Franklin being gone.

One of the great things about the people in Glenbrooke was that they knew how to gather around and support one another in tough times. Everyone they talked to offered to help in one way or another. Leah told all of them there was nothing to do. She and Seth had it taken care of, and no, no one needed to bring food to the house because Mavis was fine, and she and Seth were just leaving.

By the time Leah drove to the hospital to pick up Seth's car, it was nearly seven o'clock. They said an awkward good-bye to each other. Seth looked exhausted and in pain. He was going home to a rowdy puppy and hopefully, somehow, a good night's sleep. Leah was going home to a mess. She wanted to be angry about it, but she wasn't sure whom to blame. Bungee, for getting out? Herself, for volunteering to take Bungee home and for not making the barricade more durable? Or Seth, for having the puppy in the first place?

When she came up with that accusation, Leah knew she wasn't thinking clearly. She needed to tackle the mess, clean it up, and forget about it. However, it took Leah almost three hours to return her house to normal. She fell into bed exhausted.

The next morning she went through her Sunday school time with the toddlers in a fog. She wished she were in the service instead. It had been a long time since she had gone to the worship service. She hadn't missed it before, but now she did.

She did have a chance to sit in a pew at church that week. It was at Franklin's memorial service on Wednesday.

Collin Radcliffe called Leah that morning at work and asked if she would like him to escort her to the memorial service.

"No, thanks," Leah told him.

"I wanted to express my condolences. I know you and Franklin were close. It would mean a lot to me if I could help in any way. If you don't need a ride to the service, then please let me know if there's anything else I can do for you."

"Thanks, Collin, but I'm fine."

He sounded sincere. Leah couldn't figure out why Collin was suddenly being so attentive. When she saw him at the church, he was standing by the front door. He solemnly walked in with her as if they had arranged to meet there and sit together.

The pastor gave a wonderful tribute to Franklin Madison, a man who had lived nearly a century in Glenbrooke and who had quietly, steadfastly trusted God through many seasons.

The church was packed. Seth sat in the aisle in front of Leah, next to his parents, who had come from Boulder. After the service, Collin followed Leah out of the church. She turned to him and said, "Thanks for showing support to me, Collin, but really, I'm fine. I don't need anything. At all." The edge in her voice made it clear she wanted him to stop following her around.

Collin looked a little hurt yet he controlled his emotions well. Leah couldn't help but feel a twinge of victory as she thought, *There! How do you like having your sincere effort torn in two and the spirit of "love" crossed out?*

As soon as she thought that, she felt guilty. It was her habit to encourage people and give to them, not hurt them and take away their dignity.

Collin mumbled good-bye and turned to go. Leah reached out and stopped him with a brief touch on his arm. "I apologize for sounding so abrupt. I appreciate your concern, Collin. Thank you."

His eyes met hers, and a look of confidence washed across his face. "It's my pleasure, Leah. And please know that my expression of concern is genuine."

Leah nodded. She didn't know what to say. He had such a calming voice and such a commanding presence. She felt guilty all over again for doubting his sincerity. After all, this was Glenbrooke. Glenbrooke people stuck together in hard times. It didn't matter that he had been gone for so long. He had Glenbrooke ways in his blood. Leah knew she should trust Collin, but trusting anyone had always been a challenge for her.

Collin reached over and gave Leah's elbow a gentle squeeze. "I'll see you around, Leah."

She nodded again. "See you around, Collin."

Collin headed for his Mercedes with another glance at Leah over his shoulder and a friendly wave. She waved back and thought, *Why couldn't Collin, or any guy, have been that nice to me in high school? Does it take an extra decade to turn these local boys into men? Or was I as off-putting and porcupine-like in high school as my sisters kept telling me I was?*

Seth exited the church with his mother and father. He came over to Leah and introduced her to his parents as "this is the one I told you about."

His mother appeared to be an outgoing woman, even in the somberness of the occasion. His father resembled Seth in many ways, including his engaging smile.

"Seth tells us he would have been lost without you these past few weeks," Mr. Edwards said, as he shook Leah's hand.

She felt herself blushing and shrugged off the comment. "I didn't do much."

"You're coming to the house, aren't you?" Seth's mom asked.

"Yes, I'll be there."

Leah had arranged for all the food at the family gathering in Franklin's house. She had expected around fifty people, but nearly seventy guests came. Collin wasn't among them, which didn't surprise Leah. The invitation had circulated among close friends and family. She didn't know how close Franklin was to his lawyer. Leah did notice that Franklin's physician came as well as several home care nurses who had tended to Franklin over the years.

Despite Leah's immediate fears when she walked into the house and saw more than fifty people present, there was plenty of food to go around. And typical of Glenbrooke gatherings, there were even more stories to go around, as old-time folks recounted their favorite memories of Franklin.

"You know," one of the older gentlemen said, "a little neighbor girl used to bring Franklin flowers every year on May Day. I guess she must have done it for years because he told me once that May Day was his favorite holiday."

Leah looked down.

"That was Leah," Ida stated. "Leah Hudson. You know Leah. Why, she's standing right there in the corner. Tell him, Leah. Tell him how we brought the flowers this year, but it was too late."

All eyes turned to Leah. "I should have brought the flowers in the morning," she said quietly. The tears she had so effectively held back for days apparently had reached their limit and suddenly began to spill out. Leah felt an arm around her shoulder, and thinking it was Pastor Mike, she turned and let herself cry on his sports coat.

"Go ahead. Let the windows of your soul have a good cleaning."

Leah looked up and swallowed her tears. Everyone in the room was watching Seth comfort her. In the past, she would have pulled away from his sympathetic touch. Not this time. She buried her face in his shoulder and cried her eyes out, not caring who was watching or what they thought.

Seth wrapped both his arms around her and tenderly whispered in her ear, "Come on. Let's go in the other room."

Chapter Twenty-four

*S*eth led Leah into the kitchen and offered her a napkin to dry her eyes. "You're not somehow feeling responsible for Franklin's passing away, are you?" He let go of her and leaned back to give her some space.

"I don't know. I guess it all caught up with me."

"Go ahead and cry if it helps. You're always there for everyone else. This time, let me be there for you."

"Thanks, Seth." She looked up at him through bleary eyes. "I really appreciate it."

"Any time, George," he said warmly.

George! Does he have any idea how that nickname comforts me?

Leah wasn't sure she could believe what was happening. Seth wasn't teasing her. He wasn't on drugs. He was there, with her, by choice. In front of a crowd of people, he had willingly put his arm around her and drawn her aside to comfort her. He had called her George. Leah's tears began to subside.

"You know, you've become someone very special to me," Seth said, reaching over and catching the last of her tears as it coursed down her cheek. "Franklin told me you were the key I was looking for. I think he was right."

Leah felt her heart pounding. His confession to her in the car on the way home from the hospital hadn't been a cruel joke. He had meant it, whether he remembered all of it or not. She knew she had to decide whether she believed him. If she believed him, that meant she needed to believe something new about herself. She was of the right frame and frame of mind.

"Do you really mean that, Seth?"

"Yes, I do."

Just then Ida walked into the kitchen. "Don't mind me, you two. I'm after some more napkins."

"Right there on the counter," Seth said.

"So they are," Ida said. She seemed to search Leah's expression, trying to discern what was going on with them. "I'll just have a look in the refrigerator and see if anything else needs to be put out on the table."

Leah and Seth waited quietly until Ida was gone.

"Would you like to go somewhere?" Seth asked.

"Where? I mean, I'm supposed to clean up after everyone leaves."

"Why don't you let someone else do that for a change?" Seth suggested. "Let's go for a ride. It'll give you a chance to clear your thoughts."

"Okay," Leah heard herself say. "I'll go ask Jessica if—"

"I'll ask her," Seth volunteered. "And I'm sure my mom will be glad to help, too. You always take care of everyone else. It's time you let someone take care of you."

Leah stood in the kitchen, stunned at what was happening

with Seth. He returned after a few minutes and told her everything was set. Then he motioned to the back door and suggested they avoid walking through the crowd.

Fortunately, Seth had parked down the street so he had no problem pulling out of his parking spot. They drove past the house and took the road that led out of town.

"Where are we going?" Leah asked.

"I thought we would just drive. It's a beautiful afternoon. What happened to all that rain you said would hang around until June?"

"Don't worry. It will be back. They don't call this area the 'Great North-Wet' for nothing," Leah joked.

"I like it here," Seth said.

"You still want to stay even though you don't need to be here to be treated by Dr. Norton?"

Seth glanced at her and then back at the road. "Yes, of course I want to stay here. This is where I want to settle. Why, did you think I'd leave now that I've been given a clean bill of health?"

"Well…" Leah stalled. That was exactly what she had been thinking. More precisely, it was what she feared. She thought Seth would announce he was going back to Costa Rica. "The thought did cross my mind."

"No," Seth said decidedly. "This is where I want to be. I told my parents that last night when they tried to convince me I should go back to Boulder with them."

"Why did they want you to go to Boulder?"

Seth shrugged. "My dad thought I could find a better job there. My mom thinks the doctors are better there. I told them about the melanoma. They were pretty upset that I hadn't told them sooner. You know how it is when you're the youngest. It doesn't matter how old you are, they still think they have to take care of you."

"Not always," Leah said softy. She was the youngest, but her experience had been the opposite of Seth's.

"That's right, your situation was a little different, wasn't it?"

"But I know what you mean. Even though I was the responsible one toward the end, I still felt my parents didn't trust me to figure things out or to do things the right way. The day before my mother passed away, she asked me if I had filed my income taxes yet because April 15 was just around the corner."

"And had you worked on your taxes yet?"

Leah nodded. "I had done mine and theirs by February 15."

"My mom would have been impressed. As a matter of fact, I'm impressed. It's taken me a while to feel independent of my parents."

"I thought you said you've been on your own since high school, when you went to Sweden."

"I tried to pretend I was on my own. My mom sent me underwear in Sweden." Seth glanced at Leah with a grin.

She laughed. "Did she think they didn't sell underwear in Sweden?"

"Something like that. But we had a good talk last night. I think my parents understand why I'd like to stay here and turn the next corner of my life." Then, as if on cue, Seth turned the steering wheel and headed down a narrow, country road. Leah recognized it. It ran along the perimeter of Camp Heather Brook. She hadn't driven on that road for years, and she was amazed when they came around a bend and were met with a row of trees in full bloom.

"Look at those trees!" Leah exclaimed. "I don't know what kind they are, do you?"

"I have no idea." Seth slowed the car and looked out his window.

"They're gorgeous! And so old. Look at the blossoms. They're almost a pale lilac."

"Really? I'd call that a light pink." Seth stopped the car. "Come on, let's check them out."

Leah clambered out of the car and walked over to one of the trees. She reached up and pulled down a low branch to sniff the blossoms. It gave off the faint scent of vanilla. "This is beautiful," she said.

"Come on," Seth invited. "Let's explore some more."

"On foot?" Leah asked, when Seth took off walking into the woods behind the blooming trees.

Seth stopped and looked back at her. She had worn a black skirt with a white cotton blouse and black linen blazer to the memorial service. It wasn't her nicest outfit, but for her it was dressy. She wore practical, flat shoes simply because she always wore practical, flat shoes. That's all she owned. They were suitable for a jaunt in the woods.

Seth had on dark slacks and a light blue Oxford shirt with a tie, which he had loosened but left on. Nothing was fancy about his shoes, either.

"Aren't we a little dressed up for a hike?" Leah asked.

Seth looked at his outfit. "I thought maybe our professional appearance would frighten away the bears. They're only used to scruffy looking campers. They won't know what to do with us."

Leah laughed. This man was like medicine for her. He didn't care about dress clothes getting dirty; he always was up for an adventure; he cared about her enough to take her away from Franklin's house so she could breathe again and stop being responsible for everything. Suddenly she felt natural and easy following this man into the woods—and anywhere else he wanted to lead her.

He wasn't able to lead her very far because they hit a huge patch of what Seth called "blasted brambles."

"They're wild berries," Leah told him. "Probably blackberries, but they could be raspberries. I don't know my early spring berry brambles very well."

"Or your blooming trees," Seth added.

"Or my blooming trees," Leah repeated with a laugh.

"Why don't we venture on down the road and see if we can find a trail?" Seth suggested.

They returned to the car and drove for a long while down the bumpy road until they came to a turnaround at a dead end. Instead of heading back, Seth stopped the car and got out again.

"That looks like a trail to me," he said, leading Leah to a place where the tall spring grasses were flattened slightly. A trail did appear to lead into the woods.

"A deer trail," Leah said.

"Let's see where it leads." Seth pulled back some low branches of a cedar tree and welcomed Leah to go first.

"Since when did I become the trailblazer?" Leah asked, standing her ground with her hand on her hip.

"Fine, I'll go first." Seth let the branch sway back, just missing Leah by a fraction of an inch.

"Thanks a lot!" she spouted.

"Well, what's it going to be? Do you want to make the first move, or should I?"

Leah couldn't help but wonder if his question had a double meaning. "You," she said quickly. "You make the first move."

Seth smiled at her. "Okay. Got it. This way, if you please." He took off at his brisk hiking pace, and Leah had to work her short legs hard to keep up with him. She had left her jacket in the car this time and was glad because she warmed up quickly.

"Hey, aren't you supposed to take it easy after your surgery?" Leah asked.

"I'm feeling okay. The stitches give me grief every now and

then when I turn the wrong way. But I'm doing pretty well."

"So where are we going?"

"Onward," was Seth's answer.

They followed the narrow trail through the heart of the ancient woods. The new leaves on the trees formed a fragrant, lime green canopy over their heads. Then they came into an open area where the sunlight shot through the trees like iridescent, bronze javelins thrown from the heavens.

Seth stopped. "Here," he said. He stood in the center of the woodlands, with his hands on his hips, face toward the sky, daring the golden javelins of sunlight to spear him through the chest.

Leah drew in the fragrance of the wild violets that laced the air around them. "This is amazing!" At her feet lay an endless carpet of rich lapis-shaded bluebells and deep green moss. High overhead, brightly-colored blue jays squawked at the intruders in their enchanted world. Two squirrels sprinted across the ground about ten feet from Leah and Seth and then scampered up a tree, with their fluffy gray tails waving good-bye.

"Let's build a house right here," Seth said after several long, silent minutes.

Leah chuckled. "On our Easter hike you only wanted to build a bench at the top of the hill. Today it's a whole house! Next hike you'll envision an entire resort."

Seth stood still, studying her. Finally he said, "Exactly what is it that you don't like about me?"

Chapter Twenty-five

Leah was stunned by Seth's question. Was it true that she was standing in the woods with this wonderful man and that he was telling her he wanted her to like him? "I like everything about you," she assured him.

Seth studied her expression. "I have something to tell you." He moved over to a fallen log and sat down. Patting the space next to him, he invited Leah to sit beside him. The rotted log provided a soft, level seat. She drew near but not too close.

"I looked up your name in the Bible," Seth said. "I read everything I could find on Leah."

She felt a pinch in her stomach. "So you know I'm named after a woman who was a big disappointment."

Seth frowned and paused. "Oh, you mean how Jacob ended up marrying Leah first when he thought he was getting Rachel?"

"Genesis 29:25. 'Behold, it was Leah,'" she repeated

solemnly. "My father used to say that was the saddest verse in the Bible."

Seth looked down and rubbed his eyebrow. "That's only one small part of a verse. Many verses talk about Leah. She gave Jacob six sons and a daughter. And you know those sons became six of the twelve tribes of Israel."

Leah didn't know that. She probably should have. But, as a child, she had tuned out any Sunday school lesson when Leah was mentioned. She hadn't thought the biblical Leah had ever amounted to anything.

"The fourth son of Leah and Jacob caught my attention as I was reading," Seth went on. He reached over and took Leah's hand, intertwining his fingers with hers. This time she didn't pull away.

"Their fourth son was Judah. Leah named him that because Judah means 'praise.' The line of Christ comes through Judah, you know."

Leah nodded and thought about this revelation. All her life she had thought of her biblical namesake as unwanted, unloved, and unimportant in the great scheme of things. Yet Leah, the wife of Jacob, was a great, great, many times over great-grandmother of Jesus Christ. And Leah's more desired sister, Rachel, wasn't.

"I found out something else I thought was pretty interesting when I was reading," Seth said.

She didn't know if she could process any more. The sensation of his holding her hand and speaking to her with confidence was overpowering. Leah found herself ready to believe anything he said.

Seth continued, "Leah's first three sons were all named to reflect the state of her relationship with Jacob at the time they were born. Each time she was hoping she would gain her husband's favor because she had given him a son.'"

"What do you mean?"

"For instance, *Levi* means 'attached.' When Levi was born Leah said, 'Now my husband will be attached to me because I have borne him three sons.'"

Leah knew all too well what it was like to try hard to win the approval and favor of others. She understood what the biblical Leah must have been feeling.

Seth held Leah's hand tighter. "Then something must have happened in Leah's heart because when her fourth son was born, all she said was, 'Now I will praise the Lord.' It was as if she stopped striving and started praising God and being thankful. And that was the son on whom God chose to place his blessing. Not the firstborn son, or the second or the third. But the one Leah named 'Praise.' The lion of Judah."

Leah had so many thoughts at once. She wanted to tell Seth about her early morning encounter with God last week, how the verse Seth had left on her windshield had showed her the winter was past, and how God had been plowing up her heart to plant new seeds.

This fresh account of the biblical Leah resonated deeply within her.

"I needed to hear all this," she said softly.

A hint of bashfulness washed over Seth's face. "I hoped you wouldn't think I was lecturing you."

"No, of course not. Not at all. I want my life to change like that, too. I want to start praising God and being thankful for what he brings into my life. I've spent too many years trying to prove myself."

Seth drew her hand to his lips and kissed her fingers softly. "You don't ever have to prove anything to me, Leah."

After all Leah's tearful outbursts in the past few weeks, she was startled to find that now, when she really wanted to cry, she had no tears. Only amazement.

"Seth, I don't know what's happening, but something definitely is changing inside me. It's as if you marched into the garden of my heart, and with one mighty slash of your truth sword, you've slain the dragon that has breathed down my neck my entire life."

Now Seth looked as if he might cry. With a catch in his voice, he said, "I've never been anyone's dragon slayer before."

Leah smiled. Overhead a blue jay let out a series of sharp, squawking calls.

"Someone doesn't like us being here," she said.

"I suppose we should get back before my mother decides to send out a search party." Seth rose and drew up Leah with him.

Since she didn't consider herself to be good with words, she impulsively decided to express what she was feeling with actions. She wrapped her arms around Seth's middle and gave him a hug.

"I meant it when I said something is happening in my life. In my heart. Thanks, Seth."

He circled her with his arms. Leah let her head rest on his chest, and he drew her close. Never in her life had she felt like this.

"You know," Seth murmured, his lips lost in her hair. "You don't have to do anything for me. You don't have to give me anything. Just be who you are and let me get close to you."

"Okay," she whispered. "I will."

"I mean it," he said. "This is for real. I'm not playing games with you, Leah."

"I know. And I don't want to play games with you. It's just that it's hard for me to believe you truly could be interested in me."

Seth pulled away so they could look at each other. Leah let go. His expression was tender. "I am very interested in you."

"Why?" Leah said. "I mean—"

"Do you want a list?"

Leah shrugged.

"First, you have a long-standing relationship with the Lord, and you're interested in that relationship growing. Second, you attract me. You're beautiful."

"No, I'm not," Leah said quickly.

"Hey, this is my list. Do you mind? According to what I find attractive and desirable in a woman, you are so high, you're off the chart. Your hair is beautiful. You're just the right height. You have a great laugh. I've never gone hiking with a woman who could keep up with me. Not only do you keep up with me, but you also seem to enjoy the hike as much as I do. You fit me, Leah. You're just right in every way."

Leah felt as if her insides had turned to mush. "I think you're just right in every way, too."

Seth reached over and tilted Leah's chin up. "I've been meaning to tell you that you left something at my house the other day." A mischievous twinkle appeared in his eye. It reminded Leah of Franklin's look when he said he was making plans.

"The spinach pan? You can get that back to me any time."

"No. This was something you left on Friday after you brought me home from the hospital."

"Really?" Leah said, finding herself swimming in his deep blue eyes. "I didn't think you would remember anything that happened on Friday."

"Oh, I remember this. You left it on my cheek."

With that Seth leaned over and offered a tender, first kiss to Leah's unsuspecting lips.

Chapter Twenty-six

Floating? No, that's not it. Exhilarated? Maybe. Soaring? Yes, that's it. Soaring.

Leah was trying to describe to herself how she felt as she and Seth drove back to Franklin's house. After Seth kissed her, he said he guessed she was changing her mind about always pulling away. Leah blushed, but she didn't mind a bit. If Seth wanted to get to know her, this was part of her—the ever-blushing, candy apple cheeks.

They had lingered for a few more minutes in a warm hug before Seth uncurled his arms from her. Then he offered Leah his hand, and they began their hike back to the car. She could feel her bare legs itching from bug bites she had received while they sat on the log—bugs and mosquitoes seemed to like to nibble on her. She forced herself not to scratch the bites with a vengeance once she was seated in the passenger's seat of Seth's Subaru station wagon.

"If I still had my letterman's jacket from high school, I'd give it to you," Seth said. "Then we officially would be going together, wouldn't we?"

"What did you letter in?"

"Track. The 440 was my specialty."

A smile played across Leah's lips. "I still have my letterman's jacket. Should I give you my jacket?"

Seth laughed. "And what did you letter in?"

"You're going to laugh," Leah warned him.

"I'm already laughing."

"Discus. But mind you, it wasn't a very competitive event for our school or our state, for that matter. Especially for the women's event."

"Discus, huh? Remind me to keep my distance if you ever decide to throw things."

"Don't worry. I'm not the tantrum throwing sort."

"Would you be interested in going out to dinner with my folks when we get back? I'd sure like for them to have some more time with you."

"I'd be honored," Leah said. "How long will your parents be here?"

"They fly out in the morning. I had hoped they would be able to stay for the reading of the will, but the lawyer is out of town until Friday."

Leah wasn't sure why, but she felt a little uncomfortable when Seth mentioned the will. She remembered Ida's saying that Franklin had changed his will less than two weeks ago. It made Leah wonder if Franklin knew his life was coming to a close. She dismissed that thought when she remembered that he had planned for her to take him to the hot springs in three weeks.

A wash of remorse came over her again, the way it had at

the house when she said she wished she had brought the flowers by in the morning. Now she wished she had taken Franklin to the hot springs the very day he had asked her. Her argument to others all along was that she wanted to make an old man happy. Now it was too late. She wouldn't take Franklin anywhere ever again.

"I wish I could have taken Franklin to the hot springs," Leah said, as Seth pulled up in front of Franklin's home. Only a few cars remained out front.

"It wasn't meant to be," Seth said. He took her hand as they walked up to the front door. "You were more considerate than I was. At least you were willing to take him. I knew he was frail, though."

"And you were right. The trip would have been too much for him."

"At least he knew you were willing to take him," Seth said, opening the front door and letting go of Leah's hand so she could go in first.

"Is that you, Leah?" Ida asked as they entered. She was busying herself around the living room with a feather duster, which Leah thought was comical. The company was all gone, and no one would live in this house for a while. How funny that Ida felt she was helping by dusting. Or was she finding a way to kill time until Seth and Leah returned?

"Are you all right, Leah?" Ida asked.

"I'm fine."

Seth slipped his arm around her shoulders, as if offering a show of moral support.

Seth's mom came into the living room from the kitchen and appeared slightly surprised to see her son with his arm around Leah. She smiled at Leah and said, "We're almost finished up here. Jessica is helping Mavis put away the last of the dishes. Seth, your father went on to the hotel in Edgefield. He asked us to meet him there at six for dinner. You will be able to take me, won't you?"

"Of course. I invited Leah to come with us as well."

"Good," Mrs. Edwards said with a warm smile for Leah.

Jessica exited the kitchen with a dishtowel in her hand. "I think that's everything. Oh, Leah, you're back. Good. I'm about ready to head home. Ida, would you like me to drive you home?"

Ida looked at Leah, who had been her ride to the memorial service and then to Franklin's house. With a snap of her eyelids, Ida turned to Jessica and said, "It looks as if I will be needing a ride, thank you."

"Are you ready to go?" Jessica asked.

"I suppose."

The two of them returned to the kitchen—Jessica to put the dish towel away and Ida to stow the feather duster. It all seemed so natural to Leah, being in Franklin's house with her friends and feeling Seth's arm around her shoulders while he made small talk with his mother. Yet, at the same time, it was all so unreal. Franklin was gone. A wonderful man was showering her with attention and affection. Leah felt as if she had stepped into a parallel reality and wondered how long the two worlds could overlap. Would the dream continue and take over? Or would the old reality return and leave her alone with Hula and a handful of flowers next May Day but no doorstep to leave them on?

Seth ushered his mom and Leah to the car. Out of respect, Leah opened the door to the backseat so Mrs. Edwards could sit in the front.

"Oh, no, please, Leah," Mrs. Edwards said. "You sit in the front. I'll be comfortable in the back."

"I wouldn't," Leah said.

Seth and his mom stopped short and stared at Leah after her abrupt response.

"What I mean is, I wouldn't feel comfortable in the front seat if you were in the back. Honest. You're Seth's mom. I was raised this way. Sorry I turned this into something awkward. I'd just feel better if you sat in the front, Mrs. Edwards."

The generous smile and spontaneous hug that Seth's mom gave Leah told her she was liked and had done the right thing, even though the remark had come out bumpy.

"Please, call me Bonnie." Mrs. Edwards gave Seth a grin that reflected her definite approval of Leah. They got in the car, with Leah in the backseat and Bonnie Edwards in the front.

Leah had never been one to carry a makeup bag in her purse, but she wished she had one now. After the tromp through the forest, she felt she could use a little freshening up before meeting Seth's dad for dinner. But all she had was a comb, which she used on her hair. What she really wanted was some eye drops. The pollen in the air had gotten to her. She would love to pop out her contacts, rinse them and her eyes, and then put the contacts back in. As it was, she kept blinking in hopes of cleaning them enough to see clearly.

The conversation on the way to Edgefield was light. Mrs. Edwards was curious to learn about Leah's family and her long history in Glenbrooke. Seth glanced at Leah several times in the rearview mirror, and each time, his eyes smiled at her.

Dinner with the Edwardses turned out to be a casual affair, for which Leah was grateful. They dined in the hotel coffee shop, and she rinsed out her contacts in the restroom. She also applied a cold paper towel to the red bites on her bare legs. The beauty regime was simple, but it was enough to make her feel more comfortable with Seth's parents.

The conversation flowed easily, and Leah enjoyed Seth's parents. They both indicated they approved of her for their son, and Seth seemed proud of her.

It wasn't until the drive home with just her and Seth that she allowed herself to believe all this was really happening. She was curious about so many things, and as soon as Seth stopped talking about how much his parents liked her, Leah asked her first question. "Did you take many of your girlfriends home to meet your parents?"

"What makes you think I had a lot of girlfriends?"

"Oh, come on! I'm not that naive. Do you want me to guess which number I am? Maybe girlfriend number thirty-two? No, more like forty-seven, right?"

Seth shook his head. "How about maybe three and a half."

Leah studied his profile. "Three and a half? Am I the half?"

"No, the half was Tiffany Andrews. She was my date to the junior prom, but she asked me, and we never went out again so I'd say she was a half."

"And the other two?"

Seth extended his arm on the top of the steering wheel and casually responded, "There was Fiona in Sweden my senior year. We were together for all of three weeks before her previous boyfriend came home from the university. She told me she was getting back together with him because they 'spoke the same language,' which was, of course, true in more ways than one."

"That must have been a heartbreaker," Leah said.

"Better than a bone breaker." A sly grin crept up the edge of Seth's mouth. "Her boyfriend was huge! He could have snapped me like a dog biscuit and tossed me off some fiord. I still think Fiona made the wrong choice getting back together with him. He dominated her life, and she was this free-spirited, creative woman. I have no idea what happened to her. I always hoped she met some musician. She could have written lyrics for him."

Leah liked the way Seth spoke of this woman with such respect. "And number two?" she asked.

"Ah, number two. That would be Tessa. She's the one who broke my heart." Seth paused.

Leah didn't know if she had the right to probe. The sad truth was that she had no comparable stories to tell him. She had never had a guy return her interest in him.

"You don't have to tell me anything if you don't want to," Leah said.

"No, I don't mind. It's funny how it still hurts a little. I really fell for Tessa my senior year at college in Boulder. I thought she was the one. She had long, blond hair and was homecoming queen that year. It took me two weeks to work up the courage to ask her out. I couldn't believe it when she said yes. We went to dinner and seemed to hit it off. So I asked her out again. We went out six times. No, actually seven times. Then one of the guys I played racquetball with took me aside and told me she had spent the night in his dorm room and had slept with his roommate the night before."

Seth shook his head. "Here I'd just taken her to a movie and kissed her good night at her door. As soon as I left, she went to be with this other guy. I asked her about it, and she said I was the kind of guy she wanted to marry. But since she wasn't ready to get serious yet, she still wanted to have some fun."

"I can imagine how much that must have hurt," Leah said.

"Hurt me enough to make me boycott women for several years."

"And now? You've obviously ended your boycott."

"I settled my heart with God the last few years in Costa Rica. I knew what I wanted in a woman, in a relationship with an equal partner. That's why I was so amazed when I saw you the first time at the Little League game. It was as if God took my wish list for the perfect woman and put it all together, and there you were."

"Your wish list, huh?" Leah asked with a smile.

"You don't have a wish list?"

"Not really. But I have been known to wish upon Pluto."

"And what exactly happens when you wish upon Pluto?"

Leah turned to Seth and with a grin said, "You, I guess."

Chapter Twenty-seven

$\mathcal{M}$e, huh?" Seth said, as he stopped the car in front of Leah's house. "You wished upon Pluto, and you got me, huh? What would have happened if you wished upon Neptune?"

Leah shrugged playfully and said, "A guy who carries around a forked spear and likes seafood?"

Seth let out a deep laugh. "I hope that doesn't mean my being connected with your wish on Pluto is your way of telling me I'm a dog?" Seth got out of his side of the car and motioned for Leah to stay where she was so he could come around and open the door for her.

As he offered her a hand out, Leah answered him with, "No, but I noticed you came with a dog, or at least you got a dog the first time we did something together."

"Yes, and by the way, how was Bungee the night you had him?"

"Oh, he was great during the night," Leah said carefully, as she unlocked her front door and led Seth into the kitchen. "I took him for a long walk around the block, and he was good and tired when he went to bed."

"He sure needs a lot more attention than I've been able to give him. I've felt bad about leaving him alone in the apartment so much. And he needs a yard to run in."

"That's for sure," Leah said.

Seth went to the cupboard and pulled out Leah's coffee beans and filters as if they already had discussed his staying for coffee. They hadn't, but Leah had hoped he would come in. And here he was, in her kitchen, making coffee.

"Did I detect a hint of sarcasm there?" Seth asked. "Where does that come from?"

"I might as well tell you, your little Bungee Boy tore down the barricade I left up in the mudroom and had a free-for-all in my house."

Seth glanced around. "Anything broken?"

"No."

"Looks like you managed to clean it all up."

"It only took me three hours," Leah said dramatically. She opened her dishwasher and pulled out two coffee mugs.

"Why didn't you close the door?" Seth asked.

"I wanted Hula to be able to get away from Bungee since I had to block off the doggy door to the backyard. I thought Hula might want her space. As it was, she stayed huddled in the mudroom, and Bungee had the run of the place."

"Did he ruin anything?"

Leah had to wait a minute before answering because Seth was grinding the coffee beans. As soon as he spooned them into the filter, she could smell the rich aroma. "Not really. He just made a gigantic mess."

"I'm sorry, Leah."

"No need to apologize. I should have known Bungee is fast growing beyond the sleepy puppy stage. And I should have put up a bigger barricade."

Seth poured water into the coffeemaker and pushed the start button. It was quiet for a moment between them as they stood facing each other by the kitchen counter. Seth reached over and lightly fingered the ends of her hair. "Did I ever tell you how much I like your hair?"

"As a matter of fact, you did. More than once. However, the first time, you were slightly spacey so I wasn't sure how much of what you said was true."

"Really? What did I say?"

Leah felt her cheeks blushing.

"That good, huh?" Seth said, touching his fingers to her rosy cheeks. "What else did I say?"

"Nothing much." Leah looked down. "Just enough to let me know you were interested in me."

"And you didn't believe me, did you?"

"Well…" She hesitated, not sure if she should tell him of his mini-concert at the Dairy Queen. Any woman would question what a man said immediately after he had sung a list of hamburgers.

"Come here," Seth said, drawing Leah to him in a hug. He held her close. "Believe me, Leah. Trust me."

She wanted to. But something made her hesitate. It suddenly struck her that everything had happened so quickly and had seemed a little too perfect. Things didn't go along the lines of "perfect" or "smooth" in her life unless she did lots of preparing and planning. None of this was planned.

Leah didn't pull away from Seth on the outside; yet on the inside she began to put up a barricade. The feelings she had were similar to how she felt about Bungee. He could be in her house but only within the limits she set for him. She felt frightened to think Seth might break through and have the run of her heart. She hadn't had time to think all this through yet.

Leah guessed that Seth sensed her reluctance. He released her from his hug and held her at arm's length. "You haven't told me my number yet."

"Your number?"

"My number. Which boyfriend am I? Which number? Forty-seven? Ninety-three?"

Leah pressed her lips together and looked into his deep blue eyes. Seth seemed so sincere, so open to her. She knew she shouldn't be skittish. She had trusted him with her secret about the Glenbrooke Zorro. She could trust him with this truth.

"Seth, you're the first and only."

"Oh, come on, I find that hard to believe."

"I've never led much of a social life. Surely you guessed that."

"You know everyone in this town. They all adore you. I can't believe none of the guys I've met has come knocking on your door."

"Believe it, Seth. I've always been everyone's pal and never anyone's girlfriend."

"Their loss is my gain." He drew her close again, and Leah had the distinct impression he was about to kiss her. She turned her head, and his nose ended up in her ear. Seth let her go.

"Am I coming on too strong?" he asked gently.

"Yes," Leah said. "I mean, no. I mean…I don't know. I know you're going to say I'm too much of a skeptic, but I still can't get used to the idea that you're interested in me."

Seth took two steps back and crossed his arms in front of him. "What can I do to convince you?"

"Nothing. You don't need to do anything. I guess I need a little more time to get used to all this."

"Okay," Seth said, unfolding his arms and reaching for the coffeepot. "I'm in no hurry. We can take it as slow as you want."

Leah held up her cup, and he began to pour the coffee very slowly. "Is this slow enough for you?" he teased.

"That's perfect."

They shuffled into the living room with their coffee and a bag of cookies Leah pulled out of the cupboard. Seth sat on the recliner, and she stretched out on the couch. For the next hour and a half they talked about a dozen different topics. Leah began to feel more at ease. She scolded herself for being so paranoid about giving herself to a relationship with Seth. She guessed it was her lack of experience that made her hesitant.

When Seth left, he kept his word about taking things slowly, and he didn't kiss her good night. He promised to call her the next day at work and asked if she wanted to plan on dinner and a movie on Friday night.

Leah went to bed dreaming of Seth's kiss in the woods. The sensation of being circled in his embrace and feeling his lips on hers was intoxicating. The only thing she could compare it to was the way she had felt as a child on Easter Sunday when the pungent fragrance of lilies filled the sanctuary, and she was allowed to stand up in church and shout.

Tonight, in the stillness of her room, she felt the intoxication of Seth's touch as strongly as she remembered the scent of those Easter lilies. However, something was keeping her from standing up on the inside and shouting her declarations about Seth.

The next day Seth called her twice. First he phoned before she left for work just to say good morning and to give her the list of movies playing so she could choose which one she wanted to see Friday night.

The second time he called was late afternoon, right before she left work. He said the lawyer had phoned, asking if they could meet Monday morning for the reading of the will. Seth told Leah the lawyer would be calling her as well.

"Why?" she asked.

"You're mentioned in the will, obviously."

"What time Monday morning?"

"Nine o'clock. Do you think it will be a problem for you?"

"No, I can make arrangements."

"Good," Seth said. "I'm sure looking forward to seeing you tomorrow night."

"Me, too," Leah said and then hung up. Leah had to do some fancy schedule changing with two other employees before she could arrange to be gone for an hour Monday morning.

Seth called again on Friday afternoon and said he would pick her up at 6:30.

"I was thinking about that," she said. "Why don't I drive to your place or meet you at the restaurant in Edgefield? It would be a lot easier than your driving home after work, then driving all the way here, and then we turn around and go back to Edgefield."

Seth paused. "Are you sure? Because I don't mind coming to get you. If you wanted, I could pick you up right at work, and we could go to an early movie and then to dinner."

"No, I'd rather change out of my work clothes," Leah said. "I'll just come to Edgefield at 6:30. Where should I meet you?"

"My place, I guess. Oh, and I've been meaning to tell you, the spinach was fantastic."

"Good. I'll make you another one."

Seth chuckled. "You don't need to make me another one. I simply wanted you to know I enjoyed it."

As Leah hurried home from work Friday, she wondered if

she was overdoing it with Seth. Offering to make him spinach, insisting on driving so he wouldn't have to.

It reminded her of something Shelly had said several months ago. "Leah, you seem like the kind of woman who is only comfortable when you're in charge of things. Every once in a while it's good if you let someone else take control. Let others give to you for a change."

The comment had come during the practice for the annual church Christmas pageant when Leah was doing everything from sewing wise men costumes to coaching kids on their lines to showing up early at the performance to making sure enough chairs were set up.

Leah wondered if she actually could let herself relax with Seth tonight on this, their first official date. Could she stop being in charge?

In an effort to get herself started on the right foot, Leah decided to take a bath. It wasn't a long bath, but then she wasn't given to such luxuries so the twelve minutes she soaked in the warm tub were restful for her. Then she made liberal use of her only bottle of hand lotion. The bug bites on her legs had turned to small, red dots. Not that it mattered; she planned to wear jeans. She always wore jeans.

Leah began to dress but then wondered if her chinos might be a little nicer. She didn't know what kind of restaurant Seth planned to take her to.

What if it's formal attire only? No, Seth wouldn't like a place where he had to wear a coat and tie. I was surprised he even owned a coat and tie to wear to the memorial service. I wonder if he bought them just for the funeral?

Leah looked in her closet and decided it wouldn't hurt her to do a little shopping one of these days, too. She couldn't remember the last time she had bought herself anything other than work apparel or new tennis shoes.

She finally decided on a white cotton shirt, which she ironed vigorously so the collar would stay in place. The final vote on the pants was the jeans because the chinos looked wrinkled to her, and she didn't want to take the time to iron them. When she slipped on her black linen blazer, she thought it looked pretty good. Some sort of jewelry would improve the outfit, but her selection was limited and none of it seemed right.

While brushing her hair, which had air-dried after her bath, Leah decided to pull the top part back in a single clip. She didn't usually do anything with her hair so this seemed like a fancy change. She wondered if Seth would like it.

Her makeup routine was simple and the same every day. Tonight she experimented with some blush, which she rarely used since, in her opinion, her cheeks blushed enough on their own. The extra minutes with the mascara wand and the extra detailed flossing and brushing of her teeth all seemed to have a good effect. She felt pretty, and that was as important as anything else.

With a squirt of her only fragrance, which was a gift-sized bottle of Fresh Ocean Breeze, Leah called her good-byes to Hula and opened her front door.

There stood Collin Radcliffe, just about to ring her doorbell.

Chapter Twenty-eight

"Collin, you startled me," Leah said, catching her balance.

"Good evening, Leah. My, don't you look nice. Are you going out?"

"As a matter of fact, I was just leaving," she said, checking her watch. It was five minutes before six.

"That's a pity." Collin had on one of his expensive business suits and looked as if he had just come from the office.

"Is there something wrong?" Leah asked.

"I was hoping I might have a word with you before you met with my father Monday for the reading of Mr. Madison's will. Did you get my message?"

"No, I haven't listened to my machine yet."

"Would there be a convenient time for me to stop by tomorrow?" Collin asked.

"Tomorrow? I guess so."

"I don't want to hold you up," he said smoothly. "Here's my

card. Would you call me in the morning after nine and let me know a time that would work for you?"

"Sure." Leah took the embossed business card from him. "I'll call you."

"Good. May I walk you to your car?"

Leah found his superb manners once again put her on the defensive. This time, instead of resisting his assistance, she held her tongue and let Collin reach over and open the car door for her. She thought again of Shelly's observation that Leah only was comfortable when she was the one in control. This seemed as good a time as any for her to practice relinquishing control. Collin seemed as determined to do things for her as she was determined to do things for others.

"You'll call me tomorrow then?" he asked.

"Yes, I'll call you." She smiled at him before she drove off. Not a flirty, inviting smile, but one that expressed her decision not to resist Collin or his sudden involvement in her life. It was her way of saying, "Okay, I'll stop being the edgy, poor-me girl you knew in high school. This is the new me, the Leah who is learning to like who she is and is accepting her life as it is."

Her drive to Edgefield seemed to take only ten minutes instead of the actual thirty. She was lost in her thoughts—or more accurately, in her dreams. She saw her response to Collin as a major step in the right direction. She could be free and open in her relationships instead of controlling. It didn't matter to her at the moment if Collin wanted to talk about business or Franklin or—maybe he was considering running for mayor and wanted her support. She was a strong woman learning to soften up around the edges. And she was on her way to have a date with the most wonderful man in the world who had captured her heart. How could she possibly allow herself to enter this evening as the old, driven, misunderstood Leah?

She found herself praying aloud the last few blocks to Seth's apartment. She wanted God's blessing on her life. On this evening. On her relationship with Seth.

Parking in one of the three visitor parking spaces, Leah looked at the sticky note on her dashboard that had the Psalm 37 verses printed on it. She read the last verse aloud, "'Commit your way to the Lord, trust also in Him, and He will do it.'"

Trust in him, trust in him, Leah repeated to herself as she headed for Seth's apartment. *I'm trying, God!*

The moment she knocked on the door, it swung open, and Seth held out a bouquet of daisies.

Leah laughed. "How pretty! For me?"

"For you," he said. "I have to admit it would have felt more natural if I were the one ringing your doorbell and you were the one opening the door."

"We can try it that way," she said, playfully handing him back the flowers and pulling him outside. She went into his apartment and closed the door on him. Bungee yelped and barked and begged for Leah to come rescue him from the kitchen.

"Just a minute, Bungee Boy. I'm having a little fun with your master."

The doorbell rang. Leah deliberately waited. The doorbell rang again. "Who is it?" she called out sweetly.

"Open the door and find out," Seth said. His voice didn't sound quite as joking as she had intended this exercise to be.

She opened the door, and Seth stood there, looking more embarrassed than jovial. He held out the flowers without saying anything. His eyebrows were raised as if to say, "Are we done with this game?" Leah noticed three of his neighbors standing in the parking area. They had been loading a self-rent moving van when she had pulled up. Now all three men had stopped working and were elbowing each other and watching Seth.

"Thanks," Leah said quietly, as Seth entered the apartment and closed the door. "Sorry I sent you out the door like that. I don't know what I was thinking."

"Beginning relationship jitters?" Seth suggested.

Leah nodded. "Mind if I leave these here in water? I'll get them when we come back."

"Sure."

Leah felt awful. She had done it again. She had seized the opportunity to be the one who controlled the situation. *Why couldn't I just say thank you and take the flowers while we were both in a happy mood and excited to see each other?*

She stepped into the kitchen and greeted Bungee with enthusiasm that matched his excitement.

"Does it matter to you what I use for a vase?" she called out to Seth.

"No," he said, standing in the living room, watching her. "A bucket is under the sink, glasses are in the cupboard. I don't know which would work best for you."

Leah opted for the bucket because it was easy. Then she joined Seth on the couch.

"I don't know why I did that," she said. "I'm sorry. It was supposed to be a joke, but it didn't end up funny."

"Forget it; it's okay."

"No, it's not really okay," Leah continued. "I don't want to be like that."

"Like what?" Seth leaned back and folded his hands behind his neck, listening to her. He looked open and understanding, not upset, like he did earlier.

Leah decided not to make such a big issue out of apologizing. "I guess God is working on this one area of my life, and I keep noticing ways I need to change. It's humbling."

Seth nodded, as if he understood what she was saying.

"Shelly says I'm only comfortable in a relationship if I'm the one in control."

"Do you think that's true?" Seth asked.

"I'm sure there's some truth to it. I could make up all kinds of excuses about how I had to be that way to survive with five older sisters and in the role I played with my parents for so long. Only thing is, I don't want to go through life apologizing for who I am. I've done that far too long."

Seth's tender expression invited her to continue.

"You helped me to see that, you know," Leah said. She hadn't planned to say any of this. It was all coming up as if an underground cistern had been exposed, and she couldn't hold back the water from flowing out. "When you told me about the biblical Leah and how she started praising God instead of always trying to prove her value to others, I thought a lot about that. I've thought about how her son was the one who received the blessing. I've started to esteem my namesake more highly, and I think it's affecting how I think about myself."

"Actually," Seth said, "I think it's all in the voice inflection when you get to verse 25. You say it as if it's, 'Boo, hiss, behold, it's Leah.' I prefer to think of it this way." Seth stood and struck a pose in front of Leah like a regal town crier. He had one arm bent behind him and one bent in the front. With his chin up, he raised his left arm and dramatically announced, "Behold! It's Leah!"

Leah grinned. "You make it sound as if I've been chosen to attend a royal ball."

"Not a royal ball," Seth said, offering her his hand. "Just fish fajitas at Del Rey, and our reservation is in five minutes. Shall we?"

Leah took his hand and let him usher her out the door and to his car. She couldn't believe how easily Seth made her feel relaxed and as if her personality flaws didn't bother him. It wasn't that he didn't notice them nor have a dislike for some of them. It was more as if he had a goal, and nothing else seemed important enough to deter him from it. He was a man on a mission, Leah decided. And if his mission was to win her heart and soul, he had succeeded. She just didn't know if he realized that yet, or if she would have to find a way to express her heart to him.

As the evening progressed, Leah realized she didn't need to spell out anything for Seth. They talked and laughed freely over dinner at the Mexican restaurant Seth called his home away from home. He estimated that he had eaten there twelve times in less than a month. It was close to his apartment, inexpensive, and offered plenty of variety for a fish-eating vegetarian.

The movie they had decided on turned out to be a good choice. While they sat in the fifth row—a mutual, spontaneous decision based on both of them liking to feel as if they were part of what was happening on the screen—Seth and Leah held hands and shared a large tub of buttered popcorn.

By the time they arrived back at his apartment, the last thing Leah wanted to do was go home. She wanted to settle in with a fresh pot of coffee and sit up all night talking. However, Seth had other plans.

Chapter Twenty-nine

Lingering in his car in the apartment parking area, Seth nodded at the moving van now parked in front of the complex. "I promised one of my neighbors I'd help him move tomorrow."

"Did you get your stitches removed already?" Leah asked.

"No, which is why I couldn't help them load the van. I volunteered to drive instead."

"Oh." Leah had been dreaming of fun things they could do together on Saturday. "Where is he moving to?"

"Walnut Creek."

"Where is that?"

"Near San Francisco."

Leah looked at him with disbelief. "It'll take you all day to get there."

"So I've been told. I didn't know exactly where he was moving until after I volunteered to drive the van. We're leaving at two in the morning and driving straight through. I don't imagine I'll be back until Sunday evening."

Leah made an exaggerated pout. "I'll miss you. I was hoping we could spend some more time together this weekend."

"Me too," Seth said. "I'm glad we had tonight together. My neighbor wanted to pull out this evening as soon as he had the van loaded, but I told him I had an important meeting I couldn't cancel."

Leah thought back on how she had sent Seth out the door with his daisies in hand. The movers must have surmised quickly that his "important meeting" was with a woman who had a strange sense of humor. She wished she hadn't done that.

"I hope you understand," Seth said. "I'd invite you in for some really superb coffee, but I think I need a little sleep before I start driving."

"Definitely," Leah agreed. "I'll just run in, grab my flowers, and be on my way."

"Oh, that's right, your daisies."

"And my good-night kiss," Leah added.

Seth looked surprised. "Your good-night kiss, huh? What makes you think we were going to share a good-night kiss?"

"Just a prediction."

"Wow," Seth teased as he got out of the car, "you must be psychic."

Psychotic is more like it! she thought as he came around to open her door. *Why did I say that? My knowledge of dating etiquette is atrocious!*

They walked to his front door with an arm around each other's waist. Seth leaned his chin against her hair and said, "I suppose I'm going to have to kiss you twice tonight. Once for good night and once to soften you up extra for the huge favor I'm going to ask of you."

Leah smiled. She wouldn't mind two kisses. Not one bit.

Seth unlocked the door to his apartment, and Leah asked, "What's the favor? Or do you think you should kiss me first before you lay the tough request on me?"

Seth leaned over and kissed her on the cheek before she realized he was going to do it. She immediately felt disappointed. The first of her two kisses had been used up just like that.

"I better ask you now, and then you can decide if you still want to kiss me good night." Seth flipped on the light, and they immediately heard Bungee scampering across the linoleum floor and letting out a happy bark.

"Wait. Let me guess. You want me to baby-sit Bungee while you're gone."

Seth looked at her sheepishly. "Would you mind? I know he was a problem last time, but I bought him a long leash. I thought maybe you could anchor him in the backyard, and he could get a little exercise."

"Sure," Leah said.

"Are you positive?"

"Yes. I'll check that the barricade is strong enough to keep him in the mudroom this time, and I'll even take him for a walk or two. I'd be glad to take him for the weekend."

Seth took Leah by the elbows and pulled her close, showing her his appreciation in his kiss, which was considerably longer than the first and not on her cheek. They drew apart slowly, and Seth said, "You know, I think we're getting better at this each time."

Leah let out a nervous chuckle. "You have to consider that when you kiss someone who has as little experience as I have, there's plenty of room for improvement."

"As little experience as both of us," Seth corrected her. "I may have had two and a half girlfriends before you, but there's plenty of room for improvement in my kisses."

"That's not my opinion. I like your kisses just the way they are." She wrapped her arms around Seth in a warm hug. He held her for a minute before giving her a kiss on the side of her forehead, right where her eyebrow met her temple. "And I like yours just the way they are," he whispered.

They drew apart and smiled at each other. Neither of them initiated another kiss. It seemed to Leah that everything was right and balanced the way it was. She didn't want to do anything to disrupt the wonderful, overwhelming sense of falling in love.

"Your flowers," Seth said after a moment.

"My flowers." Leah stepped into the kitchen. "I'll take them home in the bucket, if you won't miss it."

"No, I definitely won't miss my bucket this weekend," Seth said with a laugh. He scooped up Bungee and added, "Your lasagna pan is in the cupboard there. I'll get Bungee's leash."

Leah opened the first cupboard and saw only bowls, plates, and cups. The next cupboard held papers and file folders. She was impressed Seth was so organized. For fun, she flipped through the files to see if they were alphabetized. They weren't. A file labeled Madison Property was the first file, and it came before the one labeled Car Insurance.

At least I know he's not perfect, Leah thought. She checked the lower cupboard and found her spinach casserole dish just as Seth returned with Bungee on his leash.

"You don't know how much I appreciate this," Seth said.

"I think Bungee is going to appreciate it more than you." Leah bent to greet the happy-to-be-going-anywhere puppy. "And you can show me your appreciation, Mr. B., by following the house rules this time."

"He will," Seth said. "At least I hope he will. I see you

found the pan. Would you like me to carry the flowers?"

"No, I can get them if you have the hyper-hound there."

Seth walked Leah to her car with Bungee leading the way. They settled him on the floor in front and gave each other a quick hug.

"I'll see you Monday," Seth said. "Monday morning at the reading of the will."

"Oh, that's right. Do you want to come to my house for dinner Monday night?"

"That would be great. And if you don't mind having Bungee that long, I'll pick him up then."

"That's fine. Have a safe trip." She waved good-bye, and all the way back to Glenbrooke, she planned what she would make for dinner Monday night.

When she arrived home with Bungee under her arm, sleepy Hula woke and gave Leah a look as if to say, "Oh, no, please, anything but that troublemaker again. Don't do this to me!"

"Oh, don't look at me like that, Hula! You and Bungee need to work out your differences and become good friends. You two will most likely be seeing a lot of each other in the weeks ahead. Work it out, okay? And you," she said, pulling Bungee close, "you behave!"

Bungee licked her chin. Leah closed off the doggy door and closed the door to the mudroom. "Now good night and not a peep out of either of you."

Three hours later, Leah wished they were only peeping. Bungee had taken to barking continuously when his whimpering didn't produce any results. He barked and barked until she thought his throat must be hoarse. Twice, she yelled out, "Go to sleep!" through her closed bedroom door. Then she pulled the pillow over her head and tried to ignore the ruckus.

She didn't remember falling asleep, but she did remember checking her bedside clock at three. All she knew was that once Bungee finally quieted down, she crashed.

Leah was up again at 5:30 to take Bungee outside and then plopped back into bed. She had forgotten how much work a puppy could be.

She finally woke up at nine o'clock and went to check on the dogs. They seemed fine, as if it hadn't been such a rough night for either of them. Hula was eager to get out the doggy door. Leah let her out and then fastened Bungee's leash and let him lead her down the steps and out to her backyard. With careful calculation, Leah fastened the end of Bungee's leash to the metal rail that ran along the back steps. He had enough leash to get into the mudroom if he wanted and enough to frolic on the grass, but not enough leash to reach her garden.

After providing fresh food and water for both dogs, Leah played with Bungee, giving him praise and attention. That seemed to calm him down, and she wondered why she hadn't thought to comfort him the night before. She remembered how long it had taken Hula to get used to her new surroundings when Leah had brought her home. And here poor little Bungee had been bounced between Leah's house and Seth's apartment. No wonder the little fellow was confused.

The dogs taken care of, Leah decided against what she really wanted to do, which was to go back to bed. Instead, she turned on some music and started breakfast.

A nightmare met her when she opened her lower cupboard and reached for a bag of granola-style cereal. The bag had a hole in the bottom, and on closer examination, Leah was certain a mouse had nibbled it.

"I will find you and destroy you, you destructive rodent," she muttered, getting on her hands and knees and pulling out the cupboard's contents. The plastic bag of organic, steel-cut oatmeal had an even bigger hole in it and left a trail as she pulled it out.

"Hmm, this is serious." Leah went to the bedroom and put on her glasses since she didn't want to take time to put in her contacts. She pulled up her hair and fastened it with the clip she still had in from when she had fixed her hair with such care last night. She left on her pajamas, which were flannel shorts and a long T-shirt, since she didn't care if they got ruined. To complete the ensemble, Leah slipped on a pair of garden gloves, just in case the varmint tried to chomp into one of her fingers while she was pulling everything out. A huge mess awaited her in the back of the cupboard, and she ended up throwing out everything that showed evidence of being nibbled on. She even threw away a box of graham crackers because the box hadn't been closed properly when she put it away, and she didn't know if the mouse—or mice, whichever the case might be—had managed to get into the crackers.

Once the cupboard was empty, she found neither culprits nor an obvious point of entry. Using Seth's bucket, she prepared warm, disinfected water, and still wearing the garden gloves, she grabbed a sponge and began to scrub the shelves.

The doorbell rang in the middle of her vigorous cleaning. "Come around the back," she called out. "I'm in the kitchen."

Sticking her head in the cupboard and reaching as far to the back as she could, Leah wiped down the last section of the shelf. She heard the back door close and called out, "I'm in here. Enter at your own risk."

"Doing a little spring cleaning?" a cultured voice asked behind her.

Leah bumped her head trying to get out of the cupboard fast enough to see if her suspicion was correct. It was. Her morning visitor was Collin Radcliffe. And there she sat on the kitchen floor, her glasses crooked, her hair sticking straight up from the clip in back, her garden gloves and rag-bag quality pajamas her only attire, and the fragrance of pine-scented disinfectant permeating the air.

And there stood Collin, every hair in place, wearing khaki shorts and a polo shirt. He looked as if he had just posed for pictures before the start of the U.S. Open golf tournament and was now ready to tee off.

Leah caught the sudden drip coming out her nose with the back of a garden- gloved hand and tried her best to greet Collin with a smile. There was no mistaking the look on his face. The poor man was in shock at the sight of her.

Chapter Thirty

"Mouse," Leah said simply, by way of explanation.

"Mouse?" Collin repeated.

"This is a mouse-mess. And you know what? I never expected my visitor to be you, or I wouldn't have exposed you to such a terrifying sight." She looked down and caught another drip from her nose with the back of her gloved hand.

Collin stood his ground, undaunted. "I should have called. The apology is mine. I was on my way to brunch at the country club in Baker's Grove and discovered the battery had gone out on my cell phone. I thought if you had been trying to call me this morning, you wouldn't have been able to reach me."

Leah had forgotten all about saying she would call Collin after nine that morning. "I hadn't tried yet. This took priority. How about if I call you this afternoon?"

"If that's convenient for you," Collin said. "Or, if you prefer, I'd like to invite you to join me for brunch at the country club."

Leah couldn't help but find his invitation laughable. "Okay, Collin, sure. Would you like me to go like this? Or should I maybe change into something more suitable?"

Collin didn't laugh with her. "I don't mind waiting."

"Okay," Leah answered after studying his expression for a moment. She scrunched up her nose and continued to poke fun at herself. "Why don't I just go freshen up a bit. Maybe powder my nose."

Collin still didn't laugh.

Leah slipped into her bedroom and called out, "Please help yourself to whatever you can find in the refrigerator to drink. I'm sure the mouse didn't find his way in there. Magazines are in the living room. You can change the music, if you prefer something else."

"No, I'm fine, thanks," Collin answered.

Leah was glad her bathroom had an extra door that connected to her bedroom. She could shower, wash her hair, put in her contacts, and apply some makeup before slipping into her bedroom and pulling on a pair of black, linen shorts with a belt. She chose a light blue knit shirt with collar and sleeves, just to be in the same apparel range as Collin's outfit. However, her knit shirt didn't have a pocket, let alone a fancy embroidered designer logo like Collin's.

As she buckled her watch, Leah noticed she had only been keeping him waiting for twenty minutes. That wasn't bad. Somehow she expected this all to be some kind of crazy joke and Collin would be gone when she emerged from her room.

But he was there, comfortably situated in the living room watching the sports channel. "You look terrific," he said when she joined him.

"I'd imagine anything would be an improvement over the sight you saw in the kitchen."

Collin smiled only slightly. "Shall we go?"

"Sure."

Leah wondered if she had agreed to go with Collin because she liked the idea of breakfast at the country club twenty minutes away in Baker's Grove. Or was it Collin? Was she overwhelmed with his presence in her home? His invitation for her to join him? It couldn't be because she was looking for someone to go out with. She had Seth. She was sure she was falling in love with Seth, even though she hadn't verbalized that yet.

As they sped down the road in Collin's comfortable Mercedes, he told Leah about how he had run into an old classmate of theirs when he lived in California and all the details of that person's life. Leah made the appropriate nods and "oh, reallys?" but her mind was in another place.

Is it possible Collin considers this more of a social call than a business call? Or am I delusional and pretending that all kinds of men find me attractive and want to spend time with me simply because I'm starting to feel good about myself? But Collin couldn't be interested in me. Not after the way he found me this morning on my mouse hunt! He must want something from me. Be on your guard, Leah.

"And you?" Collin was asking as Leah pulled herself out of her deep thoughts. "Are you still planning to stay in Glenbrooke, now that your folks are gone?"

"Yes, I'm pretty settled here."

"Any plans to marry soon?" Collin asked, glancing at her with his dark eyes, as he turned into the long driveway that led to the country club.

"Marry? No," Leah said cautiously. She felt as if the question was a hot potato, and she tossed it back to Collin immediately. "What about you?"

"I married almost six years ago," Collin answered.

"Oh." She didn't remember hearing about that in the local grapevine.

"But I'm currently not married."

Leah assumed he was divorced, even though he didn't offer an explanation. They were almost to the front of the impressive entrance to the country club, and Collin seemed to be concentrating on the car in front of them that was apparently going too slow for his taste.

Leah had never been here before. Classmates had gone to this country club for the prom, but she hadn't attended. A friend from work held her wedding reception here, but it was the week after Leah's father's funeral, and she couldn't leave her mother alone for the afternoon.

Leah didn't want to feel as smug as she did at this moment, but she couldn't help it. In a silly way, this was one of her high school dreams finally coming true—only better. She was riding in an expensive automobile to the white portico where uniformed valets were ready to open her door, and Collin Radcliffe was about to treat her to brunch.

Wait a minute! This isn't the prom, Leah. This is your present life. Remember? You...Seth...kisses in the woods.... God's planting new seeds in your heart. What are you doing here with Collin?

They came to a stop while waiting for the car in front of them to unload its passengers and for the valet to attend to them. Leah adjusted her posture so she was sitting up as straight as possible. Her mind was busy forming a list of questions for Collin about his motives. If he failed to answer any of them to her satisfaction, she simply would march into the country club and call a cab.

Before she could ask the first question, Collin turned to her and said, "I should tell you that my wife was in a fatal car accident two years ago in Los Angeles. She was five months pregnant at the time. I lost both of them."

The valet opened Leah's door and offered her a hand out. But she slumped against the leather seat, stunned. "I'm so sorry, Collin. I hadn't heard. I didn't know."

He shook his head and looked away. "Not many people do. I knew you would understand because of the loss you suffered with both your parents. It takes a while to recover, doesn't it?"

"Yes," Leah said simply.

The valet waited until she turned and began to get out of the car. Leah felt all her defenses lowering. Collin was someone she had known since she was a girl, just as she had known Franklin since her childhood. Collin had endured a deep and terrible blow. She did understand. She walked beside this distinguished classmate on the plush, green carpet runner, past the huge terra-cotta planters spilling over with bright flowers, and up to the entrance. It was all she could do to keep herself from slipping her arm through his and giving him several comforting pats to let him know she felt for him.

The door of the country club opened automatically, and Leah entered first, at Collin's gentlemanly gesture. They proceeded silently to the restaurant at the back of the club where the Saturday morning brunch was in full swing. Collin asked for a window seat, and they were ushered to what Leah considered the best seat in the house. Two prominent colors filled the view from the window: the crisp blue of the sky and the emerald of the golfing greens.

"Do you play golf?" Collin asked, as Leah stared out the window, taking in the serene beauty.

"No, I never have. Do you?"

"Every chance I get. You know, you're dressed the part. If you would like, we could take in nine holes after we eat."

"I might need to walk nine holes after I eat everything I saw offered on the buffet."

"We would use a cart," Collin said graciously.

"How much exercise is that?" Leah teased.

"You would be surprised." Collin smiled at her, and she found herself wanting to stare. He looked so different from Seth. Seth still had a youthful look, especially when he wore his baseball cap like the night she first saw him. Collin was a man. Suave, confident, and established. The contrast between the two was strong.

"Good morning," the waiter said. "Will you be having the buffet? Or would you like to order off the menu?"

"The buffet would be fine," Leah said, trying to match the gracious tone in the waiter's voice. Last night at the Del Rey Mexican restaurant, the waitress had a squeak when she laughed. Leah doubted anyone at the country club was allowed to squeak for any reason.

"I'll have the buffet as well," Collin answered.

The rest of their brunch progressed with continued smoothness. They talked about lots of the people they grew up with and what all of them were doing now. Leah felt as if she were with an old friend, even though she and Collin hadn't associated much while they were growing up.

"It's such a pity we're so narrowly focused as teenagers," Collin said. "If I'd known you were going to turn out this gorgeous and this much fun, I would have snatched you up our freshman year of high school and never let you go."

"Oh," was all Leah could say. She felt herself blushing and quickly buried her nose in her coffee mug, even though only a sip was left.

Gorgeous?

She knew Collin didn't mean "gorgeous." She wasn't gorgeous. Collin was a flatterer. A smoothtalker. This wasn't the simple, freckle-faced Collin she slugged in seventh grade when he said her bike was a "wimpy girlie bike." This was Collin, the lawyer from LA who drank Pelligrino sparkling water with a twist of lime.

For a brief moment, Leah allowed herself to float back to that imaginary place in her past when she was seventeen. She toyed with the idea of what it would have been like if she really were gorgeous and were dining at the country club with Collin on a date.

What would my sisters have thought of that?

Leah imagined how different the last ten years of her life would have been—and what a different person she would have been if Collin had "snatched her up."

Wait! What am I thinking? I'm becoming a different person now. I like who I am.

An image of her blue-eyed dragon slayer came to mind. Simple, earthy, living-on-a-shoestring Seth. That's the person she wanted to be snatched up by.

Leah broke off a corner of her croissant and busied herself buttering it because she didn't want to look up at Collin. She found this past week it had become increasingly difficult to make a distinction between the real and the fantasy parts of her life. Some of her realities with Seth had been more wonderful than any fantasy she ever had dared to dream up.

What am I doing here with Collin? Why am I allowing myself to think these crazy things?

Leah didn't like the feeling, as if she were losing her balance. She especially didn't like that her mind could play these kinds of games with her emotions.

"Excuse me," she said, pushing back her chair. Collin rose slightly as she stood. "I'll be right back."

As Leah asked directions to the restroom, she could almost feel Collin watching her. Had he noticed that she was short with muscular legs and a straight torso? She imagined Collin had married a tall, thin woman with a twenty-inch waist. It was still shocking to think he had lost his wife and unborn baby in a car accident.

Leah took a good look at herself in the restroom mirror. She stared at her reflection until arriving at the conclusion that she didn't know who she was. None of the old, recorded messages fit any longer. She wasn't the big failure her father and sisters had insinuated she was. Few expectations of others weighed upon her the way they used to. The soil of her soul had all been turned over. Some seeds had been planted right away. Now it was as if Leah held several bags of mixed seeds, and it was up to her to decide which ones to plant.

Do I think I'm in love with Seth simply because he was my only option? I mean, what if Collin could actually be interested in me? Is that crazy?

Leah knew she should get back to the table. Drawing in a deep breath, she decided she was going right back to her chair, sit down, and look Collin in the eye. She would ask him why he had initiated this meeting. And she wouldn't leave that chair until she knew exactly what this man's motivation was.

Chapter Thirty-one

Leah returned to the table and asked Collin her first question. "You indicated yesterday that you had something you wanted to discuss with me before the reading of the will Monday. Would this be a good time to talk about it?"

Collin leaned back in his chair and seemed to consider her question a little too long, which made her uncomfortable. Finally he said, "I think I've reconsidered. I was going to discuss a matter with you that is of the strictest confidence. However, after spending this very enjoyable time with you, I'd prefer to postpone that conversation until after the reading of the will. I'm confident my words will make more sense then."

"Are you saying you're not sure you can trust me with the confidential information?"

"Oh, no, not at all. I believe you're completely reliable."

"How is it that the urgency of your message can change simply because we've shared a meal together?"

Scratching his forehead, right between his eyebrows, Collin said, "You aren't making this easy for me." The look he gave her was the way he used to look at her on the Little League field when he pitched to her for Ranger practice games. She always could hit just about anything he tossed over the plate at her. Now she was the one pitching the fast ones over the breakfast plates.

"And exactly what is it I'm not making easy for you, Collin?"

The grown-up, cosmopolitan part of Collin took over, and he opened his hands to her in an earnest appeal. "Leah, I want you to understand I approached this case originally as a lawyer approaching a client. However, now that we've had some time together, I feel more as if this is a friend-to-friend issue. I value your friendship more than I value the prospect of gaining a new client."

Leah didn't want to play with the grown-up Collin. She wanted him to go back to being feisty, not engaging. "That's what this is?" Leah challenged. "An attempt to rustle up some business, and you thought of me as a potential client? Sorry. I don't need a lawyer."

Collin folded his arms and quietly said, "That may all change on Monday."

After that statement, Leah shut down in every way she could. If she could have figuratively taken her ball and marched home, she would have. But Collin had positioned himself as a cool, calm, civilized professional, and she knew she needed to respond in kind.

He signed for the tab and asked if she wanted to take in nine holes of golf. She declined, saying she had too big of a project with the cupboards waiting for her at home. Besides that, she had left Bungee in the backyard, and she felt she should get home to check on him.

They drove along the country road with the music from his car stereo softening the air between them. Collin spoke briefly of his credentials and listed a few of the big cases he had handled in California. None of it impressed Leah. She had no intention of feeding her imagination anything that would have dazzled a seventeen-year-old. She was fully her age and at full capacity in her ability to think rationally, with no intention of allowing herself to revert to a ridiculous fantasy world.

When they arrived at her house, Collin said he thought he was doing what was best for her. Then he said one line that nearly toppled her over the edge of frustration. "I need you to trust me on this, Leah. Everything will make sense Monday. We'll talk then, okay?"

Leah simply answered, "I'll see you at your father's office at nine on Monday."

Stomping into the backyard, she found Bungee contentedly gnawing on a doggy chew that he must have retrieved from the mudroom. Hula was stretched out in the shade, apparently catching up on the sleep she had lost the night before. That didn't sound like such a bad idea to Leah, but she had a major mess waiting for her in the kitchen.

She spent the rest of the day organizing her cupboards. She had to go to the store to buy some mousetraps, and while she was in the checkout line, she overheard two women in the line next to hers. One was saying she was on her way to pick up her new car. Leah gathered from the conversation that the woman had been in an accident. She was raving about how much she received in the settlement and how great her lawyer was.

"Did you go through a law firm in Eugene?" the other woman asked.

"No, right here in Glenbrooke. Radcliffe and Sloane. My lawyer was the younger Radcliffe. The son who recently moved here. He's really terrific."

"Did they charge you an outrageous fee?" the other woman asked.

"Only fifty dollars, which he said was for processing some papers."

The other woman went on to say what a bargain that was and all about how high the lawyer fees had been for her cousin when he was in an accident.

Leah left the grocery store wondering if Collin Radcliffe was really the dashing hero this woman had made him out to be. Was it possible he *was* out to protect Leah's rights and did have her best interests in mind?

She didn't want to think about it. She wished Seth were home. He would help her make sense of everything. By nine o'clock Sunday night, Leah still hadn't heard from Seth. She tried to call him several times, but when he didn't answer, she tried not to worry about something having gone wrong on his trip. It was more likely that it took him longer to drive back than he had estimated. Or perhaps he was sleeping and not answering the phone because he was so exhausted.

Whatever the reason, all she could hope was that Seth would show up at the lawyer's office Monday morning. She didn't want to face Collin Radcliffe alone. If Seth were there, she felt certain it would be easy to stay focused and not start thinking crazy thoughts about Collin being interested in her.

On Monday morning, Leah wore a nice skirt and jacket. It was the same outfit she had worn to Franklin's memorial service. She decided she needed to go shopping that week because her wardrobe was far too limited for this crazy life that had fallen into her lap. Women in California no doubt arrived at their lawyer's office wearing silk dresses with their nails done in a color that matched. Leah knew she would never go that far, but it wouldn't hurt her to own a decent-looking outfit.

When she entered the efficient, air-conditioned office, Andrea Brown met her at the front desk. Andrea's son was the tallest of the Glenbrooke Rangers. The two women chatted comfortably for a few moments before Andrea offered Leah some coffee.

"No thanks. Am I early?"

Andrea checked her watch. "Only by a few minutes. Why don't you go on into Mr. Radcliffe's office."

Knocking twice and then opening the polished wood door, Andrea ushered Leah into a large office and invited her to take a seat on the leather sofa. Collin, who was seated in one of the four wingback chairs, rose politely as she entered. He held an open file of papers in his hand.

"Sure you don't want any coffee?" Andrea asked.

"No thanks."

Andrea left, closing the door behind her.

Collin smiled at Leah and asked about her kitchen cleaning.

"I caught the mouse yesterday," she said. "Let's hope he doesn't have any pals."

"Yes," Collin said politely.

Leah felt certain that Collin Radcliffe had never lived where rodent infestation was a problem.

Fortunately, someone knocked on the door so she didn't have to come up with any more small talk. Collin's father, whom everyone called "Radcliffe Senior," walked in. A large, striking man with white hair and a white moustache, he shook Leah's hand and placed a large file on the edge of the desk.

"Franklin and I went back for years," the distinguished gentleman said. "He will certainly be missed in this community."

Leah thought that was an odd thing for Radcliffe Senior to

say since Franklin had led such a quiet life. He had very few visitors aside from Leah and had never been involved in local politics or civic events. Perhaps he simply represented the last living tie to Cameron Madison and the founding of Glenbrooke.

"We're going to wait for Mr. Edwards before we begin," Radcliffe Senior explained.

"Do you mean no other relatives are coming?" Leah asked.

"No," Radcliffe Senior said.

"That surprises me."

"Does it?" the white-haired gentleman asked, pulling one of the wingback chairs closer. "Why so?"

"Several of his relatives came to the memorial service from out of town. I thought this would be an important meeting for them as well."

"No, only you and Mr. Edwards."

Collin added to his father's comment, "It's unfortunate so few of those relatives came from out of town to see Mr. Madison before the memorial service."

Leah was beginning to feel uncomfortable. She had imagined several people would attend the meeting. Unless, of course, Franklin had nothing to will to anyone, and they all knew it. She wasn't sure why she was here. And it concerned her that Seth hadn't arrived yet.

"Could I get a drink of water?" she asked.

Collin immediately rose. "I'll get it for you."

She smiled nervously at Radcliffe Senior. She felt as if she had been called to the principal's office and was waiting to find out what she had done wrong.

"Collin told me he had an enjoyable time with you on Saturday," Radcliffe Senior said. He looked cool, calm, confident. After all, this was his domain. She was the fish out of water here.

"Yes, it was nice. I hadn't been to the country club before."
As soon as she said it, Leah realized how much of a hick that
made her sound like. "The brunch was scrumptious," she
added, trying to sound a little more sophisticated.

*Oh, brother! "Scrumptious"? Where did I pick up that cutesy
word?*

Just then the door opened, and Andrea appeared with Seth
beside her. Leah felt like springing up and running into his
arms. He apologized for being late and greeted Leah as formally
as he greeted Radcliffe Senior.

Leah noticed Seth was in his PDS uniform, and she
guessed he was slipping this meeting in between deliveries.
She also noticed he looked extremely tired.

"Here you are, Ms. Hudson," Collin said, handing her a
cold bottle of sparkling mineral water. "May I bring you anything, Mr. Edwards?"

Seth held up his hand. "I'm fine." He smiled warmly at
Leah but then sat in one of the wingback chairs, leaving Leah
alone on the couch and feeling deserted.

"Let's get down to business," Radcliffe Senior said. He
began to read through the papers in the file. It all sounded like
blurry double-talk to Leah. When he finished the first page,
Radcliffe Senior looked up and said, "Are you with me so far?"

Leah glanced at Seth and then back at Radcliffe Senior. "I'm
sorry, but I'm not catching a lot of this. Would it be possible for
us to follow along on copies of what you're reading?" Leah navi-
gated complicated lab reports and monstrous stacks of insurance forms on a regular basis, but she always had the words to
look at, not just listen to.

"I would like that as well," Seth said.

"Basically, I just read you some of the preliminary information with respect to the estate of Franklin R. Madison,"
Radcliffe Senior said. "In an effort to save time, perhaps you

would allow me to continue. Andrea has prepared copies, and she will present them to you before you leave."

"But if the copies are already prepared," Leah stated, "I don't see why—"

"Actually, Dad," Collin interrupted. He leaned forward and granted Leah a gracious expression of apology for cutting her off. "I think we can tell these two the bottom-line of the will. We're among friends here."

Radcliffe Senior looked at his son with startled disfavor. It appeared he was a man of the old school who always went by the book, line by line.

Without waiting for his father's blessing, Collin said, "Leah, you are to receive the contents of Franklin's safe-deposit box, which has been kept sealed at the bank. Mr. Edwards, you are to receive the rest of Franklin's estate, which includes his house, fifty acres of woodlands, and $250,000 in treasury bills."

Leah turned to Seth. He looked as if he was in shock. She couldn't blame him. Fifty acres, a house, and a quarter of a million dollars was quite a fortune, especially when no one suspected Franklin still had such holdings.

"However," Collin continued, his voice going up a notch in volume. "There is one stipulation. Franklin Madison made it clear when he changed his will earlier this month, that the only way Mr. Edwards could receive his inheritance was under one condition."

Seth seemed to have lost his voice, but Collin was pausing and dramatically waiting for the inevitable question.

Leah jumped in. "What condition?"

Collin stood and turned to his father, as if inviting Radcliffe Senior the privilege of delivering the punch line. It seemed as if the two lawyers had choreographed the meeting to elicit the maximum shock from Seth and Leah.

"The condition," Radcliffe Senior began, "simply put, is that you, Seth Edwards, must legally marry Leah Hudson before the property, house, and funds are transferred to your name."

Chapter Thirty-two

$\mathcal{L}$eah and Seth exchanged stunned glances.

"The estate will be held in trust for a year," Collin explained. "If, at the end of that time, you and Ms. Hudson are not legally married, the entire estate will be donated to the Glenbrooke Historical Society."

Leah couldn't move. *What was Franklin thinking? Why would he make such a condition? Did the old fox even consider that he was making plans for other people and controlling their lives without including them in the decision?*

"Leah, are you all right?" The voice was coming from Seth, but it sounded far away.

She turned and saw he was still in the chair, less than three feet from her. "Yes. Are you okay?"

Seth nodded. "Did you know about any of this?"

"No, I had no idea."

"This is the first I've heard any of this," Seth said.

"That's how Franklin wanted it," Radcliffe Senior said. "You'll find all the details in the document, Mr. Edwards. Andrea has prepared a copy for you. Now you can see why I didn't want you looking at the papers until after we had a chance to go over them with you."

"Thank you," Seth said with a nod. He was still looking at Leah. His face had turned pale. With his right hand he kept rubbing his jaw line.

"Do you have any questions?" Radcliffe Senior asked.

"A dozen," Seth answered numbly. "But perhaps I should read the papers for myself and then set up another appointment with you."

"That would be fine. Andrea can make the appointment for you."

Radcliffe Senior stood next to Collin, who was still standing from when he rose to make the shocking announcement. It appeared that Leah and Seth were being dismissed.

Seth caught the cue and stood. Leah rose as well, but Collin stepped closer to her and said, "I wonder if you might stay a few more minutes, Leah. We need to give you the key to the safe-deposit box and discuss a few other items."

"All right."

"I'll see you later," Seth said, walking slowly to the door. "I'll call you."

"Okay," Leah said, trying hard to give him a smile. It seemed all her smiles were buried under an avalanche of stunned emotions. The best she could offer was a simple raised hand in a parting wave.

Seth exited the office, and Radcliffe Senior followed him out, closing the door behind him. Collin sat down and leaned forward, as if he were about to offer Leah confidential information. "Perhaps you realize that Franklin Madison listed you in his will many years ago."

Leah shook her head and began to speak quickly, as if she had to defend herself. "No, I didn't know. We never talked about it. I never expected anything. To be honest, I was convinced he didn't own anything besides his house. I had no idea about the treasury bills or the property."

"He did in fact own some property," Collin said.

"Where is the property? Here in Glenbrooke? Is it from Cameron Madison's original landholdings? Because Seth thought Franklin might still own land, but I didn't think so."

Leah noticed that Collin's eyebrows rose on her last statement. "What else did Mr. Edwards have to say about Franklin's estate?"

"Nothing." Leah felt the need to slow down and watch her words. "I'm sure Seth is just as shocked as I am that Franklin had so much."

"Leah," Collin leaned toward her and rubbed his hands together. "This is what I wanted to discuss with you the other day. You see, I don't think you realize it, but all of this was in your name in Franklin's will until a few short weeks ago."

"In my name?"

"After Naomi passed away, Franklin changed his will. We have all the paperwork in his file. He willed everything he had to you."

"But why?"

"I asked my father, and he said Franklin's reasons were private. We may never know. Or perhaps the safe-deposit box holds an explanation for you. Regardless of the reason, for nearly twenty years, you were heir to his entire estate. Don't you agree that it's suspicious that a distant nephew would come into town and suddenly the will is changed?"

Leah wasn't ready to accuse Seth of anything. "Were you the one who went to Franklin's house two weeks ago to change his will?"

"No, unfortunately, my father was out of town. Franklin met with my father's partner, Mr. Sloane. Their meeting was strictly professional with no explanations given. Franklin might have offered more of an explanation if my father had been the lawyer he was working with since the two of them had known each other for so long. I thought you might have some insight because I don't understand why everything was changed to Seth's name."

"I think that should be obvious," Leah said. "He's a relative. Franklin liked him. Seth has very little. He would benefit greatly from such an inheritance."

Collin looked at Leah, his eyes level with hers. "And you don't find this a bit suspicious?"

"No."

"Don't you see that all this would have been yours?"

Leah shrugged. It hadn't sunk in yet, but she didn't see why this was such a big issue. Leah was more eager to receive the key and get out of there so she could find out what was in the safe-deposit box.

"I'd like to represent you in this case," Collin said, reaching into his suit coat pocket to pull out one of his business cards.

"I have several of your cards, Collin," Leah said impatiently. "And I don't have a case."

"Oh, but you do, Leah. If we can prove that Seth influenced Franklin unduly to change his will, or if we can prove that Franklin wasn't in his right mind when he made the change, then the estate will revert back to you."

"But I don't want Franklin's estate!"

Collin leaned back in the chair and pressed his fingers

together. He drew the index fingers to his lips as if in deep contemplation.

Leah rose to her feet and said, "If that's all, I think I should get back to work."

Collin rose and looked down on Leah. His voice was calm. "I apologize, Leah. This is what I was making reference to on Saturday. You're not like other women, and I'm approaching this the wrong way. Would you be so kind as to sit for just another moment? I feel there's something important for you to know."

Leah sat down but not very quickly.

Collin took a seat next to Leah on the couch. He seemed to be searching for the right words. When he met her gaze, his expression was sincere and concerned. "Leah, you know me. I'm from here. You were with me when I fell off the boulders at Heather Creek and broke my arm."

"That's right," Leah said, a smile creeping across her lips. "We went fishing together that one time."

Collin nodded and smiled. He seemed pleased finally to have initiated a shared memory that brought a smile to Leah's face. "We were fishing for frogs," Collin corrected her. "The creek was thick with them that year, remember?"

"Oh, yeah. I got in trouble for leaving my dad's bucket at the creek when I took off on my bike to go for help. Do you remember how I told you to stay there and put your feet up?"

Collin chuckled.

"I don't know where I got the idea that if you thought your arm was broken you should raise your feet. How old were we? Nine?"

"At least nine. Maybe ten."

"I'd forgotten all about that," Leah said.

"It was a little harder for me to forget," Collin said, leaning forward. "This is exactly the point I wanted to make, Leah. We go back quite a few years. I trusted you to go for help that day, and now I'm asking you to trust me. I can help you with this."

Leah felt herself calming. It was easy to melt into the softness of the leather couch under Collin's dark gaze.

"I didn't want to have to disclose this to you," Collin continued, "but it seems the only way to help you understand. We have reason to believe that Seth Edwards is, for lack of a better word, an opportunist. We ran a check on him last week, and I'm afraid the results weren't very promising." Collin reached for the file he had left on the coffee table. He opened it to the first page and showed it to Leah.

The paper was a credit report showing that Seth Edwards had filed bankruptcy and backed out of almost $30,000 in credit card debt.

"But he was in Costa Rica for the last four years."

"Are you sure?"

Leah thought quickly. She didn't have any proof. The melanoma and the tan skin were the closest she could come to proving he had been in the tropics.

"This paper details his police record with the Colorado police. As you can see, it's for possession of illegal drugs."

"Police record? Colorado? Collin, you must have the wrong Seth Edwards. Where did you get this information?"

"From a very reliable service we've used for years." Collin closed the file. "I see I don't have to subject you to the rest of the information listed here. The question for you is whether you truly know Seth Edwards or not. Is he reliable? Has he been telling you the truth?"

Leah sat back in stunned silence.

"Let me help you consider the facts," Collin said. "As a friend. You've only known Seth Edwards for a few weeks. I'm sure he's told you exactly what he wanted you to believe. As I see it, he'll be eager to marry you, but once the estate is his,

Franklin added no provision for cancellation on any grounds. In other words, Seth could very well marry you, take every-thing, and disappear."

Collin reached over and took Leah's hand in his. "We go way back, Leah. I would hate to see any man do that to you. Especially if one of the most precious treasures he takes with him is your heart."

Leah needed air. She couldn't breath. She couldn't think. Pulling her hand away from Collin's, she stood up and said, "I need to get back to work, Collin."

He stood beside her and said, "You can see why I didn't want to drop all this on you on Saturday. I was enjoying being with you too much. Please call me." He began to reach into his pocket and then stopped and pulled out his hand. "That's right, you already have my card. Consider me a friend, Leah. That's all. A friend who cares and can help you through this. I'm sure a woman like you could find good use for a quarter of a million dollars."

Leah all but fled the law office. She drove like a crazy per-son toward the hospital and then realized she couldn't work in her state of mind. She needed to think. Suddenly, she knew where she could go.

Turning at the next corner, Leah put her foot to the accel-erator pedal and headed for the Victorian mansion on the top of Madison Hill.

Chapter Thirty-three

I can see how you would feel that way," Jessica said sympathetically, as she and Leah slowly rocked together in the porch swing. "That was an awful lot of information to take in."

"Maybe I don't exactly feel like I'm going crazy," Leah said, retracting her previous statement with a sigh. "That might have been an exaggeration. I'm overwhelmed; that's more accurate. I feel overwhelmed, and I don't know who to trust."

"You have to trust God," Jessica said simply.

"I know, but I mean, I don't know if Collin is telling me the truth about Seth."

"That's my point," Jessica said. Her smile accentuated the faint, half-moon scar on her upper lip. "God knows which one is trustworthy. Let him reveal it to you. Trust him."

"That's much easier said than done," Leah muttered, taking a sip from her iced tea glass. "I saw the credit report. The name was definitely Seth Edwards."

Jessica didn't comment. Leah had hoped Jessica would say something like, "There has to be more than one Seth Edwards in the world. They must have gotten the wrong one." But Jessica just closed her eyes, and Leah had the impression her friend was praying for her. Leah didn't know why Jessica hadn't invited her to pray aloud the way they had when, months ago, they had prayed together regularly.

Leah slowly drank her iced tea and forced herself to breathe deeply. She felt herself calming down and a sense of peace coming over her. Forming her own, silent prayer, Leah asked God for wisdom and direction. She told him she wanted to trust him but was having a hard time, in case he hadn't noticed.

Jessica opened her eyes and smiled at Leah. "I have a very good lawyer in Los Angeles. Greg Fletcher. If it would be of any help, I'd be glad to forward the papers to him and ask him to check into the situation for you."

"Do you mean forward Franklin's will or the file on Seth?"

"Do you have the file on Seth?"

"No."

"Then just the will," Jessica said. "Maybe Greg won't see anything in it. I don't know. I'm not sure how Greg could help, but if you think you would like me to contact him, I'd be glad to."

"I would. It's my right to obtain a second opinion. We encourage patients to do that all the time with doctors."

"I'll get his number," Jessica said. "If you tell his secretary you're my friend, she'll make sure he calls you as soon as possible."

Jessica went inside and left Leah alone in the swing. The late morning sky was stuffed with clouds. Only remnants of blue showed through. It was warm, not hot. The hanging geraniums were still dripping from when Jessica had watered them just as Leah pulled into the driveway and frantically ran up the steps.

This house on Madison Hill has become such a place of comfort and blessed retreat in my life. Then Leah recognized an ironic twist. *How strange that it was built by the man who started all this property-ownership, land-rights, inheritance business. Never in a million years would I have guessed I would be linked to this property in such a bizarre way.*

The air was filled with the scent of coming rain. Everything was still except for the sound of a slow moving honeybee, drunk on the sweetness of his cargo. Leah spotted the bee in the hydrangea bush and felt sympathetic for his dilemma. He had so many blossoms from which to choose. The flowers were adorned in their finest, soft pink gowns like enticing belles of the ball, torturing the one bewildered bee with their wild-scented pollen.

Suddenly a thought came to Leah with clarity and strength. If she did have the money from Franklin's estate, she could live in a house like this. A quarter of a million dollars could buy a lot of beauty and peace. Not to mention how incredible it would be for the Glenbrooke Zorro to have such resources available. Leah felt certain she could make good use of the money. And if the fifty acres were the woodlands she thought they were, the land that bordered Camp Heather Brook, Leah could give that land to Shelly and Jonathan, and they could build their tree house camp. As far as Franklin's house was concerned, she could fix it up and rent it out. Glenbrooke had few rentals in that neighborhood.

The opportunities seemed as bountiful as the blossoms available to that bewildered honeybee. Leah hadn't seen it from this angle at the lawyer's office, but it was beginning to make sense. Maybe this was something worth fighting for, on the off-chance Seth really was a rogue. Franklin never would have put such a qualification in the will if he had known what his nephew really was like.

"Wait a minute," Leah said to herself. "What am I saying?" She pressed the cold, iced tea glass to her cheek in an effort to shock herself into thinking more clearly.

How can I even think of Seth that way? What if Collin ran the report on the wrong Seth Edwards? What if Seth truly loves me and is an honest, God-fearing man? If we marry, the inheritance will be mine as well. I don't need to pull it away from Seth and claim it all for myself.

The front door opened, and Jessica appeared with one of her ubiquitous three-by-five note cards. "Greg's number," she said, handing it to Leah. "And a verse for the day to give you some encouragement."

Leah looked at the reference. When she saw it was Psalm 37:4, she said, "You gave me this one before. I've even memorized it. 'Delight yourself in the LORD; and He will give you the desires of your heart.'"

"I thought it might be a good reminder to you in the midst of all the confusion."

"Thanks," Leah said, rising to go. "And thanks for being here for me. I don't know what I'd do without you."

Jessica hugged her. "Keep me updated, okay? I'll be praying my little heart out for you."

As Leah drove to work, she thought about how much she depended on Jessica's prayers. It was astounding to think that Jessica might very well be the only person in the world who prayed for her. Where would she be if Jessica hadn't been praying all this time?

The realization prompted Leah to pray herself. And she had plenty to pray about. Her biggest concern was what she should do that night when Seth showed up at her house for dinner. Should she come right out and ask him about the credit and police reports? What would he say? If Seth had managed to lie so convincingly to her for these past few weeks, wouldn't he continue to lie and convince her of whatever he wanted?

When Leah arrived at work, she pushed all thoughts of the intense morning from her mind. She had to. The hospital was busy, and she was half a day behind with no backup support from Mary.

Of the many phone messages her coworker from ER had taken while covering Leah's desk that morning were messages from Alissa, Seth, and Collin. Leah chose not to return either man's calls, but on the way home, she dialed Alissa's number on the cell phone.

"A Wing and a Prayer Travel," Alissa answered the phone.

"Hi, it's Leah. I received a message that you called earlier today."

"Yes, I have good news for you. Or interesting news. Before I tell you what it is, I want to remind you that you gave away the last vacation package that fell in your lap. You might want to reconsider this one."

"What? Did the radio call you to say I'd won their grand drawing? Around the world for two?"

"Not quite that glamorous. The trip I'm talking about is to Hamilton Hot Springs for the weekend. They called today since I had made the arrangements for Franklin, and this was the phone number listed. They wanted to know if any of the party of three wanted to schedule a massage. I tried to cancel the whole reservation, but they said they required two weeks' notification, and since it's for this weekend, they couldn't refund the money."

"What do you mean this weekend? I was supposed to take Franklin the last weekend in May."

"Really? The last weekend? He told me it was this weekend when he set up the reservations. I wonder if he was confused."

Leah's heart began to pound. This was exactly the kind of evidence Collin was looking for to build a case against Franklin's changing the will.

"Are you still there?" Alissa asked.

"Yes, I'm here. Go ahead. What were you saying?"

"I was saying, the trip is paid for. It's in your name. Why don't you go up for the weekend and treat yourself for once? It's not too late for me to schedule a massage for you."

"A massage? I don't need a massage."

"But you could use some time away," Alissa said.

Leah couldn't argue with that. "Okay, tell me what I need to do."

"Just show up at the hot springs on Friday, any time after three. I have a brochure and a map, if you need it."

"Yes, I need a map. I'll come by tomorrow to pick it up."

"Good for you," Alissa said. "I think Franklin wanted this for you even more than he wanted it for himself."

Yeah, well, I know what he really wanted. He wanted to play matchmaker with Seth and me in the same place where he shared romantic memories with Naomi.

"You have two rooms reserved, so why not take some friends, if you don't feel like being by yourself."

"Can't you cancel one room if I keep the reservation on the other?"

"Possibly but not likely. The second room still is listed in Franklin's and Seth's names. Franklin was hopeful when he made the reservation that Seth would go with you, although Franklin told me Seth wasn't sure he wanted to go."

Leah sighed. "No, he didn't want to go. Seth didn't think Franklin should go either. Nothing is ever easy, is it? Let's drop the whole topic of Seth going. I'll go. That's that."

Alissa paused on her end of the line, apparently not sure what to make of Leah's comment.

"I'll see you tomorrow," Leah said. "Thanks for letting me know about this, Alissa. You're right. I should get away now."

Leah pushed the End button on her cell phone. When she turned the corner to her street, the first thing she saw was a PDS truck parked in front of her house.

Chapter Thirty-four

*L*eah turned off the car's engine and sat in front of her house looking for the PDS truck's driver. She didn't see anyone at her front door. Seth might have gone around the back of the house to pick up Bungee. Maybe he was avoiding her after the meeting this morning. She wondered if he needed time to sort out this turn of events as much as she did.

Leah realized how awkward it would be to see Seth, now that they suddenly were expected to get married. Before today she hadn't even allowed herself the luxury of daydreaming about such an outcome to their growing relationship, but now it was set, established by someone who hadn't asked them what they thought of the idea.

Ironic, Leah thought as she compared the similarity between this situation and the account of Jacob and Leah in Genesis. To obtain Rachel, Jacob had to take Leah. For Seth to inherit the estate, he had to take Leah. She didn't like the comparison one bit.

What concerned her even more, as she sat in her car, alone with her tormenting thoughts, was the possibility that Collin was right. What if Seth had known all along that the original will was in Leah's name? What if he had been romancing her to gain all that Franklin had left to her? What if Seth never cared for her, and it was all a lie? He could hire his own lawyer to refute the conditions, find a way to cut the marriage clause out of the will, and take the entire estate for himself.

Leah didn't know what to think or who to believe. She successfully had pushed it all away at work, but now that she was home the situation's complexities came rushing at her with a fresh urgency. She needed some answers.

Leah punched the phone number for Jessica's lawyer into her cell phone. She reached a voice mail message inviting her to dial a pager or leave a message. Leah left a brief message and then dialed the pager as well, giving her home phone number.

She knew that, if she ate something, her energy level might be restored. That's when she saw Jack from PDS crossing the street and jogging back to his truck. The older couple across the street were waving good-bye to him. Jack called out a cheerful hello to Leah and drove off down the street.

You can now enter your home safely, Leah. Seth is not lurking in the backyard ready to spring on you.

Once in the house, the first thing Leah did was change into shorts and a T-shirt. Then she went into the backyard to check on Bungee and Hula. She found Hula in the mudroom, lapping up the few drops left in the bottom of her water dish.

"Poor girl. I should have realized you were sharing your water. Would you like some dinner, too? It looks like Bungee cleaned you out."

As Leah filled the water and food dishes, she called for Bungee to come in through the doggy door. A moment later a very dirty bundle of fun came bounding in.

"I thought you might come when the word 'dinner' was mentioned." Leah roughed him up behind the ears. "How did you get so dirty, Bowser?" She looked out the window and felt relieved to see her garden was still intact. He must have been digging along the side of the house to have such a snootful of dirt.

Leaving the dogs to their dinner, Leah went out the back door and located where Bungee had been digging. He had made a royal mess, but it was just dirt along the side of the house, and he hadn't disturbed anything. If he had to dig, that was a good place to do it. Leah turned on the hose to water her garden. The sight of tiny green sprouts sticking up in straight, neat rows made her smile.

Maybe I don't want a big mansion on a hill. Maybe this is all I need to feed my soul. A little place of my own. A little garden.

Leah turned the hose onto the grass and began to water the lawn. The tormenting thoughts of Seth, Collin, and Franklin's estate had followed her to the garden sanctuary, and they didn't seem eager to leave. Leah knew the main conflict was deciding whom she was going to believe. It still seemed impossible to her that Seth could have filed bankruptcy and had a police record. She preferred to believe the research was incorrect. A different Seth Edwards had shown up on Collin's report. It had to be.

Still, there was the nagging thought that women more intelligent and less trusting than Leah had been duped by men before. She could have fallen into a great big trap.

What have I fallen into, God? A trap? Or a pocket of grace? What do I do now?

Oddly, all Leah could think about was the poster behind Alissa's desk of the gondola in Venice. *Yes, I would like to run away and float down a serene canal right now. Is that what you're telling me, God? I should buy a one-way ticket to Italy? Say the word, and I'm there! Ciao, baby!*

Leah thought of how pleasant it would be to sit back in that gondola and let someone else do the navigating through these challenging canals before her. She felt as if she was doing all the rowing and steering, which had been her pattern in the past. But this time she had no idea where she was going. Only uncharted waters lay ahead.

Bungee began to wrestle with the dripping garden hose, delighted with the spray of water that soaked his underside.

"Not a bad idea, Bungee. Come here. I'm going to hose you down and get all that mud off you before Seth comes for you."

Leah held Bungee down and washed him off. Once all the mud was gone, she unfastened the leash, picked him up, and took him inside to towel him off. Blocking the doggy door, she then instructed Bungee to stay put and stay clean while she changed and started dinner.

Closing the door to the mudroom, she turned to see Seth standing in her kitchen with a bouquet of red roses.

"The front door was unlocked," he said. "I guess you didn't hear me knock."

Without saying a word, Leah examined everything about Seth in an effort to determine if he was trustworthy. He looked stable. Sincere. Honest. Could he really be out to deceive her?

"I, um…" Leah felt weak and unable to respond to Seth and the gorgeous bouquet. "I'm all wet," she finally managed to say. "Let me go change. I'll be right back."

She fled to her bedroom, closed the door, and crumpled onto her bed. There she cried what seemed like a thousand salty tears. It was all such a cruel joke. A guy, who was perfect for her in every way, was standing in her kitchen waiting for her with a bouquet of red roses. It was the dream she had given up long ago when she realized all "the good ones" were taken.

Who am I supposed to believe? Which canal do I paddle down?

The fear of the unknown paralyzed Leah. If it weren't for her cold, soggy T-shirt, she might have stayed in that position a lot longer. Pulling herself to her feet, she drew on the strength and determination that had been her banner traits in demanding situations. She took a deep breath and changed her clothes. Then, washing her face and quickly brushing her hair, Leah returned to the kitchen.

Seth had managed to find Leah's one and only large vase and had arranged the flowers for her. They dominated the kitchen counter. The daisies he had given her on Friday were still fresh and filled a jar on her small kitchen table.

"How are you doing?" Seth asked cautiously, as Leah stood staring at the roses.

When she didn't answer, he took several steps closer to her with his arms open, inviting a hug.

Leah pulled back and put up her hand. "I'm still processing all this, Seth."

"Tell me about it." Seth scratched his forehead. "It's unbelievable, isn't it?"

"Yes." Leah cautiously made her way past Seth to the small kitchen table where she lowered herself onto a chair. "It's pretty overwhelming, all right."

Seth joined her at the table and moved the daisies so they could see each other more clearly. "Can I get you something to drink, Leah?"

"No. I mean, I should be getting you something to drink." She hopped up and went to the refrigerator. "Juice? Milk? Water?"

"Just water," Seth said. He had gotten up and was standing

beside her. "I can get it. Are you sure you're okay?"

"Yes, I'm okay." Leah heard the edge in her own voice and headed into the living room, as if the soft furniture would offer her comfort at this moment of confusion. Part of her wanted to order Seth to leave her house. Another part of her wanted to fall into his arms and beg him never to let go.

Seth joined her with two glasses of water, both with ice. He placed them on the coasters on top of the suitcase coffee table. Then, as if he sensed Leah's need for a little breathing space, he sat in the recliner, letting her have the love seat to herself.

They sat for several long minutes without speaking. Seth sipped his water.

"Seth," she said at last, "I have to ask you something. Did you know that you weren't in Franklin's will until he changed it two weeks ago?"

"No, I had no idea. I told you at the law offices. I didn't even know he changed the will."

"Did you know what was in his will before he changed it?"

Seth hesitated and looked down. He gazed up at Leah. "Yes, I did. Franklin told me. I didn't ask. He told me. On Easter."

A random phrase Seth had used several days ago suddenly came back to Leah. *Franklin said you are the key to my future happiness.*

"So you knew he had a large estate."

"No, I didn't. I thought it was just the house and the land. I didn't know about the treasury bills."

"The land?" Leah echoed. "You knew about the land?"

Seth leaned back and rubbed his hand across his jaw line. "I was going to tell you when the time was right, but it got a little awkward."

"A little awkward?" Leah repeated. Her memory flashed on the file folders she had seen in Seth's cupboard. She remembered now that the first rather full file had been labeled Madison Property. At the time, she hadn't made the connection.

"I hired a person to run a title search, and all the papers came in right after Franklin passed away. It felt awkward for me to tell you the results of my research on the heels of his death. I was going to tell you the day of his memorial service. I had studied the map, and I thought I'd take you to the property and tell you there."

"The woodlands," Leah whispered.

Seth nodded. "Once we got there, you were still pretty distraught. It was such a beautiful place. What you and I shared that day was so intimate and incredible to me that I felt it would ruin the moment if I started to talk about Franklin's estate. I knew we were meeting with the lawyer Monday, and I thought it best to wait until then."

Leah let his words sink in. Something still felt unbalanced. "You knew about the land, but you didn't tell me."

Seth nodded. "I should have. Then it wouldn't have come as such a surprise to you at the law office."

"And you knew I was listed as heir to Franklin's estate."

Seth nodded again.

"Why didn't you tell me that? You knew I didn't know anything about it."

Seth shrugged. "I don't know, Leah. I guess a few other dimensions of our relationship seemed more important to me. Not to mention that the melanoma surgery pretty much occupied my attention for awhile. To be honest, I was waiting for you to bring it up so it would feel more natural."

Leah felt her lower lip curve inward. "None of this feels natural to me."

"I know," Seth said. "I understand this is all surprising. It's surprising for both of us. But, Leah, I've thought about it all day, and I think Franklin had the right idea. His methods were a little wacky, but Franklin knew that you and I were really good for each other."

Leah studied his expression, trying to determine if she could trust his words.

"Not only that," Seth continued, "but I think the conditions of the will are... well, they're good."

"Good?" Leah repeated.

Seth readjusted his position and leaned forward with his hands folded. "I know this has to be the world's most backward, crazy, unromantic proposal in history, but Leah, honey, I think we should get married."

Chapter Thirty-five

Leah stared at Seth in disbelief. All of Collin's cautions about Seth's eagerness to marry her and to take possession of the inheritance came rushing back. She couldn't believe Collin's predictions had come true before the sun had even set that day.

Seth rose with a timid expression on his face. He opened his arms, welcoming Leah to come to him and to accept his proposal.

Leah couldn't move. "Seth, I have to ask you a question. And you have to promise me you will answer honestly."

"Of course." He lowered his arms and sat next to Leah on the love seat.

She looked him in the eye. "Seth, is it true that you filed bankruptcy with a credit-card debt in excess of $30,000?"

Seth's mouth dropped open. "Where did you hear that?"

"Just answer me. Yes or no."

Seth's eyes widened, as if he felt terror at her discovering this information. He swallowed and in a low voice said, "Yes, but—"

"And do you have a record with the Colorado police for illegal drug possession?"

"Well," Seth hesitated. "Kind of, but, you see…"

Leah felt her cheeks turning a fiery red as all the pieces began to come together. "You originally told me you came to Glenbrooke to seek the favor of your great-uncle so you could inherit—"

"I was only kidding, Leah! I didn't think Franklin owned anything."

"But now you know the inheritance is substantial. And I'm your only obstacle to obtaining it, aren't I?" Leah couldn't make herself wait to hear his answer. She sprang from the love seat, marched to the mudroom, and scooped up Bungee and his leash.

"Leah, it's not like that!" Seth called out as he followed her.

Shaking all over, Leah plowed her way back into the kitchen where Seth stood looking pale.

"Let me explain," he pled.

Yanking the roses from the vase, she thrust the flowers and the puppy into Seth's arms.

"Please leave," she growled.

"Leah, wait!"

"I mean it, Seth. Leave me alone!" She began to push him toward the front door.

"But, Leah, you have to let me explain!"

"No, I don't!" Leah shouted, yanking open the door and pushing Seth outside. "And I don't have to trust you, either!"

She knew her hand hit the spot on his back where the stitches had been because he winced and pulled away.

"Leah, this isn't fair!"

"No, it's not!" she cried, as the tears cascaded down her cheeks. "Just go!"

With a slam that rattled the morning-glory stained glass window, Leah locked the door and locked her heart to Seth Edwards. She leaned her back against the door while her heart raced and her lungs painfully pushed out great gasps of air.

Just then two steady knocks sounded on the door. She felt their vibrations against her back. "I said go away, and I mean it!"

"Leah," the smooth, professional voice called from the other side of the door. "Leah, it's Collin. May I come in?"

Leah hesitated before unlocking the door and opening it cautiously. Behind Collin she could see Seth standing beside his car with Bungee squirming in his arms and the roses spilling onto the street. Seth looked dumbfounded.

"Are you all right?" Collin asked.

Leah looked away. "I don't know."

"May I come in?"

Leah didn't know how to respond. She really wanted to be alone. Before she could think of what to say, Seth called out, "Is this where you got the information, Leah?" He still held Bungee under his arm, but the roses were now strewn on the ground.

"It doesn't appear that my client is interested in discussing this with you at the moment, Mr. Edwards." Collin stood between Leah and Seth, pulling his frame to its full height and speaking louder than was necessary in a quiet neighborhood like Leah's.

"What else did he tell you, Leah?" Seth persisted, his voice-level matching Collin's. Bungee started to bark. "Don't you see what's happening here? He's trying to turn you against me, Leah. Why are you believing him?"

Bungee kept barking.

Leah peered around Collin's broad frame and was about to

state that she had seen the evidence herself. But Collin spoke even more firmly than the first time. "I have to ask you to leave the premises, Mr. Edwards, unless you wish for my client to add harassment to the case she already has against you."

"What case against me?" Seth shouted. Bungee barked louder.

"Good night, Mr. Edwards," Collin stated, taking Leah by the elbow and ushering her into the house.

Leah didn't protest. Nor did she try to stop Collin when he firmly closed the door on Seth and Bungee.

"Come sit down," Collin said, leading Leah to the love seat. "May I get you something to drink?"

Leah sank onto the seat, shaking her head wearily. Something inside her urged her to run to the front door and let Seth back in. Maybe they could straighten everything out if the three of them could talk calmly. But Leah was not calm. She felt overwhelmed with weakness and vulnerability. She couldn't stand up and walk all the way to the front door if her life depended on it. All this was out of character for her. She knew how to be strong in any situation. She had proved that over the years. Now, she felt only weakness.

Collin lowered his large frame next to hers and put his arm along the back of the sofa. She didn't like Collin's taking her under his wing; yet she felt powerless to do anything at the moment.

"I'm sorry you had to find this out, Leah. Although I'm certain it's better to find out now than later."

Leah lowered her head into her hands, breathing deeply.

"This is too big for you to handle alone," Collin continued smoothly. "You need to give yourself some time. Then, when you're ready, I'm here for you. I can prepare the case to have the inheritance returned to you. You will only have to be involved at a minimal level. I can take care of everything."

"I don't care about the money, Collin, or the land, or any of it. I just feel so confused."

"I know," Collin said, placing his hand on her shoulder. "Unfortunately, I see this all too often in my line of work. You'll be glad later that it came out in the open so soon."

Leah wanted to cry, but no tears came.

"Is there any way you can get away for a few days?" Collin asked. "It would be good for you to separate yourself from all this. Let me start handling the case."

Leah told him about the reservations Franklin had made at the hot springs and how she was planning to go on Friday.

"Would it be possible for you to leave earlier?"

"I don't think so. Alissa wasn't able to cancel the reservations."

"The reservations can't be cancelled, but are they transferable?"

"I wouldn't know."

"It's easy enough to find out." Collin pulled an incredibly small cell phone from his breast pocket and asked information to connect him with Hamilton Hot Springs.

Leah wasn't sure why, but she liked the idea of leaving town for a few days. She felt too overwhelmed to stay here. She needed to be alone to think and pray.

"What you're telling me is that you *can* transfer the reservations?" Collin said into the phone. "Yes, I'd like to transfer the reservation for Leah Hudson to tonight."

"Tonight!" Leah squeaked out.

Collin put up his hand to silence her. "Right," he said into the phone. "She will arrive close to eleven tonight."

"I can't go tonight," Leah told Collin as soon as he hung up. "I have to make arrangements at work and...I don't know. I have to pack."

"You start to pack. I'll make a few calls."

"But work," Leah protested. "I can't call in sick."

"Have you ever?"

"No."

"Have you ever used all your sick days or vacation days?" Collin asked.

"No."

Collin reached over and placed his large hand on her forehead. "You feel feverish," he declared. "As your legal advisor, I'm recommending that you consider the next few days as sick days due to stress and fatigue. You need to take some time to recover. I can make the calls for you. I know several people in hospital administration. Now go. Start to pack."

Leah numbly obeyed. In some ways, it all made perfect sense. She pulled a battered suitcase from the back of her closet and began to fill it with everything her foggy brain thought she might need at a resort. She had nothing especially nice to pack, but then, what did that matter? She was going to be alone and to soak in the mineral pools. It wasn't as if this were a cruise to Alaska or anything.

Collin tapped on her closed bedroom door just as she threw in her toothpaste and a bottle of contact lens solution.

"I'm almost ready," she called out, lugging the ugly old suitcase to the front door. Collin stood there, holding out an envelope to her.

"I forgot, and I do apologize. This is the key to the safe-deposit box. I failed to give it to you this morning at my office. That's why I came over this evening."

Leah had nearly forgotten about the safe-deposit box. "It doesn't matter. The bank is probably closed by now."

"I made a few calls," Collin said. "Robert is still there. He said he would wait for us if we came over in the next few minutes. Here, let me carry that for you."

Leah handed Collin her suitcase and made a quick check

on Hula, giving her more food and water and a calm talking to as she hugged the dog around its neck. Then, locking her front door, Leah headed for her car only to find that Collin was loading her suitcase into his Mercedes' trunk.

Chapter Thirty-six

What are you doing?" Leah asked Collin, as he closed the Mercedes' trunk with her suitcase tucked inside.

"I'm driving you to Hamilton."

"It's four hours one way."

"I reserved a room for myself," Collin said. "I'll drive back in the morning. When you're ready to come home in a few days, you can call me, and I'll come pick you up. It's not a problem, Leah."

Without protesting, Leah got in his car, and the two of them drove to the bank. The truth was, Leah didn't know what to think of anything anymore. Her life had become a frantically twirling carousel, and all she could do was hold on tight as the ride went up and down and round and round faster and faster.

Robert, the bank president, and two tellers who were still doing paperwork were the bank's only occupants. Robert led Leah and Collin to the vault where Collin handed Leah the key and indicated he would wait for her in the bank's lobby so she could open the box in private.

Leah thought of how she would rather have waited until after her retreat at the hot springs to retrieve whatever was in the safe-deposit box. She wasn't ready for any more surprises. For all she knew, a check for a million dollars drawn on a secret Swiss bank account could be waiting for her. Or two tickets to the movies.

However, Collin was steering her life at the moment, and so she entered the bank vault holding in her hand the sum total of what she had inherited from Franklin Madison—a key.

Robert took Leah's key and used one of his own to open door of the safe-deposit box. Inside was a long, metal box with a handle. Robert pulled out the box and handed it to her. "You can open it in this room here," he said, pointing to a small private room she hadn't noticed before. He then quietly left.

As she opened the box's lid, inside she saw a plain, eight-by-ten manila envelope, folded in half and wedged into the flat, narrow box. Leah lifted the envelope. It was fairly light. And thin. She pinched the metal tabs on the back and was about to open the envelope when something stopped her.

She stood for a silent moment in the privacy of the room. *I don't want to know. Not yet. I want to give my heart a chance to settle.*

She folded the envelope and tucked it in her purse. As she walked back into the vault, Robert appeared and put the box into its slot, using his key and hers to lock it in place.

"Everything okay?" Collin asked when she joined him in the bank lobby.

Leah interpreted his question to mean, "What was in the box, and is there anything I should know about, now that I'm your attorney?"

"Everything is fine. Thank you."

Collin and Leah thanked the bank president and walked to Collin's Mercedes in silence.

"Any surprises?" Collin asked, as he opened Leah's car door for her.

She slid in without answering.

Collin got in and started the engine. "Not that you have to tell me. It is private, of course. You do know that I'm available if you need consultation on anything you found in the safe-deposit box. Franklin has turned out to be a man of surprises, and I want to make sure he didn't overwhelm you with another one."

Leah smiled to herself. Collin's voice carried the same tone of the little boy she had once left on the boulders at Heather Creek with his feet propped up.

"Collin, I don't know what was in the box." Leah decided that honesty was the best way to handle his questions. Especially considering this web she found herself caught in.

"It was empty?" Collin surmised.

"No, there was an envelope. But I didn't open it. I want to wait until after I've had time to clear my thoughts. I want to be prepared for whatever I find."

Collin nodded slowly, as he pulled the car onto the main highway. "Sounds wise."

For almost a mile neither of them spoke. Then Collin said, in the same tone as the freckled face boy Leah once had a crush on, "I suppose you're one of those people who actually can wait until Christmas morning to open her presents."

"Of course," Leah said. "Why? Can't you?"

"Nope. Never have been able to." With a chuckle Collin added, "The first Christmas we were married, my wife put three presents under the tree a week before Christmas. First chance I had, I unwrapped all three, saw what they were, and taped them back up."

"Did you get caught?"

Collin nodded and grinned. "And was she ever mad! Every year after that she hid my presents at her friend's house and refused to bring the gifts home until Christmas morning. Christmas was *her* holiday, and she wasn't going to let me spoil her fun."

Leah smiled and felt herself beginning to relax. "You must miss her a lot. Especially at Christmas."

Collin shot her a quick, startled look as if Leah had overstepped a boundary. "Yes," he said. Then, with a lopsided tone to his voice, he added, "When do you miss your parents the most?"

Leah had to think about that for a moment. "I'm not sure. For so many years my life revolved around being available to meet their needs. It might sound heartless, but I don't miss that part. I miss funny little things like reading the Sunday comics together and the way my mom used to hum to herself when she was cooking dinner."

"The loss of special people in our lives changes us, doesn't it?" Collin's voice had switched back to the wise-advisor tone.

Leah felt a tight lump in her throat. "Yes, it does." She was thinking of Seth. *Ever since he stepped into my life I was changing for the better. Was it all a hoax? How will I change now that he's gone?*

They reached the freeway, and Collin headed north. "Would you mind, Leah, if I put on some music?"

"No, please do." She would be glad for the focus to be off their conversation. It felt as if she might lose her emotional equilibrium at any moment.

Collin pressed a few buttons, and suddenly they were surrounded by the magnificent voice of an Italian tenor. Leah leaned back in the plush leather seat and closed her eyes. What filled her ears was the most romantic, heart-stirring music she had ever heard.

And once again, the image of the gondola in Venice came to mind. Leah imagined she was settled in the soft cushions while the rich voice of this passionate Italian tenor sang over her. She didn't have to steer or direct or decide which canal to go down. All she had to do was nestle in this pocket of grace.

Casually opening one eye slightly, Leah glanced at Collin's profile as he drove. *Is he the gondolier I've been waiting for and dreaming of?* Leah snapped her eyes shut. *Where did that thought come from?*

A wave of confusion washed over her stronger than ever. She suddenly wasn't sure why she was going anywhere with Collin Radcliffe. Leah wanted to rest in this pocket of grace, but somehow it wasn't right.

Collin shouldn't be directing and controlling which way I go, should he?

A sense of remorse over losing Seth hit her with force. Leah squeezed her eyes shut and turned her face to the window. While the Italian tenor sang his heart out, Leah cried silently, refusing to think of this exercise as "washing the windows of her soul."

Chapter Thirty-seven

*W*hen Leah awoke the next morning in her luxurious room at Hamilton Hot Springs, she blinked several times to make sure this wasn't part of a long, bizarre dream she had been floating in and out of. Even without her glasses on, she knew the fireplace set into the far wall was real. She could feel the extra fluffy down comforter. That was real, too. So was the silken, sheer canopy draped over the four-poster bed. She was at Hamilton Hot Springs, and there wasn't a fleck of avocado green or harvest gold in sight. Franklin's resort was a luxury spa.

This was all so foreign. She might as well have been dropped on Mars. Leah had no idea what to do in this place. She decided to dress and go downstairs to the restaurant for breakfast. As she pulled her clothes from her suitcase, Leah remembered how smoothly everything had happened last night. Collin drove for several hours while she silently cried herself to sleep under the spell of the Italian tenor's luxurious sounds. When Collin stopped for gas, Leah woke, and they ate at a drive-through restaurant. The rest of the way they talked about sports, music, and Collin's mother, who recently had sold one of her oil paintings to a museum in Minneapolis.

Collin didn't ask anything of Leah. He didn't bring up the topic of the safe-deposit box. He didn't talk business at all. After he saw Leah to her room at the resort, he said good night and asked her if she needed his number so she could call in a few days when she was ready to return home.

Leah sheepishly had to admit that she didn't have any of his business cards with her. Collin instantly produced a card from his pocket and disappeared down the hallway.

As Leah dressed this morning, she guessed that Collin already had left to drive home. She supposed he hadn't called her room to tell her he was leaving so that she could sleep in. It made her think of the sacrifices Collin was making on her behalf.

With bittersweet irony, Leah thought of the verse Seth had left on her windshield. The one she had thought was the valley of nuts. Leah was certain that if Collin hadn't intervened, she would have tumbled into that valley of nuts by now.

It was good to be here. Alone. Away from it all.

Leah checked her purse to make sure the envelope from Franklin's safe-deposit box was still there. She didn't feel ready to open it. Not yet.

Throwing a few things into the backpack she had brought with her, Leah decided to go for a walk. She stopped at the restaurant downstairs and asked if she could order a sandwich to go.

"Certainly," the hostess said. "Any particular kind of sandwich?"

"Wheat bread, no meat, lots of lettuce and tomato."

"We have a vegetarian special on a toasted basil and garlic bagel," the hostess offered.

"Perfect. And whatever kind of juice you have that comes in a bottle."

As Leah waited on the bench just inside the restaurant, she thumbed through a brochure that described the various mineral pools at the Hamilton spa. She already could imagine how good those therapy pools were going to feel when she returned from her hike. On the backside of the brochure was a map of a two-mile loop that led through the woodlands down to a small lake.

Leah took off on her hike with zest. Right away she noticed that she was hiking at a pace faster than she normally went. Her two hikes with Seth evidently had affected her hiking speed.

How could I have allowed myself to so easily fall in love with Seth? Weren't there hints along the way that he was setting me up?

Leah couldn't think of any. Everything about him had appeared genuine, even down to the lack of furniture in his apartment. She remembered the insurance papers Mary had showed her in Seth's file that were all in Spanish. Those documents couldn't have been false. Collin had suggested Seth had lied to her about being in Costa Rica, but Leah had seen the doctor's report on letterhead from a Costa Rican hospital.

Okay, so Seth isn't a complete liar. He was in Costa Rica. But maybe Collin was right. Maybe Seth had to flee the country because of the drug charges.

Leah picked up her pace as the trail led through an open meadow, laced with tiny blue wildflowers and tall white field daisies. They reminded her of the daisies Seth had given her last Friday, and how she had pushed him outside his own apartment and made him stand there, ringing the doorbell. Yesterday she had shoved the roses back at him. It occurred to Leah that both gestures were expressions of a woman who was trying to be in control. She winced; that wasn't the kind of person she wanted to be.

Hiking past the meadow, Leah entered a cool, green woodland. With only the company of the sound of twigs crunching under her feet as she marched onward, Leah silently asked forgiveness again for trying to control her life instead of allowing God to be at the helm.

Suddenly she stopped walking. She drew in a deep draught of the moist earth and the mossy trees. Woodlands were so soothing and restorative. The faint scent of wild violets rose to circle her, reminding her of the day Seth had held her in his arms in the woodland. She thought back on how he had talked of building a house on the very spot where the sun poured through the trees.

And to think that Seth took me to the fifty acres of woodland that Franklin owned, and that he kissed me there, knowing all along the significance of that plot of earth we stood on. And yet he didn't tell me. Did he really expect me to believe that our time together was more important than the information he had on the property and the will?

Pushing herself onward, Leah thought about how she would include that bit of information in her next talk with Collin so he could use it in the case he would build against Seth.

Am I sure I want to build a case against Seth?

She knew Collin probably could win the case if she gave him the right information. Then all of Franklin's money and land would revert to her.

And then what? I build myself a castle in the woodland and live there all by myself for the rest of my life? What kind of reward is that?

A wooden bench appeared on the trail ahead, just at the

woods' edge. Leah sat down so she could remove her shoe and shake out a pebble. The gesture reminded her again of Seth and their Easter morning hike.

"Okay, enough of the memories of Seth!" she said aloud. Overhead several birds sang out, and Leah listened. Theirs was a song of springtime.

See! The winter has past…the season of singing has come.

Sitting quietly for some time, Leah rehearsed the past month's events. Yes, the winter season of her life had passed. Yes, she was close to the Lord again and feeling sensitive to his Spirit. Her heart felt clean. No unconfessed junk to clog it up.

Yet I don't feel right. This is supposed to be the season of singing, but I don't have a song to sing. I want to enter into the season of Judah, of praise, like Leah in the Bible when she started to praise God instead of trying to prove herself, and yet I don't know how to do that.

Leah cleared her throat and attempted to sing. It was a noble effort, although not a successful one. She gave up and let the birds do the singing.

By the time she reached the lake, she felt emotionally exhausted and more than ready for her lunch. Several ducks floated on the placid, blue-gray waters of the kidney-shaped body of water before her. One of them headed her way when he saw her sitting down with food in her hand. Leah tore off a pinch of her bagel and tossed it to the friendly local. That was all his cronies needed to feel they had been invited to a company picnic.

With great honking and comical waddling, the army of freeloading ducks came after Leah. She relinquished the top half of her bagel, standing and tearing it up piece by piece. She tried to eat as much as she could while sharing the bottom of her falling apart sandwich. As soon as the bagel was gone, it began to rain.

Without a single "thank you" honk, the line of waddling tails hotfooted it back into the lake and frolicked in the rain.

Leah pulled down her baseball cap and began to tromp uphill in the rain. The hike back was much more difficult than the walk that had sloped downward to the lake. All the way, as she huffed along, she heard birds singing.

Singing in the rain, she thought with a grin. *Wish I could sing. I just don't have a song. Maybe the season of singing hasn't come to me yet. Why not? What's missing?*

Leah stomped her boots on the front mat before entering the lobby of the resort. She was chilled and wet and eager to soak in one of the mineral pools. Hurrying to her room, she pulled on her bathing suit and covered up with the luxurious robe provided in her room. The elevator at the end of the hall took her to the mineral pools where a resort staff member offered her a towel and pointed out the specifics of each pool.

Leah chose the bubbling hot tub of 103-degrees and slowly lowered herself into the inviting cauldron. All her tension melted, as instantly she was warmed and soothed after her hike in the rain.

She didn't want to think about anything. She wished her mind could shut down and float for a while the way her body was floating in the relaxing spa. But jumbled thoughts kept popping up in her mind. Thoughts of Seth. Thoughts of Collin. Thoughts of Jessica's description of being nestled in a pocket of grace.

Leah's eyelids flew open. *Jessica! I called her lawyer yesterday, and he's expecting me to call him back.* Leah knew she didn't have to call him, but she also knew it would nag at her since she had said she would. She would call and leave a message that she no longer needed a second opinion.

Feeling sufficiently poached, Leah decided to get out of the steaming spa and ask the resort assistant on duty if she could use a phone in the pool area. She knew that if she got that call off her mind, she could relax some more.

Rising from the hot mineral water, Leah was about to reach for her towel on a nearby lounge chair when someone held it out to her. She looked up to see Collin Radcliffe offering her the towel with a pleasant smile on his face.

Chapter Thirty-eight

*W*hat are you doing here? I thought you had gone home."
Leah quickly wrapped the thick, white towel around herself.

Collin shrugged. "When I woke up this morning, I thought about how long it's been since I've given myself a vacation. So I made a few calls, did a little shopping for some clothes, and decided to take it easy for a day or two." He was wearing a spa robe, and his hair was wet. "Have you tried the steam sauna yet? It's exceptionally good for the sinuses."

Leah felt deceived. Collin had just as much right to be here as she did; yet her private space was being invaded. She didn't know why she felt such a strong sense of distrust for Collin after all he had done for her, but she did.

"No, I, ah…" Leah reached for her robe. "I haven't been in the sauna yet, but I need to go back to my room right now." She felt awkward admitting she was going to call another lawyer so she added, "I forgot to do something."

"Well, I'll be here." Collin settled in a lounge chair and smoothed back his wet hair with a hand towel. "If you feel like coming back to the pools, that is."

"Okay," Leah mumbled.

"And if you don't have any plans for dinner, I'd love to have you join me. I made reservations at The Loft for six o'clock. Their specialty is prime rib."

"I don't eat red meat."

"Oh. Salad bar, perhaps?"

"I'll let you know," Leah said after a pause.

"Okay. Good. I'll call your room later to see what works best for you."

"Thanks." Leah turned to go.

"Oh, Leah?"

She looked over her shoulder at him.

"Any surprises with the contents of Franklin's envelope?"

Leah felt her jaw clenching. "I don't know."

Collin raised his hands in a gesture of apology. He didn't offer any more comments.

As Leah walked briskly to the elevator, her emotions ran at a frenzied pace. The moment she entered her room, the phone was ringing.

Come on, Collin, give me a little space here!

Opting for a warm shower to remove the scent of the mineral pools before calling Jessica's lawyer, Leah let the phone ring and turned the water on full force.

Once she had showered, changed, and dried her hair, she felt more centered. She called Jessica and wrote down the number for her lawyer. She also told Jessica what had happened with Seth and that she was at the hot springs. Leah thought it best not to mention Collin was there as well.

"I spoke with my lawyer today," Jessica said. "Greg said he

tried to call you several times and that people at work told him you had taken a few sick days. I was concerned about you. I'm glad you called."

"I'm going to call Mr. Fletcher now," Leah said. "I didn't think I needed a second lawyer's opinion, but maybe I do."

"Sounds wise," Jessica said. "Are you sure you're okay?"

"I think so. I went for a hike this morning, and that helped to clear my thoughts. Only you know what? I tried to sing, and I don't have a song."

Jessica paused. "What do you mean?"

"You know, 'See! The winter is passed…the season of singing has come.' I know that winter has passed. God has done amazing springtime planting in my life, but I'm not singing yet."

After another pause Jessica said slowly, "Well, I don't know if you're the one who is supposed to be singing."

Before Leah could process that comment, she heard a knock on the door. "I have to go, Jess. I'll call you later."

Leah hung up and hurried to the door, certain Collin would be standing there. She didn't want to talk to him. Not yet.

"Room service," the voice behind the door called out.

Leah opened the door and smiled at the uniformed woman. "I've already had my room cleaned, thank you."

"I'm here to restock the minibar," the woman said.

"I haven't even opened it."

"Okay. Thank you."

Just then the phone rang again, and once again, Leah let it ring. "I'm not ready for you to smooth talk me, Collin," she muttered. "Let me have some space."

She flipped the gas lighter switch on the wall, and instantly the logs in the fireplace began to heat up, taking the chill off the room.

Leah checked the clock. 4:20. She dialed the number for Gregory Fletcher, and his assistant answered.

"Yes, Leah," the assistant said. "Mr. Fletcher is available. He asked that I put you through if you called."

"Leah, hello, this is Greg Fletcher."

"I'm sorry you had to make several calls today trying to track me down. I just spoke with Jessica, and she told me."

"No problem," Greg said. "How can I help you?"

"I'm not exactly sure," Leah said, adjusting her position on the end of the bed. "I have a lawyer who is helping me with an inheritance situation, but I'm thinking I might need a second opinion."

"Yes, Jessica told me your lawyer was Collin Radcliffe."

"That's right."

Mr. Fletcher paused.

Leah sensed something in his silence. "Do you know Collin?"

"Yes. His office used to be in the same building as mine. As a matter of fact, one of my clients married his first wife."

"Collin told me about her," Leah said. "It was tragic the way he lost her and their child in the car accident."

"Their child?" Greg echoed.

"Yes, Collin said his wife was five months pregnant at the time of the accident."

"His wife?"

"Yes." Leah didn't like the tone in Greg's voice. "She was his wife, wasn't she? I mean they were married, right?"

"Actually, Collin and DeeDee had been divorced for two years before she married my friend, Bryan. She was carrying Bryan's child when she died."

Leah could only think of one response. "Oh. I'm so sorry."

"Yes. Well, Collin is a competent lawyer. He tends to get what he goes after so I'm sure he'll work hard for you."

Now Leah was the one pausing. "Mr. Fletcher, would it be

all right if I called you back? I think I need a little time to pull my thoughts together."

"Certainly. You have my numbers. Feel free to call me when you're ready to talk."

"You've already helped me more than you can know."

Leah sat on the edge of the bed staring into the fire that danced in the fireplace.

Collin lied. He slanted the details so I'd feel sympathy for him. I can't trust him. If he lied about his "wife," he also could have lied about Seth and Seth's records.

Leah felt her heart racing. She might have condemned Seth unfairly. *But why did Seth admit to the bankruptcy and the police record?*

Suddenly she felt very sure that Collin had slanted the facts in Seth's file to manipulate her opinion of Seth. She had been brutally unfair not to let Seth explain.

How could I have been so blind? For all I know, Collin is the one scheming to marry me after I claim Franklin's fortune and then dump me and take it all. What was it Mr. Fletcher just said? "Collin tends to get what he goes after."

"Well, he's not getting me!" Leah spouted, jumping up and heading for the door. She planned to march down to the mineral pools and tell Collin exactly what she thought of him. However, an urgent knock on the door caused her to pause for a moment.

So much the better! I'm ready for you now, Collin! Leah's fingers flew to unclasp the locks, and she yanked open the door, spewing out the first thing that came to her. "I don't take it very well when people lie to me!"

"So I noticed." The man at her door stood with his arms covering his face as if expecting Leah to throw something at him. "But I haven't lied to you about anything." He lowered his arms.

"Seth!" Leah rushed to him and threw her arms around him. "Seth, I can't believe you're here. Will you forgive me? I'm so sorry. Please forgive me."

"Of course I forgive you," he said. "Now will you forgive me?"

"Forgive you? For what?"

"For not telling you what you wanted to know when you wanted to know it."

"You didn't do anything wrong. I was the one who had it all mixed up. I misunderstood everything." Leah pulled back and looked up at his unshaven face and his red eyes. "Seth, you look exhausted. Come in. How did you know I was here?"

Seth went over to a chair by the fireplace. "I called you last night a dozen times. Then I called you again this morning at work. They told me you were out sick. I went by your house, and when you weren't there I guessed that if I could find Collin, I'd find you since you were with him last night."

Leah sat on the raised hearth and reached over to take Seth's hands in hers.

"Collin's secretary told me he was staying here. I called the front desk, and they said you were registered here, too. I know people at work must think I'm a maniac, but I turned in my truck at noon and said I had to leave on an emergency. I drove straight here, and when I arrived, I tried to call your room from the lobby."

"I thought it was Collin. That's why I didn't answer."

"I think the hotel operator slipped up when she told me there was no answer in room 145. That's how I found out your room number. I hope you don't mind my barging in on you like this. I was so concerned."

"I'm glad you're here, Seth."

His expression softened. "I'm glad I'm here, too. Leah, I apologize for handling everything so poorly yesterday. The roses and the suggestion that we get married.... I can imagine how that must have looked to you. I don't know why it seemed like a good idea."

Leah searched his expression for the deeper meaning behind his words.

"No, no! I don't mean that marrying you isn't a good idea. I mean coming on so strong like that after we've only known each other a few weeks. I can see how it would seem as if I were reacting to the condition of the will. I didn't realize that at the time. I didn't understand why you were so upset. And then all that information you had about the bankruptcy and the police record. How did you find out about that?"

"Collin."

Seth's expression turned grim. "What else did he tell you?"

"He has a whole file on you, but that was all he showed me."

Seth let go of Leah's hand. He began to pace the floor. "Man, that is really the lowest. Let me guess. He wanted to find a way to get the will switched back into your name only."

Leah nodded. "Tell me about the police record, Seth."

"It was in college. I had three roommates my senior year. One of the guys I didn't know until he moved into our apartment. He borrowed my car on a pretty consistent basis, which was fine. We all helped each other out. But then, because of Warren's excessive parking violations, my car was impounded, and the police found some drug paraphernalia under the seat. Warren said he was holding it for a friend, but it was all recorded in my name because it was my car."

Leah shook her head. "That's awful." She felt worse than ever for doubting Seth.

"And the bankruptcy issue is a very painful subject for me."

"You don't have to tell me about it if you don't want to,

Seth. I trust you." Leah was surprised to hear those last three words come out of her mouth. Trust was such an issue to her she might as well have just said, "I love you."

"No, I don't mind telling you. It was stupidity on my part. I received a credit card in the mail my last year of college. You know how they do those promotional deals. I activated it, but then I never used it. I kept it in my desk drawer at the apartment. When I moved out, I didn't notice it was missing. That is, until a credit bureau tracked me down in Costa Rica and said I'd run up debt of more than $28,000 plus more than a year's interest at 22 percent."

Leah let out a low whistle.

"I told them my card had been stolen, but I had nothing to stand on because I hadn't reported it lost or stolen. I had no way of paying it off. I had nothing. I followed my dad's lawyer's advice and filed bankruptcy."

"Seth, I'm so sorry. I'm sorry I doubted you and jumped to conclusions."

He moved over to the hearth beside Leah and drew her close. His voice mellowed. "What matters now is that we've cleared all this up. We're together. I couldn't sleep last night thinking I'd lost you, Leah."

"I trust you, Seth," Leah said firmly.

He drew away and looked into her eyes. She knew he understood the deeper meaning behind her words. "And I love you," he answered.

"I'll never let someone else influence my opinion of you again."

"Speaking of 'someone else,'" Seth said. "Is he still here at the hotel?"

"Yes, he's at the mineral pools now."

"I'd like to have a word with him," Seth said sharply.

"So would I. It just so happens I've learned that Collin has been manipulating all kinds of facts."

The phone's ringing interrupted Leah. She knew Collin was calling to see if she would take him up on his dinner invitation. "Seth, do you trust me?"

Seth's clear blue eyes opened wide. "Yes."

"Then don't say anything when I answer the phone. I have an idea."

Chapter Thirty-nine

Leah hung up the phone and said to Seth, "We have an appointment to meet Collin for dinner at six o'clock."

"What did he say when you asked him to change the reservations to three people instead of two?"

"Nothing. I think it confused him, but I don't think he suspects you're the third party."

Seth checked his watch. "It's five o'clock now. I have some clothes in my car. I should probably change before dinner."

"Why don't you use my shower, and I'll go downstairs? A library is on the other side of the gift shop. I saw in the brochure that they serve tea in the library until six."

"You don't mind my taking over your space?"

Leah couldn't help but think how different it felt to have Seth in her "space" compared to Collin crowding in on her.

"No, I like having you here. You feel like you belong in my space."

Seth smiled. "And you belong in my space. In my galaxy. In my universe."

Leah laughed. "Does this mean we've ended up on Pluto together?"

Seth kissed her on the end of her nose. "And who says wishes don't come true?"

Leah's heart felt full. She knew what needed to come next for her. Grabbing her purse, she gave the room key to Seth. "I'll be in the library. I have some reading to do."

"I'll walk you down so I can get the stuff from my car."

Hand in hand, Leah and Seth headed for the elevator. Seth let go and pushed the down button. Then he put his arm around Leah's shoulders. "Did I ever tell you that you're exactly the right height?"

Leah put her arm around Seth's middle and said, "We do fit together nicely, don't we?"

"Perfectly." He leaned over and gave Leah a tender kiss on the lips.

The elevator door opened, and Leah shyly pulled away. Then she froze. Before them stood Collin Radcliffe in the elevator.

"Seth," Collin said with a nod. "Leah."

Neither Seth nor Leah responded right away.

The door began to close, and Collin stepped out, dressed in his poolside apparel. "I take it this is our mystery guest for dinner." Collin's voice was anything but friendly.

"If you want to cancel dinner, that's fine," Leah said. "We both wanted to talk a few things through with you." For good measure, she added, "Before we drive home together this evening."

Collin straightened his shoulders. "Fine." The smooth, professional tone had returned to his voice. "You have to eat anyway; might as well eat before you hit the road. It's a long drive."

"Yes, it is," Seth agreed. "But I'm sure the ride home for me will be much less stressful than the journey here."

Leah caught Seth's deeper meaning and gave his side a squeeze since her arm was still around his middle.

"I'll see you both at six," Collin said, excusing himself and walking past them.

Seth pushed the elevator button again, and the door opened. They entered and rode to the lower level in silence.

"I'm not afraid of him," Leah said, as Seth walked her to the library. "I don't trust him."

"You don't have to trust Collin. The only one you have to trust completely is Christ. I know that's been hard for you over the years, but he's the only one who won't ever let you down." Seth gave Leah's shoulder a squeeze and headed through the lobby for the parking lot.

Leah watched him go and then entered the small library through the thick wooden doors. She was the only one there. A crackling fire rose from the large fireplace, which was lined with gray and brown river rock. Built-in bookshelves ran from the floor to the ceiling on the two opposite walls. In front of Leah stood a long marble-top table decked out with a silver platter of tiny sandwiches, strawberries dipped in white chocolate, and sugar cookies in the shape of flowers with light pink and purple frosting.

Shelly would love this. So would Lauren. And Jessica.

Leah poured herself a cup of tea from the brass urn in the center of the table. It felt strange to be the only one in the library and the only one at this tea. But this was good. She wanted to be alone with the fire, a soothing cup of tea, and the envelope from Franklin's safe-deposit box.

She settled herself on the comfortable, forest green sofa that faced the fireplace. After eating two strawberries and taking a sip of tea, she pulled the folded manila envelope from her purse. The nervous fear of the unknown had left her. The confusion over how to respond to so many surprises no longer hung over her. Leah knew that whatever was in the envelope was something Franklin had wanted her to have, and that alone made it special.

Reaching her hand into the flat envelope, Leah pulled out three postcards. One was of the Austrian Alps, the second of the Seine River in Paris, and the third of a gondola docked against a red-and-white-striped pole. The gondolier stood on the dock, complete with a wide-brimmed straw hat with a blue ribbon hanging down its back. He leaned casually against the pole and indicated with his hand that his gondola was available for the next rider.

Seth's postcards. A nostalgic smile danced across Leah's lips. She thought of all the times she had held those postcards at Franklin's house and how she had whispered to the gondolier that one day she would ride in his gondola.

Leah flipped over the cards. If she had read them before, she didn't remember any of Seth's messages to his great-uncle. The postcard from Paris held three scribbled lines: one about the weather, one about the Mona Lisa in the Louvre, and a final line about the weather again.

The postcard from the Austria Alps read,

Thanks so much for the money you wired me in Munich. My mom wrote and said you were going to send me some traveling money. It came at just the right time because I was down to my last two deutsche marks. I'm going to Italy tomorrow. They say it's cheaper to eat there.

Leah smiled broadly as she read the back of the postcard from Venice.

I looked up the verse you sent with the money, and I've thought about it a lot. I agree. It is the blessing of the Lord that makes us rich, and He adds no sorrow to it.

Leah gazed into the cheery fire and tried to remember where she had heard that phrase before. It wasn't from one of Jessica's three-by-five cards. For some reason, she could hear Mavis's voice when she thought of the verse.

Then she remembered. It was the last thing Franklin had said to Leah the day she visited him before he passed away. Mavis had noted he had been saying it ever since the lawyer had come to change the will.

"The blessing of the Lord makes us rich, and He adds no sorrow to it," Leah whispered into the firelight. "I agree with that." She felt a settled confidence that Seth believed that as well. His life so far was evidence that he had not lived to gain riches. Seth impressed her as someone who was living for God's blessing, not man's. That was certainly how Franklin had lived.

Leah read the last lines of the postcard.

Thanks again for the money. Here's one of my favorite verses for you to look up. Zeph. 3:17.
    Seth

The double doors of the library opened, and Leah turned to see Seth entering. He was clean-shaven and wearing fresh clothes. She smiled as he grabbed a strawberry before coming over to sit beside her on the couch.

"What do you have there?" he asked.

"Do you recognize these?" Leah held up the postcards.

It took Seth a moment. He turned one over and viewed his own handwriting. A smile came across his face. "Where did you get them?"

"Franklin's safe-deposit box."

"Those were in his safe-deposit box?"

"Yes, that's all that was in it. He kept these on his coffee table for years, and I would always stare at them. I had a private conversation going with this gondolier." She handed Seth the postcard.

He read the back. "'The blessing of the Lord makes us rich.' So that's where I first heard that verse."

"And what's the verse in Zephaniah?" Leah asked.

"That's been my favorite since I was a kid. You probably know it, too. 'The LORD thy God in the midst of thee is mighty, he will save, he will rejoice over thee with joy, he will rest in his love, he will joy over thee with singing.'"

Leah didn't know that verse. "Wait, what was the last part again?"

"'He will joy over thee with singing.'"

Leah took the postcard from Seth and stared at the picture of the gondolier. She felt her lungs squeeze and the pulse pound in her throat.

"Are you okay?" Seth asked.

"I'm not supposed to sing," she said in a whisper. "That's what Jessica said today. I'm not supposed to be the one singing."

"I don't follow you."

Tears rushed to Leah's eyes, as she held the postcard for Seth and tried to explain what had just become so clear. "The gondolier. It's the Lord. He's been inviting me to rest in this pocket of grace for so long, but I've been the one doing all the steering. My whole life I had to be in control, even if I didn't know which canal to go down."

Seth reached over and wiped away a tear. He looked at her compassionately; yet his expression showed he didn't have a clue what she was rambling on about.

"It's from your verse, Seth. 'The winter is past and the season of singing has come.' Only I'm not the one who's supposed to do the singing. Jesus is the Gondolier of my life. He wants me to rest in his pocket of grace while he decides which canal to take me down."

The tears came in a steady cascade. "Do you understand what I'm saying at all? It's my season of Judah. I choose to praise God instead of trying to prove myself good enough for him. I finally get it! I don't have to steer the boat and sing the songs and do everything. Jesus is the Gondolier. I rest. Here." She pointed at the pillows cushioning the gondola. "He steers, he leads, and he sings over me. That's what I never understood. He's the one who does the singing."

Seth opened his arms, and Leah leaned against his chest, sobbing. She felt so free. Pulling away, with a ripple of laughter, she said, "Honest, Seth, I never in my life have cried as much as I have this last month."

"You know how I feel about your tears." Seth stroked her hair.

"It's just that I never understood before. Not the way I understand now. He sings over me!"

Chapter Forty

$\mathcal{L}$eah wasn't sure if Seth completely understood what she was saying. It didn't matter. She understood. And her relationship with the Lord would never be the same.

Drying her tears and composing herself, Leah tucked the postcards back into her purse and tried another sip of her tea, which had cooled too much for her to drink.

Seth checked his watch. "Almost six."

"I'm ready," Leah said.

She and Seth strolled to The Loft restaurant with their arms around each other. Collin was already seated.

Leah resisted the urge to control the conversation. She sat back in her chair and opened her menu, as if this were just dinner with two friends.

Collin waited until they had ordered before saying, "I don't know that much needs to be said at this point. It's obvious, Leah, you've made some choices about whom to trust."

Leah remembered Seth's words from earlier in the lobby. "Collin, I've learned a few things today. One is that Christ is the only one I can trust completely. He's the only one who won't ever let me down. Humans make mistakes all the time."

Collin's expression registered his surprise. "Perhaps as a professional advisor, I should mention it can be risky to trust your future to people who have made mistakes in the past."

"I think it's even riskier to trust people who manipulate the truth."

Collin looked intrigued.

"I don't want to play any games, Collin. I just need to say that I felt it was unfair of you to try to gain my sympathy by telling me that your wife had been killed in a car accident. I happen to know you had been divorced for two years when she died, and the child she was carrying wasn't yours."

Collin squinted at Leah as if he couldn't believe she had detective powers that could uncover such information. Seth appeared equally surprised.

"I'm sure it was still a very painful experience for you," Leah continued. "But if you plan to stay in Glenbrooke and continue your father's practice, I think it would help you to know that the people your father has served for years are honest people who expect the truth. That's all, Collin, just tell the truth."

Collin paused, studying Leah. "You are an exceptional woman, Leah Hudson. I said it before, and I'll say it again. It's my loss I didn't recognize that when we were in high school."

Leah felt her candy apple cheeks doing what they loved to do. Yet she didn't try to hide their blushing. She looked openly at Collin and said, "I don't think I knew who I was in high school. But I know who I am now, and I hope we can be friends. I'd like the three of us to be friends."

Collin's appearance softened. "I'd like that as well, Leah."

Seth spoke up. "Before I'd be real comfortable with that, I think you and I have a few things to settle. First, I understand you have a file on me. I'm sure it's legal or else you wouldn't have it."

Glancing at Leah, Seth continued, "I told Leah everything, and I would like you to know that I have nothing to hide. Everything I said in your office yesterday was true. I didn't know the will had been changed. I didn't come to Glenbrooke in search of my great-uncle's fortune. I came here for medical reasons. I agree with Leah that I, like all the other people of Glenbrooke, expect honesty and decency from a man in your position. I look forward to your display of those qualities as we continue to do business together."

Collin looked at Leah and then back at Seth. He hesitated before saying, "My apologies. To both of you."

The waiter arrived with their food, and Seth asked if he could offer a prayer.

They ate quietly for a few minutes before Collin said, "If I might add my own swan song here, I'd like to say a few things. I moved back to Glenbrooke looking for something. I think you've both helped me to see what that was. I missed the honesty and integrity I grew up with. I guess some of my old business ways followed me back home. Consider your words taken to heart. I appreciate your honesty. Both of you. I'd highly value a friendship with you."

Leah felt relieved. She also was impressed that Collin had responded so well.

After that the conversation flowed more easily and freely. Collin agreed to destroy the file he had on Seth. Then, because Leah knew Collin was still probably dying to know, she told him about the postcards being the only treasure in the safe-deposit box. She pulled them from her purse and showed them to him.

"'It's the blessing of the Lord that makes us rich,'" Collin read. "I remember hearing Franklin say that once when I went with my father to pay him a visit."

"'And He adds no sorrow to it,'" Seth added.

Collin nodded somberly, turning over the postcards and examining each of the pictures. Leah couldn't help but smile when he studied the postcard from Venice. She knew that no one else would ever see what she saw in that picture. She already had plans to frame it so she would always remember what had become so clear to her today, that the Gondolier daily invites her to ride with him while he does all the work and chooses the right canals. And most importantly, that he expresses his delight by singing over her.

"So you two are heading back to Glenbrooke tonight?" Collin asked.

Seth and Leah both nodded.

"Is there anything I can do for either of you?"

Seth said, "No, thanks."

Leah was about to echo the same answer, but then she had a thought. "Actually, Collin, you could do one thing for me."

"Name it."

Twenty minutes later, Seth and Leah were on the road in his Subaru station wagon, heading south for Glenbrooke.

"Ready for this?" Leah asked.

Seth nodded. Leah held Seth's portable CD player in her lap and inserted the CD she had borrowed from Collin. Into the air floated the rich, romantic voice of an Italian tenor, singing his heart out.

Leah pulled the paper insert from the CD case and told Seth, "This says the title of this song in English is 'I'll Go with You.'"

Seth smiled at her. "It's true, George. I will go with you."

"And I'll go with you," Leah said, reaching over and slipping her hand into his.

Leah leaned back and closed her eyes. She could clearly picture a charming cottage tucked away in the clearing of a certain woodland where the sunbeams shot through the trees like bronzed javelins thrust from the heavens. She reveled in thoughts of Seth's kisses in the golden light of those woodlands. Bungee would have a yard to play in.

Leah looked over at Seth, wondering what he was thinking. She couldn't keep back the smile that had broken out as she studied the profile of the man with whom she knew she would spend the rest of her life.

"I was thinking," Seth said, glancing at Leah.

"Yes?"

"You don't have to say anything right away. Take all the time you want to think about it."

"Yes?" Leah waited for Seth to finish. She felt as if the Gondolier was steering their course home to Glenbrooke, and she and Seth had fallen together into this pocket of grace. As the soaring notes of the Italian love song showered over them, Leah whispered under her breath, "Oh, Lion of Judah, keep singing over us. Sing over us with joy!"

"I was wondering," Seth said. "What would you think of a honeymoon in Venice?"

Dear Reader,

During my teen years, which were spent in southern California, every Fourth of July my family visited friends at the beach. The summer I was fourteen, I was sitting on the beach watching the waves when "Uncle" Bob leaned over and said, "You do know, don't you, that the Lord sings over you?"

I had no idea what he was talking about. I did know that Bob was full of surprises. He wrote clever poetry, and his wife, Madelyn, decorated their beachfront home with his original oil paintings of their favorite Hawaiian locations. He had hung a swing from their vaulted ceiling for their three children. And he was one of the first God-lovers I ever met.

As the summer sun poured over us that July afternoon, I squinted at Uncle Bob in response to his remark. He added with a nod, "It's true. The Lord sings over you, Robin. It's in the Bible so I know it's true." He quoted Zephaniah 3:17, "He will joy over thee with singing."

I felt as if I had been handed a secret key that unlocked one of the mysteries of God. The Lord sings over me!

That knowledge became sweeter than just knowing that God loved me. It was deeper than believing Christ had died for me. It was more promising than trusting that one day Christ would return and take me to be with him.

The Lord sings over me! God takes delight in being with me!

My soul's response was to promise to always take delight in him. His singing over me became evidence that God liked me. He was the eternal romancer. The relentless lover. The one who always wants me back.

As I wrote about Leah, I felt she represented so many women I know who haven't yet realized God takes delight in them simply because they are his daughters. I wanted Leah to discover this truth and to realize it wasn't up to her to direct her life down each "canal" she came to. I like the way she yielded to the Gondolier and finally settled into his pocket of grace. I want to live like that every day.

My friend, you do know, don't you, that the Lord rejoices over you with singing? It says so in his Book so I know it's true.

Always,

Robin Jones Gunn

P.S. You are invited to come visit me online at www.robingunn.com or write to Robin Jones Gunn, c/o Multnomah Publishers P.O. Box 1720, Sisters, Oregon 97759

My son decided he liked spinach when he was in third grade. The school's cafeteria served spinach once a week, and none of the other kids could believe my son actually ate it. He came home one day with a story about how he not only ate all his spinach, but he also powered down most of the other kids' servings. They hailed him as having performed some kind of inhuman feat. (In third grade, I guess we all take whatever fame we can get.)

I asked my son what made the school spinach so good, and he said it was "all mixed up with cheese in in." I began to experiment with a spinach soufflé recipe until he said it was just as good as the cafeteria spinach. It's still his favorite. I make it every Thanksgiving, Christmas, and a dozen other times during the year. And, I have to say, it doesn't feel like a feat at all to pack away a considerable amount of spinach—even if no third-graders are surrounding you and cheering you on.

I think Leah would have come up with the same recipe, which is why I call it "Leah's Spinach."

I must tell you I really goofed on this easy recipe once. We were having company for dinner, and in my haste, I bought frozen collard greens instead of spinach. It wasn't until our poor company dug in and took the first bite that I realized something was wrong. I'll never forget the look on that poor guy's face! So whatever you do, don't substitute chopped collard greens. It makes for a bitter surprise.

LEAH'S SPINACH

6 boxes frozen, chopped spinach (10-ounce size)
6 large eggs
1 cup monterey jack cheese, grated
3 slices bread, crumbled into crumbs
few pats of butter
salt and pepper

Thaw the spinach and drain excess water. Place spinach in oven-safe soufflé bowl (or casserole dish). Mix in the grated cheese. Add a few shakes of salt and pepper. In a separate bowl, beat all six eggs and pour over spinach and cheese and mix together. Cover mixture with breadcrumbs and dot with a few pats of butter. Bake for 30 minutes in a 350-degree oven.

IDA'S LEMONADE

Berries are plentiful in the Northwest each summer so it's easy to think of creative ways to include berries in our summer menu. Here's a recipe for fresh lemonade with berries, one of Ida's secret ingredients.

1 1/2 cups berries, washed and hulled
1 cup fresh-squeezed lemon juice (about 6 lemons)
3/4 cup sugar
4 cups cold water

Combine the berries, lemon juice, and sugar in a blender or food processor. Blend until smooth. Pour into a large pitcher. Add cold water and squeeze half a lime over the top. Stir well and add ice. Ah, the joys of summer!

THE GLENBROOKE SERIES

by Robin Jones Gunn

COME TO GLENBROOKE...

A QUIET PLACE WHERE SOULS ARE REFRESHED

Imagine a circle of friends who enter into each other's lives during that poignant season when love comes their way. Imagine the sweetness of having those friends to depend on as the journey into marriage and motherhood begins.

Meet the women of Glenbrooke: Jessica, Teri, Lauren, Alissa, Shelly, Meredith, Leah, and Genevieve. When their lives intersect in this small town, the door to friendship is opened and hearts come in to stay.

Perfectly crafted, heartwarming, and rich in truth, Robin's Glenbrooke novels have delighted half a million readers with their insights and charm. All souls looking to be refreshed are warmly invited to come to Glenbrooke.

SECRETS
Glenbrooke Series #1
Beginning her new life in a small Oregon town, high school English teacher Jessica Morgan tries desperately to hide the details of her past.

1-57673-420-X

WHISPERS
Glenbrooke Series #2
Teri went to Maui hoping to start a relationship with one special man. But romance becomes much more complicated when she finds herself pursued by three.

1-57673-327-0

ECHOES
Glenbrooke Series #3
Lauren Phillips "connects" on the Internet with a man known only as "K.C." Is she willing to risk everything...including another broken heart?

1-57673-648-2

SUNSETS
Glenbrooke Series #4
Alissa loves her new job as a Pasadena travel agent. Will an abrupt meeting with a stranger in an espresso shop leave her feeling that all men are like the one she's been hurt by recently?

1-57673-558-3

CLOUDS
Glenbrooke Series #5
After Shelly Graham and her old boyfriend cross paths in Germany, both must face the truth about their feelings.

1-57673-619-9

WATERFALLS
Glenbrooke Series #6
Meri thinks she's finally met the man of her dreams...until she finds out he's movie star Jacob Wilde, promptly puts her foot in her mouth, and ruins everything.

1-57673-488-9

WOODLANDS
Glenbrooke Series #7
Leah Hudson has the gift of giving, but questions her own motives, and God's purposes, when she meets a man she prays will love her just for herself.

1-57673-503-6

WILDFLOWERS
Glenbrooke Series #8
Genevieve Ahrens has invested lots of time and money in renovating the Wildflowers Café. Now her heart needs the same attention.

1-57673-631-8

TEA AT GLENBROOKE

- Authored by: *Robin Jones Gunn*
- Artist: *Susan Mink Colclough*

Snuggle into an overstuffed chair, sip your favorite tea, and journey to Glenbrooke…"a quiet place where souls are refreshed." Writing from a tender heart, Robin Jones Gunn transports you to an elegant place of respite, comfort, and serenity—a place you'll never want to leave! Look forward to a joyful reading experience, lavishly illustrated by Susan Mink Colclough, that captures the essence of a peaceful place.

ISBN 1-58860-023-8

Sisterchick n.: a friend who shares the deepest wonders of your heart, loves you like a sister, and provides a reality check when you're being a brat.

SISTERCHICKS ON THE LOOSE!

Zany antics abound when best friends Sharon and Penny take off on a midlife adventure to Finland, returning home with a new view of God and a new zest for life.

ISBN 1-59052-198-6

SISTERCHICKS DO THE HULA!

You can't cancel an adventure you've dreamed of for this long... An unexpected pregnancy only multiplies Waikiki's wackiness for two middle-aged Sisterchicks who are dying to let their hair down.

ISBN 1-59052-226-5

SISTERCHICKS IN SOMBREROS!
Coming October 2004

Two Canadian sisters inherit beachfront property in Mexico and take off on an adventure to claim their inheritance. With the help of a few locals, the Canadian cuties figure out what to do with their less-than-desirable legacy.

ISBN 1-59052-229-X

Visit www.letstalkfiction.com today!

Fiction Readers Unite!

You've just found a new way to feed your fiction addiction. Letstalkfiction.com is a place where fiction readers can come together to learn about new fiction releases from Multnomah. You can read about the latest book releases, catch a behind-the-scenes look at the your favorite authors, sign up to receive the most current book information, and much more. Everything you need to make the most out of your fictional world can be found at www.letstalkfiction.com. Come and join the network!

CELEBRATE HER BECOMING A WOMAN!

Gentle Passages

Guiding Your Daughter | Robin
| Jones
into Womanhood | Gunn

Every woman who has an adolescent daughter recognizes her own forgotten questions and insecurities mirrored in those bright young eyes. How can she let her know that she understands these changes, too strange and intimate for her daughter to mention? How can she make the passage into womanhood not a shameful, unpleasant experience but a harmonious and joyful one—an invitation to a treasured role in God's eyes? Robin Jones Gunn shares stories of how this uncertain transition can become the loveliest time in the life of a mother and daughter, inspiring women with special traditions to carry on for generations to come.

ISBN 1-57673-943-0

CELEBRATING THE MOMENTS
THAT LAST FOREVER

Focusing upon the special bond between a mother and child, this unique gift book offers lilting poetry, poignant prose, spiritual insights, romantic photographic images, inspiring quotations, and heart-warming journal entries. A delightful companion to women of every age and background celebrating the vast and myriad joys of motherhood!

ISBN 1-57673-914-7

ENJOY ANOTHER DELIGHTFUL ROMANCE SERIES WITH GAYLE ROPER'S SEASIDE SEASONS!

SPRING RAIN
Seaside Seasons Book 1

Leigh Spenser is thrown into conflict when her son's estranged father comes home to Seaside, New Jersey, to comfort his brother dying of AIDS, forcing them to face powerful emotions neither wants to acknowledge. But it's not until their son is kidnapped that Leigh and Clay discover the answers they've been looking for all their lives.

ISBN 1-57673-638-5

SUMMER SHADOWS
Seaside Seasons Book 2

Abby Patterson witnesses a hit-and-run accident but has amnesia and can't remember it. She determines to discover what really happened, endangering herself and her landlord, Marsh Winslow. Marsh, a writer of Westerns, fights the phantoms of his past even as Abby fights chronic pain and struggles with how to honor her overbearing parents.

ISBN 1-57673-969-4

AUTUMN DREAMS
Seaside Seasons Book 3

Cassandra Merton has her hands full with aging parents, a teenage niece and nephew, and a rich bachelor who arrives at her bed-and-breakfast to contemplate his future. When a troubled employee unknowingly endangers Cass, who is taken hostage by a gunman, Dan Harmon realizes his love for Cass.

ISBN 1-59052-127-7

WINTER WINDS
Seaside Seasons Book 4

Pastor Paul Trevelyan hasn't seen the woman he loves in six years. When he's given a second chance with her, he longs to make it work this time. The trouble is, if he doesn't win her back, it could cost him his job—and his happiness. Church discord and a sinister luggage mix-up force the stubborn spouses to take a new look at each other...

ISBN 1-59052-279-6

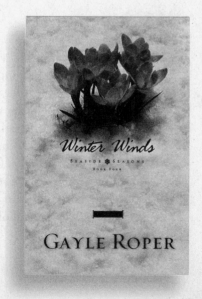